# Livingstone's
# Companions

# LIVINGSTONE'S COMPANIONS

*Stories by*

NADINE GORDIMER

NEW YORK / THE VIKING PRESS

First published in 1971 by The Viking Press, Inc.
625 Madison Avenue, New York, N.Y. 10022
Published simultaneously in Canada by
The Macmillan Company of Canada Limited
SBN 670-43570-8
Library of Congress catalog card number: 78-158415
Printed in U.S.A. by Vail-Ballou Press, Inc.

The following stories appeared originally in *The New Yorker:* "The Life of the Imagination," "Why Haven't You Written?" "A Meeting in Space" (under the title "Say Something African"), "An Intruder (under the title "Out of the Walls"). "Abroad" and "No Place Like" appeared in *The Southern Review*, and other stories appeared in *The Atlantic, Encounter, London Magazine,* and various other American and British magazines.

*For Hugo*

# CONTENTS

*Livingstone's
Companions*

# LIVINGSTONE'S COMPANIONS

In THE HOUSE that afternoon the Minister of Foreign Affairs was giving his report on the President's visit to Ethiopia, Kenya, and Tanzania. "I would like to take a few minutes to convey to you the scene when we arrived at the airport," he was saying, in English, and as he put the top sheet of his sheaf of notes under the last, settling down to it, Carl Church in the press gallery tensed and relaxed his thigh muscles—a gesture of resignation. "It's hard to describe the enthusiasm that greeted the President everywhere he went. Everywhere crowds, enormous crowds. If those people who criticize the President's policies and cry neo-colonialism when he puts the peace and prosperity of our country first—"

There were no Opposition benches since the country was a one-party state, but the dissident faction within the party slumped, blank-faced, while a deep hum of encouragement came from two solid rows of the President's supporters seated just in front of Carl Church.

". . . those who are so quick to say that our President's policies are out of line with the OAU could see how enthusiastically the President is received in fellow member states of the OAU, they would think before they shout, believe me. They would see it is they who are out of line, who fail to understand the problems of Pan-Africa, they who would like to see our crops rot in the fields, our people out of work, our development plans come to a full stop"—assent swarmed, the hum rose—"and all for an empty gesture of fist-shaking"—the two close-packed rows were leaning forward delightedly; polished shoes drummed the floor—"they know as well as you and I will not free the African peoples of the white-supremacy states south of our borders."

The Foreign Minister turned to the limelight of approval. The President himself was not in the House; some members watched the clock (gift of the United States Senate) whose graceful copper hand moved with a hiccup as each minute passed. The Speaker in his long curly wig was propped askew against the tall back of his elaborate chair. His clerk, with the white pompadour, velvet bow and lacy jabot that were part of the investiture of sovereignty handed down from the British, was a perfect papier-mâché blackamoor from an eighteenth-century slave trader's drawing-room. The House was panelled in local wood whose scent the sterile blast of the air-conditioning had not yet had time to evaporate entirely. Carl Church stayed on because of the coolness, the restful incense of new wood—the Foreign Minister's travelogue wasn't worth two lines of copy. Between the Minister and the President's claque the dialogue of banal statement and deep-chested response went on beamingly, obliviously.

". . . can assure you . . . full confidence lies in . . ." Suddenly the Speaker made an apologetic but firm gesture to attract the Minister's attention: "Mr. Minister, would it be convenient to adjourn at this point . . . ?"

The claque filed jovially out of the House. The Chamberlain came into the foyer carrying his belly before turned-out thighs, his fine African calves looking well in courtier's stockings, silver buckles flashing on his shoes. Waylaid on the stairs by another journalist, the Minister was refusing an interview with the greatest amiability, in the volume of voice he had used in the House, as if someone had forgotten to turn off the public address system. With the feeling that he had dozed through a cinema matinee, Carl Church met the glare of the afternoon as a dull flash of pain above his right eye. His hired car was parked in the shade of the building—these were the little ways in which he made some attempt to look after himself: calculating the movement of the sun when in hot countries, making sure that the hotel bed wasn't damp, in cold ones. He drove downhill to the offices of the broadcasting station, where his paper had arranged telex facilities. In the prematurely senile building, unfinished and decaying after five years, the unevenness of the concrete floors underfoot increased his sensation of slowed reactions. He simply looked in to see if there was anything for him; the day before he had sent a long piece on the secessionist movement in the Southern Province and there just might be a word of commendation from the Africa desk. There *was* something: "100 YEARS ANNIVERSARY ROYAL GEO-GRAPHICAL SOCIETY PARTY SENT SEARCH FOR LIVINGSTONE STOP YOU WELL PLACED RETRACE STEPS LIVINGSTONES LAST JOURNEY SUGGEST LAKES OR INTERIOR STOP THREE THOUSAND WORDS SPECIAL FEATURE 16TH STOP THANKS BARTRAM."

He wanted to fling open bloody Bartram's bloody door—the words were in his mouth, overtaking each other. *Church is out there, he'll come up with the right sort of thing. Remember his "Peacock Throne" piece?* Oh yes. He had been sent to Iran for the coronation of the Shahanshah, he was marked down to have to do these beautiful, wryly understated sidelights. Just as a means of self-expression, between running about after Under Ministers and party bosses and driving through the bush at a hundred in the shade to look at rice fields planned by the Chinese and self-help pig farms run by the Peace Corps, and officially nonexistent guerrilla training camps for political refugees from neighbouring countries. He could put a call through to London. How squeakily impotent the voice wavering across the radio tele-

phone. Or he could telex a blast; watch all the anticipated weariness, boredom and exasperation punching a domino pattern on
clean white tape.

Slowly pressure subsided from his temples. He was left sulkily
nursing the grievance: don't even realize the "lakes and interior"
are over the border! In the next country. Don't even know that.
The car whined up the hill again (faulty differential this one had)
to the office full of dead flies and posters of ski slopes where the
airline agency girl sat. There was a Viscount the next day, a local
Dakota the day after. "I'll wait-list you. You're sure to get on.
Just be at the airport half-an-hour early."

He was there before anybody. Such a pretty black girl at the
weigh-bay; she said with her soft, accented English, "It looks
good. You're top of the list, don't worry, sir." "I'm not worried,
I assure you." But it became a point of honour, like the obligation to try to win in some silly game—once you'd taken the
trouble to get to the airport, you must succeed in getting away.
He watched the passengers trailing or hurrying up with their
luggage and—smug devils—presenting their tickets. He tried
to catch the girl's eye now and then to see how it was going. She
gave no sign, except, once, a beautiful airline smile, something she
must have learnt in her six weeks' efficiency and deportment
course. Girls were not beautiful, generally, in this part of Africa;
the women of Vietnam had spoilt him for all other women, anyway. In the steps of Livingstone, or women of the world, by our
special correspondent. But even in his mind, smart phrases like
that were made up, a picture of himself saying them, Carl A.
Church, the foreign correspondent in the air-conditioned bar
(when asked what the American-style initial stood for, the story
went that he had said to a bishop, "Anti, Your Grace"). Under
his absurdly tense attention for each arrival at the weigh-bay
there was the dark slow movement of the balance of past and
present that regulates the self-estimate by which one really man-
ages to live. He was seeing again—perhaps for the first time

since it happened, five? six? years ago—a road in Africa where the women were extremely beautiful. She was standing on the edge of the forest with a companion, breasts of brown silk, a water-mark of sunlight lying along them. A maroon and blue *pagne* hid the rest of her. On a sudden splendid impulse he had stopped the car (that one had a worn clutch) and offered her money, but she refused. Why? The women of that country had been on sale to white men for a number of generations. She refused. Why not? Well, he accepted that when it came to women, whom he loved so well, his other passion—the desire to defend the rights of the individual of any colour or race—did not bear scrutiny.

Now a blonde was up at the weigh-bay for the second or third time; the black girl behind it was joined by an airline official in shirtsleeves. They consulted a list while the blonde went on talking. At last she turned away and, looking round the echoing hall with the important expression of someone with a complaint to confide, this time came and sat on the bench where he waited. Among her burdens was a picture in brown paper that had torn over the curlicues of the gilt frame. Her thin hands had rings thrust upon them like those velvet Cleopatra's needles in the jewellers'. She puts on everything she's got, when she travels; it's the safest way to carry it. And probably there's a pouch round her middle, containing the settlement from her last ex-husband. Carl Church had noticed the woman before, from some small sidetrack of his mind, even while she existed simply as one of the lucky ones with a seat on the plane. She was his vintage, that's why; the blond page-boy broken into curling locks by the movement of her shoulders, the big red mouth, the high heels, the girlish floral beach-dress—on leaves during the war, girls his own age looked like that. But this one had been out in the sun for twenty years. Smiled at him; teeth still good. Ugly bright blue eyes, cheap china. She knew she still had beautiful legs, nervous ankles all hollows and tendons. Her dead hair tossed frowsily. He thought, tender to his own past: she's horrible.

"This's the second morning I've sat here cooling my heels."
Her bracelets shook, dramatizing exasperation. "The second day
running. I only hope to God I'm on this time."

He said, "Where're you trying to get to?" But of course he
knew before she answered. He waited a moment or two, and
then strolled up to the weigh-bay. "Still top of the list, I hope?"
—in an undertone. The airline man, standing beside the black
beauty, answered brusquely, "There's just the one lady before
you, sir." He began to argue. "We can't help it, sir. It's a com-
passionate, came through from the town office." He went back
and sat down.

She said, "You're going on the same plane?"

"Yes." Not looking her way, the bitch, he watched with hope
as boarding time approached and there were no new arrivals at
the weigh-bay. She arranged and rearranged her complicated
hand luggage; rivalry made them aware of one another. Two
minutes to boarding-time, the airline girl didn't want him to
catch her eye, but he went over to her just the same. She said,
cheerfully relieved of responsibility, "Doesn't look as if anyone's
going to get a seat. Everybody's turned up. We're just check-
ing."

He and the blonde lady were left behind. Hostility vanished as
the others filed off down the Red Route. They burst into talk at
once, grumbling about the airline organization.

"Imagine, they've been expecting me for days." She was de-
fiantly gay.

"Dragging out here for nothing—I was assured I'd get a seat,
no trouble at all."

"Well, that's how people are these days—my God, if I ran
my hotel like that. Simply re-lax, what else can you do? Thank
heaven I've got a firm booking for tomorrow."

A seat on tomorrow's plane, eh; he slid out of the conversation
and went to look for the reservations counter. There was no need
for strategy, after all; he got a firm booking, too. In the bus back
to town, she patted the seat beside her. There were two kinds of
fellow travellers, those who asked questions and those who talked

about themselves. She took the bit of a long cigarette holder between her teeth and quoted her late husband, told how her daughter, "a real little madam," at boarding school, got on like a house on fire with her new husband, said how life was what you put into it, as she always reminded her son; people asked how could one stand it, up there, miles away from everything, on the lake, but she painted, she was interested in interior decorating, she'd run the place ten years by herself, took some doing for a woman.

"On the lake?"

"Gough's Bay Hotel." He saw from the stare of the blue eyes that it was famous—he should have known.

"Tell me, whereabout are the graves, the graves of Livingstone's companions?"

The eyes continued to stare at him, a corner of the red mouth drew in proprietorially, carelessly unimpressed. "My graves. On my property. Two minutes from the hotel."

He murmured surprise. "I'd somehow imagined they were much further north."

"And there's no risk of bilharzia *whatever*," she added, apparently dispelling a rumour. "You can water-ski, goggle-fish— people have a marvellous time."

"Well, I may turn up someday."

"My dear, I've never let people down in my life. We'd find a bed somewhere."

He saw her at once, in another backless flowered dress, when he entered the departure lounge next morning. "Here we go again"—distending her nostrils in mock resignation, turning down the red lips. He gave her his small change smile and took care to lag behind when the passengers went across the runway. He sat in the tail of the plane, and opened the copy of Livingstone's last journals, bought that morning. *Our sympathies are drawn out towards our humble hardy companions by a community of interests, and, it may be, of perils, which make us all friends.* The book rested on his thighs and he slept through the hour-and-a-half's journey. Livingstone had walked it, taking ten months and recording his position by the stars. This could be the lead for his story, he thought: waking up to the recognition of the habits of his mind like the same old face in the shaving mirror.

The capital of this country was hardly distinguishable from the one he had left. The new national bank with air-conditioning and rubber plants changed the perspective of the row of Indian stores. Behind the main street a native market stank of dried fish. He hired a car, borrowed a map from the hotel barman, and set out for "the interior" next day, distrusting—from long experience —both car and map. He had meant merely to look up a few places and easy references in the Journals, but had begun to read and gone on half the night. *A wife ran away, I asked how many he had; he told me twenty in all: I then thought he had nineteen too many. He answered with the usual reason, "But who would cook for strangers if I had but one?"* . . . *It is with sorrow that I have to convey the sad intelligence that your brother died yesterday morning about ten o'clock* . . . *no remedy seemed to have much effect. On the 20th he was seriously ill but took soup several times, and drank claret and water with relish.* . . . *A lion roars mightily. The fish-hawk utters his weird voice in the morning, as if he lifted up to a friend at a great distance, in a sort of falsetto key.* . . . *The men engaged refuse to go to Matipa's, they have no honour.* . . . *Public punishment to Chirango for stealing beads, fifteen cuts; diminished his load to 40 lbs.* . . . *In four hours we came within sight of the lake, and saw plenty of elephants and other game.* How enjoyable it would have been to read the journals six thousand miles away, in autumn, at home, in London. As usual, once off the circuit that linked the capital with the two or three other small towns that existed, there were crossroads without signposts, and place names that turned out to be one general store, an African bar, and a hand-operated petrol pump, unattended. He was not fool enough to forget to carry petrol, and he was good at knocking up the bar owners (asleep during the day). As if the opening of the beer refrigerator and the

record player were inseparably linked—as a concept of hospitality if not mechanically—African jazz jog-trotted, clacked
and drummed forth while he drank on a dirty veranda. Children
dusty as chickens gathered. As he drove off the music stopped in
mid-record.

By early afternoon he was lost. The map, sure enough, failed to
indicate that the fly-speck named as Moambe was New Moambe,
a completely different place in an entirely different direction
from that of Old Moambe, where Livingstone had had a camp,
and had talked with chiefs whose descendants were active in the
present-day politics of their country (another lead). Before setting
out, Carl Church had decided that all he was prepared to do was
take a car, go to Moambe, take no more than two days over it,
and write a piece using the journey as a peg for what he did
know something about—this country's attempt to achieve a
form of African socialism. That's what the paper would get, all
they would get, except the expense account for the flight, car,
and beers. (The beers were jotted down as "Lunch, Sundries,
Gratuities, £3. 10." No reason, from Bartram's perspective, why
there shouldn't be a Livingstone Hilton in His Steps.) But when
he found he had missed Moambe and past three in the afternoon
was headed in the wrong direction, he turned the car savagely in
the road and made for what he hoped would turn out to be the
capital. All they would get would be the expense account. He
stopped and asked the way of anyone he met, and no one spoke
English. People smiled and instructed the foreigner volubly, with
many gestures. He had the humiliation of finding himself twice
back at the same crossroads where the same old man sat calmly
with women who carried dried fish stiff as Chinese preserved
ducks. He took another road, any road, and after a mile or two
of hesitancy and obstinacy—turn back or go on?—thought
he saw a signpost ahead. This time it was not a dead tree. A sagging wooden finger drooped down a turn-off: GOUGH'S BAY LAZITI
PASS.

The lake.

He was more than a hundred miles from the capital. With a

sense of astonishment at finding himself, he focused his existence, here and now, on the empty road, at a point on the map. He turned down to petrol, a bath, a drink—that much, at least, so assured that he did not have to think of it. But the lake was farther away than the casualness of the sign would indicate. The pass led the car whining and grinding in low gear round silent hillsides of white rock and wild fig trees leaning out into ravines. This way would be impassable in the rains; great stones scraped the oilsump as he disappeared into steep stream-beds, dry, the sand wrung into hanks where torrents had passed. He met no one, saw no hut. When he coughed, alone in the car he fancied this noise of his thrown back from the stony face of hill to hill like the bark of a solitary baboon. The sun went down. He thought: there was only one good moment the whole day; when I drank that beer on the veranda, and the children came up the steps to watch me and hear the music.

An old European image was lodged in his tiredness: the mirage, if the road ever ended, of some sort of Southern resort village, coloured umbrellas, a street of white hotels beside water and boats. As the road unravelled from the pass into open bush, there came that moment when, if he had had a companion, they would have stopped talking. Two, three miles; the car rolled in past the ruins of an arcaded building to the barking of dogs, the horizontal streak of water behind the bush, outhouses and water tanks, a raw new house. A young man in bathing trunks with his back to the car stood on the portico steps, pushing a flipper off one foot with the toes of the other. As he hopped for balance he looked round. Blond wet curls licked the small head on the tall body, vividly empty blue eyes were the eyes of some nocturnal animal dragged out in daylight.

"Can you tell me where there's a hotel?"

Staring, on one leg: "Yes, this's the hotel."

Carl Church said, foolishly pleasant, "There's no sign, you see."

"Well, place's being redone." He came, propping the flippers against the wall, walking on the outside edges of his feet over the remains of builders' rubble. "Want any help with that?" But Carl Church had only his typewriter and the one suitcase. They struggled indoors together, the young man carrying flippers, two spearguns and goggles. "Get anything?" "Never came near the big ones." His curls sprang and drops flowed from them. He dropped the goggles, then a wet gritty flipper knocked against Carl Church. "Hell, I'm sorry." He dumped his tackle on a desk in the passage, looked at Carl Church's case and portable, put gangling hands upon little hips and took a great breath: "Where those boys are when you want one of them—that's the problem." "Look, I haven't booked," said Church. "I suppose you've got a room?"

"What's today?" Even his eyelashes were wet. The skin on the narrow cheekbones whitened as if over knuckles.

"Thursday."

A great question was solved triumphantly, grimly. "If it'd been Saturday, now—the weekends, I mean, not a chance."

"I think I met someone on the plane—"

"Go on—" The face cocked in attention.

"She runs a hotel here . . . ?"

"Madam in person. D'jou see who met her? My step-father?" But Carl Church had not seen the airport blonde once they were through customs. "That's Lady Jane all right. Of course she hasn't turned up here yet. So she's arrived, eh? Well thanks for the warning. Just a sec, you've got to sign," and he pulled over a leather register, yelling, "Zelide, where've you disappeared to—" as a girl with a bikini cutting into heavy red thighs appeared and said in the cosy, long-suffering voice of an English provincial, "You're making it all wet, Dick—oh give here."

They murmured in telegraphic intimacy. "What about number 16?" "I thought a chalet." "Well, I dunno, it's your job, my girl—" She gave a parenthetic yell and a barefoot African came from the back somewhere to shoulder the luggage. The young man was dismantling his speargun, damp backside hitched up on the reception desk. The girl moved his paraphernalia patiently aside. "W'd you like some tea in your room, sir?"

"Guess who w's on the plane with him. Lady Godiva. So we'd better brace ourselves."

"Dickie! Is she really?"

"In person."

The girl led Carl Church out over a terrace into a garden where rondavels and cottages were dispersed. It was rapidly getting dark; only the lake shone. She had a shirt knotted under her breasts over the bikini, and when she shook her shaggy brown hair—turning on the light in an ugly little outhouse that smelled of cement—a round, boiled face smiled at him. "These chalets are brand new. We might have to move you Saturday, but jist as well enjoy yourself in the meantime." "I'll be leaving in the morning." Her cheeks were so sunburned they looked as if they would bleed when she smiled. "Oh what a shame. Aren't you even going to have a go at spear-fishing?" "Well, no; I haven't brought any equipment or anything." He might have been a child who had no bucket and spade; "Oh not to worry, Dick's got all the gear. You come out with us in the morning, after breakfast—okay?" "Fine," he said, knowing he would be gone.

The sheets of one bed witnessed the love-making of previous occupants; they had not used the other. Carl Church stumbled around in the dark looking for the ablution block—across a yard, but the light switch did not work in the bathroom. He was about to trudge over to the main house to ask for a lamp when he was arrested by the lake, as by the white of an eye in a face hidden by darkness. At least there was a towel. He took it and went down in his pants, feeling his way through shrubs, rough grass, over turned-up earth, touched by warm breaths of scent, startled by squawks from lumps that resolved into fowls, to the lake. It held still a skin of light from the day that had flown upward. He entered it slowly; it seemed to drink him in, ankles, knees, thighs, sex, waist, breast. It was cool as the inside of a mouth. Suddenly hundreds of tiny fish leapt out all round him, bright new tin in the warm, dark, heavy air.

*. . . I enclose a lock of his hair; I had his papers sealed up soon after his decease and will endeavour to transmit them all to you exactly as he left them.*

Carl Church endured the mosquitoes and the night heat only by clinging to the knowledge, through his tattered sleep, that soon it would be morning and he would be gone. But in the morning there was the lake. He got up at five to pee. He saw now how the lake stretched to the horizon from the open arms of the bay. Two bush-woolly islands glided on its surface; it was the colour of pearls. He opened his stale mouth wide and drew in a full breath, half-sigh, half-gasp. Again he went down to the water and, without bothering whether there was anybody about, took off his pyjama shorts and swam. Cool. Impersonally cool, at this time. The laved mosquito bites stung pleasurably. When he looked down upon the water while in it, it was no longer nacre, but pellucid, a pale and tender green. His feet were gleaming tendrils. A squat spotted fish hung near his legs, mouthing. He didn't move, either. Then he did what he had done when he was seven or eight years old, he made a cage of his hands and pounced—but the element reduced him to slow motion, everything, fish, legs, glassy solidity, wriggled and flowed away and slowly undulated into place again. The fish returned. On a dead tree behind bird-splattered rocks ellipsed by the water at this end of the beach, a fish-eagle lifted its head between hunched white shoulders and cried out; a long whistling answer came across the lake as another flew in. He swam around the rocks through schools of fingerlings as close as gnats, and hauled himself up within ten feet of the eagles. They carried the remoteness of the upper air with them in the long-sighted gaze of their hooded eyes; nothing could approach its vantage; he did not exist for them, while the gaze took in the expanse of the lake and the smallest indication of life rising to its surface. He came back to the beach and walked with a towel round his middle as far as a baobab tree where a black man with an ivory bangle on either wrist was mending nets, but then he noticed a blue bubble on the verge—it was an infant afloat on some plastic beast, its mother in attendance—and turned away, up to the hotel.

He left his packed suitcase on the bed and had breakfast. The dining-room was a veranda under sagging grass matting; now, in the morning, he could see the lake, of course, while he ate. He was feeling for change to leave for the waiter when the girl padded in, dressed in her bikini, and shook corn flakes into a plate. "Oh hullo, sir. Early bird you are." He imagined her lying down at night just as she was, ready to begin again at once the ritual of alternately dipping and burning her seared flesh. They chatted. She had been in Africa only three months, out from Liverpool in answer to an advertisement—receptionist/secretary, hotel in beautiful surroundings. "More of a holiday than a job," he said. "Don't make me laugh"—but she did. "We were on the go until half-past one, night before last, making the changeover in the bar. You see the bar used to be here—" she lifted her spoon at the wall, where he now saw mildew-traced shapes beneath a mural in which a girl in a bosom-laced peasant outfit appeared to have given birth, through one ear, Rabelaisian fashion, to a bunch of grapes. He had noticed the old Chianti bottles, by lamplight, at dinner the night before, but not the mural. "Dickie's got his ideas, and then she's artistic, you see." The young man was coming up the steps of the veranda that moment, stamping his sandy feet at the cat, yelling towards the kitchen, blue eyes open as the fish's had been staring at Carl Church through the water. He wore his catch like a kilt, hooked all round the belt of his trunks.

"I been thinking about those damn trees," he said.

"Oh my heavens. How many's still there?"

"*There* all right, but nothing but blasted firewood. Wait till she sees the holes, just where she had them dug."

The girl was delighted by the fish: "Oh pretty!"

But he slapped her hands and her distractibility away. "Some people ought to have their heads read," he said to Carl Church.

"If you can tell me why I had to come back here, well, I'd be grateful. I had my own combo, down in Rhodesia." He removed the fish from his narrow middle and sat on a chair turned away from her table.

"Why don't we get the boys to stick 'em in, today? They could've died after being planted out, after all, ay?"

He seemed too gloomy to hear her. Drops from his wet curls fell on his shoulders. She bent towards him kindly, wheedlingly, meat of her thighs and breasts pressing together. "If we put two boys on it, they'd have them in by lunch-time? Dickie? And if it'll make her happy? Dickie?"

"I've got ideas of my own. But when Madam's here you can forget it, just forget it. No sooner start something—just get started, that's all—she chucks it up and wants something different again." His gaze wavered once or twice to the wall where the bar had been. Carl Church asked what the fish were. He didn't answer, and the girl encouraged, "Perch. Aren't they, Dickie? Yes, perch. You'll have them for your lunch. Lovely eating."

"Oh what the hell. Let's go. You ready?" he said to Church. The girl jumped up and he hooked an arm round her neck, feeling in her rough hair.

"Course he's ready. The black flippers'll fit him—the stuff's in the bar," she said humouringly.

"But I haven't even got a pair of trunks."

"Who cares? I can tell you I'm just-not-going-to-worry-a-damn. Here Zelide, I nearly lost it this morning." He removed a dark stone set in Christmas-cracker baroque from his rock-scratched hand, nervous-boned as his mother's ankles, and tossed it for the girl to catch. "Come, I've got the trunks," she said, and led Carl Church to the bar by way of the reception desk, stopping to wrap the ring in a pink tissue and pop it in the cash box.

The thought of going to the lake once more was irresistible. His bag was packed; an hour or two wouldn't make any difference. He had been skin-diving before, in Sardinia, and did not expect the bed of the lake to compare with the Mediterranean, but if the architecture of undersea was missing, the fish one could get at were much bigger than he had ever caught in the Mediterranean. The young man disappeared for minutes and rose again between Carl Church and the girl, his Gothic Christ's body sucked in below the nave of ribs, his goggles leaving weals like duelling scars on his white cheekbones. Water ran from the tarnished curls over the bright eyeballs without seeming to make him blink. He brought up fish deftly and methodically and the girl swam back to shore with them, happy as a retrieving dog.

Neither she nor Carl Church caught much themselves. And then Church went off on his own, swimming slowly with the borrowed trunks inflating above the surface like a striped Portuguese man-of-war, and far out, when he was not paying attention but looking back at the skimpy white buildings, the flowering shrubs and even the giant baobab razed by distance and the optical illusion of the heavy waterline, at eye-level, about to black them out, he heard a fish-eagle scream just overhead; looked up, looked down, and there below him saw three fish at different levels, a mobile swaying in the water. This time he managed the gun without thinking; he had speared the biggest.

The girl was as impartially overjoyed as she was when the young man had a good catch. They went up the beach, laughing, explaining, a water-intoxicated progress. The accidental bump of her thick sandy thigh against his was exactly the tactile sensation of contact with the sandy body of the fish, colliding with him as he carried it. The young man was squatting on the beach, now, his long back arched over his knees. He was haranguing, in an African language, the old fisherman with the ivory bracelets who was still at work on the nets. There were dramatic pauses, accusatory rises of tone, hard jerks of laughter, in the monologue. The old man said nothing. He was an Arabized African from far up the lake somewhere in East Africa, and wore an old towel turban as well as the ivory; every now and then he wrinkled back his lips on tooth-stumps. Three or four long black dugouts had come in during the morning and were beached; black men sat motionless in what small shade they could find. The baby on his blue swan still floated under his mother's surveillance—she turned a

visor of sunglasses and hat. It was twelve o'clock; Carl Church
merely felt amused at himself—how different the measure of
time when you were absorbed in something you didn't earn a living by. "Those must weigh a pound a piece," he said idly, of the
ivory manacles shifting on the net-mender's wrists.

"D'jou want one?" the young man offered. (*My graves*, the
woman had said, *on my property*.) "I'll get him to sell it to you.
Take it for your wife."

But Carl Church had no wife at present, and no desire for loot;
he preferred everything to stay as it was, in its place, at noon by
the lake. Twenty thousand slaves a year had passed this way, up
the water. Slavers, missionaries, colonial servants—all had
brought something and taken something away. He would have a
beer and go, changing nothing, claiming nothing. He plodded to
the hotel a little ahead of the couple, who were mumbling over
hotel matters and pausing now and then to fondle each other. As
his bare soles encountered the smoothness of the terrace steps he
heard the sweet, loud, reasonable feminine voice, saw one of the
houseboy-waiters racing across in his dirty jacket—and quickly
turned away to get to his room unnoticed. But with a perfect instinct for preventing escape, she was at once out upon the
dining-room veranda, all crude blues and yellows—hair,
eyes, flowered dress, a beringed hand holding the cigarette away
exploratively. Immediately, her son passed Church in a swift,
damp tremor. "Well, God, look at my best girl—mm-мнн . . .
madam in per-son." He lifted her off her feet and she landed
swirling giddily on the high heels in the best tradition of the
Fred Astaire films she and Carl Church had been brought up on.
Her laugh seemed to go over her whole body. "Well?" "And so,
my girl?" They rocked together. "You been behaving yourself in
the big city?" "Dickie—for Pete's sake—he's like a spaniel—"
calling Carl Church to witness.

A warm baby-smell beside him (damp crevices and cold cream)
was the presence of the girl. "Oh Mrs. Palmer, we were so worried you'd got lost or something."

"My dear. My you're looking well—" The two vacant, inescapable blue stares took in the bikini, the luxuriously inflamed skin, as if the son's gaze were directed by the mother's. Mrs. Palmer and the girl kissed but Mrs. Palmer's eyes moved like a lighthouse beam over the wall where the bar was gone, catching Carl Church in his borrowed swimming trunks. "Wha'd'you think of my place?" she asked. "How d'you like it here, eh? Not that I know it myself, after two months . . ." Hands on hips, she looked at the peasant girl and the mildewed outlines as if she were at an exhibition. She faced sharply round and her son kissed her on the mouth: "We're dying for a beer, that's what. We've been out since breakfast. Zelide, the boy—"

"Yes, he *knows* he's on duty on the veranda today—just a minute, I'll get it—"

Mrs. Palmer was smiling at the girl wisely. "My dear, once you start doing their jobs for them . . ."

"Shadrach!" The son made a megaphone of his hands, shaking his silver identification bracelet out of the way. The girl stood, eagerly bewildered.

"Oh it's nothing. Only a minute—" and bolted.

"Where is the bar, now, Dickie?" said his mother as a matter of deep, polite interest.

"I must get some clothes on and return your trunks," Carl Church was saying.

"Oh, it makes a world of difference. You'll see. You can move in that bar. Don't you think so?" The young man gave the impression that he was confirming a remark of Church's rather than merely expressing his own opinion. Carl Church, to withdraw, said, "Well, I don't know what it was like before."

She claimed him now. "It was here, in the open, of course, people loved it. A taverna atmosphere. Dickie's never been overseas."

"Really *move*. And you've got those big doors."

She drew Church into the complicity of a smile for grownups, then remarked, as if for her part the whole matter were calmly accepted, settled, "I presume it's the games room?"

Her son said to Church, sharing the craziness of women,

"There never was a games room, it was the lounge, can you see a lot of old birds sitting around in armchairs in a place like this?"

"The lounge that was going to be redecorated as a games room," she said. She smiled at her son.

The girl came back, walking flat-footed under a tray's weight up steps that led by way of a half-built terrace to the new bar. As Carl Church went to help her she breathed, "What a performance."

Mrs. Palmer drew on her cigarette and contemplated the steps: "Imagine the breakages."

The four of them were together round beer bottles. Church sat helplessly in his borrowed trunks that crawled against his body as they dried, drinking pint after pint and aware of his warmth, the heat of the air, and all their voices rising steadily. He said, "I must get going," but the waiter had called them to lunch three times; the best way to break up the party was to allow oneself to be forced to table. The three of them ate in their bathing costumes while madam took the head, bracelets colliding on her arms. He made an effort to get precise instructions about the best and quickest route back to the capital, and was told expertly by her, "There's no plane out until Monday, nine-fifteen, I suppose you know that." "I have no reason whatever to doubt your knowledge of plane schedules," he said, and realized from the turn of phrase that he must be slightly drunk, on heat and the water as much as beer.

She knew the game so well that you had only to finger a counter unintentionally for her to take you on. "I told you I never let anyone down." She blew a smokescreen; appeared through it. "Where've they put you?"

"Oh, he's in one of the chalets, Mrs. Palmer," the girl said. "Till tomorrow, anyway."

"Well, there you are, re-lax," she said. "If the worst comes to the worst, there's a room in my cottage." Her gaze was out over the lake, a tilting, blind brightness with black dugouts appearing like sunspots, but she said, "How're my jacarandas coming along? Someone was telling me there's no reason why they shouldn't do,

Dickie. The boys must make a decent trench round each one and
let it *fill up* with water once a week, *right* up, d'you see?"

*The effect of travel on a man whose heart is in the right place
is that the mind is made more self-reliant; it becomes more confident of its own resources—there is greater presence of mind.
The body is soon well-knit; the muscles of the limbs grow hard
as a board . . . the countenance is bronzed and there is no dys-
pepsia.*
    Carl Church slept through the afternoon. He woke to the feel-
ing of helplessness he had at lunch. But no chagrin. This sort of
hiatus had opened up in the middle of a tour many times—lost
days in a blizzard on Gander airport, a week in quarantine at
Aden. This time he had the Journals instead of a Gideon Bible.
*Nothing fell from his lips as last words to survivors. We buried
him to-day by a large baobab tree.* There was no point in going
back to the capital if he couldn't get out of the place till Monday. His mind was closed to the possibility of trying for
Moambe, again; that was another small rule for self-preservation:
if something goes wrong, write it off. He thought, it's all right
here; the dirty, ugly room had as much relevance to "spoiling"
the eagles and the lake as he had had to the eagles when he
climbed close. On his way down to the lake again he saw a little
group—mother, son, receptionist—standing round the grave-
side of one of the holes for trees. Dickie was still in his bathing
trunks.
    Church had the goggles and the flippers and the speargun, and
he swam out towards the woolly islands—they were unattain-
ably far—and fish were dim dead leaves in the water below him.
The angle of the late afternoon sun left the underwater deserted,
filled with motes of vegetable matter and sand caught by oblique
rays of light. Milky brilliance surrounded him, his hands went
out as if to feel for walls; there was the apprehension, down
there, despite the opacity and tepidity, of night and cold. He shot
up to the surface and felt the day on his eyelids. Lying on the
sand, he heard the eagles cry now behind him on the headland,

where trees held boulders in their claws, now over the lake. A
pair of piebald kingfishers squabbled, a whirling disk, in midair,
and plummeted again and again. Butterflies with the same black
and white markings went slowly out over the water. The Arabized fisherman was still working at his nets.

Some weekend visitors arrived from the hotel, shading their
eyes against the sheen of the lake; soon they stood in it like stat-
ues broken off at the waist. Voices flew out across the water after
the butterflies. As the sun drowned, a dhow climbed out of its
dazzle and dipped steadily towards the beach. It picked up the
fisherman and his nets, sending a tiny boat ashore. The dhow lay
beating slowly, like an exhausted bird. The visitors ran together
to watch as they would have for a rescue, a monster—any sign
from the lake.

Carl Church had been lying with his hand slack on the sand as
on a warm body; he got up and walked past the people, past the
bao-bab, as far along the beach as it went before turning into an
outwork of oozy reeds. He pushed his feet into his shoes and
went up inland, through the thorn bushes. As soon as he turned
his back on it, the lake did not exist; unlike the sea that spread
and sucked in your ears even when your eyes were closed. A
total silence. Livingstone could have come upon the lake quite
suddenly, and just as easily have missed it. The mosquitoes and
gnats rose with the going down of the sun. Swatted on Church's
face, they stuck in sweat. The air over the lake was free, but the
heat of day cobwebbed the bush. *We then hoped that his youth
and unimpaired constitution would carry him through . . . but
about six o'clock in the evening his mind began to wander and
continued to. His bodily powers continued gradually to sink till
the period mentioned when he quietly expired . . . there he rests
in sure and certain hope of a glorious Resurrection.* He thought
he might have a look at the graves, the graves of Livingstone's
companions, but the description of how to find them given him
that morning by the young man and the girl was that of people
who know a place so well they cannot imagine anyone being unable to walk straight to it. A small path, they said, just off the

road. He found himself instead among ruined arcades whose whiteness intensified as the landscape darkened. It was an odd ruin: a solid complex of buildings, apparently not in bad repair, had been pulled down. It was the sort of demolition one saw in a fast-growing city, where a larger structure would be begun at once where the not-old one had been. The bush was all around; as far as the Congo, as far as the latitude where the forests began. A conical anthill had risen to the height of the arcades, where a room behind them must have been. A huge moon sheeny as the lake came up and a powdery blue heat held in absolute stillness. Carl Church thought of the graves. It was difficult to breathe; it must have been hell to die here, in this unbearable weight of beauty not shared with the known world, licked in the face by the furred tongue of this heat.

Round the terrace and hotel the ground was pitted by the stakes of high heels; they sounded over the floors where everyone else went barefoot. The shriek and scatter of chickens opened before a constant coming and going of houseboys and the ragged work gang whose activities sent up the regular grunt of axe thudding into stumps, and the crunch of spade gritting into earth. The tree-holes had been filled in. Dickie was seen in his bathing trunks but did not appear on the beach. Zelide wore a towelling chemise over her bikini, and when the guests were at lunch, went from table to table bending to talk softly with her rough hair hiding her face. Carl Church saw that the broken skin on her nose and cheeks was repaired with white cream. She said confidentially, "I just wanted to tell you there'll be a sort of beach party tonight, being Saturday. Mrs. Palmer likes to have a fire on the beach, and some snacks—you know. Of course, we'll all eat here first. You're welcome."

He said, "How about my room?"

Her voice sank to a chatty whisper, "Oh it'll be all right, one crowd's cancelled."

Going to the bar for cigarettes, he heard mother and son in there. "Wait, wait, all that's worked out. I'mn'a cover the whole thing with big blow-ups of the top groups, the Stones and the Shadows and such-like."

"Oh grow up, Dickie my darling, you want it to look like a teenager's bedroom?"

Church went quietly away, remembering there might be a packet of cigarettes in the car, but bumped into Dickie a few minutes later, in the yard. Dickie had his skin-diving stuff and was obviously on his way to the lake. "I get into shit for moving the bar without telling the licensing people over in town, and then she says let's have the bar counter down on the beach tonight—all in the same breath, that's *nothing* to her. At least when my stepfather's here he knows just how to put the brake on."

"Where is he?"

"I don't know, something about some property of hers, in town. He's got to see about it. But he's always got business all over, for her. I had my own band, you know, we've even toured Rhodesia. I'm a solo artist, really. Guitar. I compose my own stuff. I mean, what I play's original, you see. Night club engagements and such-like."

"That's a tough life compared with this," Church said, glancing at the speargun.

"Oh, this's all right. If you learn how to do it well, y'know? I've trained myself. You've got to concentrate. Like with my guitar. I have to go away and be *undisturbed*, you understand—right away. Sometimes the mood comes, sometimes it doesn't. Sometimes I compose all night. I got to be left *in peace*." He was fingering a new thick silver chain on his wrist. "Lady Jane, of course. God knows what it cost. She spends a fortune on presents. You sh'd see what my sister gets when she's home. And what she gave my stepfather—I mean before, when they weren't married yet. He must have ten pairs of cuff-links, gold, I don't know what." He sat down under the weight of his mother's generosity. Zelide appeared among the empty gas containers and beer crates outside the kitchen. 'Oh, Dickie, you've had no lunch. I don't think he ever tastes a thing he catches." Dickie squeezed her thigh and said coldly, "S'best time, now. People don't know it. Between now and about half-past three."

There had always been something more than a family resemblance about that face; at last it fell into place in Church's mind. Stiff blond curls, skull ominously present in the eye sockets, shiny cheekbones furred with white hairs, blue-red lips, and those eyes that seemed to have no eyelids, to turn away from nothing and take in nothing: the face of the homosexual boy in the Berlin twenties, the perfect, impure master-race face of a George Grosz drawing.

"Oh Dickie, I wish you'd eat something. And he's got to play tonight." They watched him lope off lightly down the garden. Her hair and the sun obscured her. "They're both artistic, you see, that's the trouble. What a performance."

"Are you sorry you came?"

"Oh no. The weather's so lovely, I mean, isn't it?"

It was becoming a habit to open Livingstone's Journals at random before falling stunned-asleep. *Now that I am on the point of starting another trip into Africa I feel quite exhilarated: when one travels with the specific object in view of ameliorating the condition of the natives every act becomes ennobled.* The afternoon heat made him think of women, this time, and he gave up his siesta because he believed that daydreams of this kind were not so much adolescent as—worse—a sign of approaching age. He was getting—too far along, for pauses like this; for time out. If he were not preoccupied with doing the next thing, he did not know what to do. His mind turned to death, the graves that his body would not take the trouble to visit. His body turned to women; his body was unchanged. It took him down to the lake, heavy and vigorous, reddened by the sun under the black hairs shining on his belly.

The sun was high in a splendid afternoon. In half-an-hour he missed three fish and began to feel challenged. Whenever he dived deeper than fifteen or eighteen feet his ears ached much more than they ever had in the sea. Out of training, of course. And the flippers and goggles lent by the hotel really did not fit properly. The goggles leaked at every dive, and he had to surface quickly, water in his nostrils. He began to let himself float aimlessly, not diving any longer, circling around the enormous boulders with their steep polished flanks like petrified tree-trunks. He was aware, as he had been often when skin-diving, of how active his brain became in this world of silence; ideas and images interlocking in his mind while his body was leisurely moving, enjoying at once the burning sun on his exposed shoulders and the cooling water on his shrunken penis—good after too many solitary nights filled with erotic dreams.

Then he saw the fish, deep down, twenty feet maybe, a yellowish nonchalant shape which seemed to pasture in a small forest of short dead reeds. He took a noble breath, dived with all the power and swiftness he could summon from his body, and shot. The miracle happened again. The nonchalant shape became a frenzied spot of light, reflecting the rays of the sun in a series of flashes through the pale blue water as it swivelled in agony round the spear. It was—this moment—the only miracle Church knew; no wonder Africans used to believe that the hunter's magic worked when the arrow found the prey.

He swam up quickly, his eyes on the fish hooked at the end of the spear, feeling the tension of its weight while he was hauling it and the line between spear and gun straightened. Eight pounds, ten, perhaps. Even Dickie with his silver amulets and bracelets couldn't do better. He reached the surface, hurriedly lifted the goggles to rid them of water, and dived again: the fish was still continuing its spiralling fight. He saw now that he had not transfixed it; only the point of the spear had penetrated the body. He began carefully to pull the line towards him; the spear was in his hand when, with a slow motion, the fish unhooked itself before his eyes.

In its desperate, thwarted leaps it had unscrewed the point and twirled loose. This had happened once before, in the Mediterranean, and since then Church had taken care to tighten the spearhead from time to time while fishing. Today he had forgotten. Disappointment swelled in him. Breathlessness threatened to burst him like a bubble. He had to surface, abandoning the gun in order to free both arms. The fish disappeared round a boulder with the point of the harpoon protuding from its open belly amid flimsy pinkish ribbons of entrails; the gun was floating at mid distance between the surface and the bed of the lake, anchored to the spear sunk in dead reeds.

Yet the splendour of the afternoon remained. He lay and smoked and drank beer brought by a waiter who roamed the sand, flicking a napkin. Church had forgotten what had gone wrong, to bring him to this destination. He was *here;* as he was not often fully present in the places and situations in which he found himself. It was some sort of answer to the emptiness he had felt on the bed. Was this how the first travellers had borne it, each day detached from the last and the next, taking each night that night's bearing by the stars?

Madam—Lady Jane in person—had sent down a boy to pick up bottle tops and cigarette stubs from the water's edge. She had high standards. (She had said so in the bar last night. "The trouble is, *they'll* never be any different, they just don't know how to look after anything.") This was the enlightenment the discoverers had brought the black man in the baggage he portered for them on his head. This one was singing to himself as he worked. If the plans that were being made in the capital got the backing of the World Bank and the UN Development Fund and all the rest of it, his life would change. Whatever happened to him, he would lose the standard that had been set by people who maintained it by using him to pick up their dirt. Church thought of the ruin—he'd forgotten to ask what it was. Lady Jane's prefabricated concrete blocks and terrazzo would fall down more easily.

He had had a shirt washed and although he was sweating under the light bulb when he put it on for dinner, he seemed to have accustomed himself to the heat, now. He was also very sunburned. The lady with the small child sat with a jolly party of Germans in brown sandals—apparently from a Lutheran Mission nearby—and there was a group of men down from the capital on a bachelor binge of skin-diving and drinking who were aware of being the life of the place. They caught out at Zelide, her thick feet pressed into smart shoes, her hair lifted on top of her head, her eyes made up to twice their size. She bore her transformation bravely, smiling. "You are coming down to the beach, arnch you?" She went, concerned, from table to table. Mrs. Palmer's heels announced her with the authority of a Spanish dancer. She had on a strapless blue dress and silver sandals, and carried a little gilt bag like an outsize cigarette box. She joined the missionary party: "*Wie geht's*, Father, have you been missing me?" Dickie didn't appear. Through the frangipani, the fire on the beach was already sending up scrolls of flame.

Church knew he would be asked to join one group or another and out of a kind of shame of anticipated boredom (last night there had been one of those beer-serious conversations about the possibility of the end of the world: "They say the one thing'll survive an atomic explosion is the ant. The ant's got something special in its body, y'see") he went into the empty bar after dinner. The little black barman was almost inaudible, in order to disguise his lack of English. There was an array of fancy bottles set up on the shelves but most of them seemed to belong to Mrs. Palmer's store of *objets d'art:* "Is finish'." Church had to content himself with a brandy from South Africa. He asked whether a dusty packet of cigarillos was for sale, and the barman's hand went from object to object on display before the correct one was identified. Church was smoking and throwing darts as if they were stones, when Dickie came in. Dickie wore a dinner jacket; his lapels were blue satin, his trousers braided, his shirt tucked and frilled; his hands emerged from ruffles and the little finger of the left one rubbed and turned the baroque ring on the finger beside it. He hung in the doorway a moment like a tall, fancy doll; his mother might have put him on a piano.

Church said, "My God, you're grand," and Dickie looked down at himself for a second, without interest, as one acknowledges one's familiar working garb. The little barman seemed flattened by Dickie's gaze.

"Join me?"

Dickie gave a boastful, hard-wrung smile. "No thanks. I think I've had enough already." He had the look his mother had had, when Church asked her where her hotel was. "I've been drinking all afternoon. Ever since a phone call."

"Well you don't look it," said Church. But it was the wrong tone to take up.

Dickie played a tattoo on the bar with the ringed hand, staring at it. "There was a phone call from Bulawayo, and a certain story was repeated to me. Somebody's made it their business to spread a story."

"That's upsetting."

"It may mean the loss of a future wife, that's what. My fiancée in Bulawayo. Somebody *took the trouble* to tell her there's a certain young lady in the hotel here with me. Somebody had nothing better to do than make trouble. But that young lady is my mother's secretary-receptionist, see? She works here, she's *employed*, just like me. Just like I'm the manager."

From country to country, bar to bar, Church was used to accepting people's own versions of their situations, quite independently of the facts. He and Dickie contemplated the vision of Dickie fondling Zelide in the garden as evidence of the correctness of his relations with the secretary-receptionist. "Couldn't you explain?"

"Usually if I'm, you know, depressed and that, I play my guitar. But I've just been strumming. No, I don't think I'll have any more tonight, I'm full enough already. The whole afternoon."

"Why don't you go to Bulawayo?"

Dickie picked up the darts and began to throw them, at an angle, from where he sat at the bar; while he spoke he scored three bull's eyes. "Huh, I think I'll clear out altogether. Here I earn fifty quid a month, eh? I can earn twenty pounds a night —*a night*—with a personal appearance. I've got a whole bundle of my own compositions and one day, boy!—there's got to be one that hits the top. One day it's got to happen. All my stuff is copyright, you see. Nobody's gonna cut a disc of my stuff without my permission. I see to that. Oh I could play you a dozen numbers I'm working on, they're mostly sad, you know —the folk type of thing, that's where the money is now. What's a lousy fifty quid a month?"

"I meant a quick visit, to put things straight."

"Ah, somebody's mucked up my life, all right"—he caught Church's eye as if to say, you want to see it again?—and once again planted three darts dead-centre. "I'll play you some of my compositions if you like. Don't expect too much of my voice, though, because as I say I've been drinking all afternoon. I've got no intention whatever of playing for them down there. An artist thrown in, fifty quid a month, they can think again." He ducked under the doorway and was gone. He returned at once with a guitar and bent over it professionally, making adjustments. Then he braced his long leg against the bar rail, tossed back his skull of blond curls, began a mournful lay—broke off: "I'm full of pots, you know, my voice"—and started again, high and thin, at the back of his nose.

It was a song about a bride, and riding away, and tears you cannot hide away. Carl Church held his palm round the brandy glass to conceal that it was empty and looked down into it. The barman had not moved from his stance with both hands before him on the bar and the bright light above him beating sweat out of his forehead and nose like an answer exacted under interrogation. When the stanza about death and last breath was reached, Dickie said, "It's a funny thing, me nearly losing my engagement ring this morning, eh? I might have known something"— paused—and thrummed once, twice. Then he began the song over again. Carl Church signalled for the brandy bottle. But suddenly Mrs. Palmer was there, a queen to whom no door may be closed. "Oh show a bit of spunk! Everyone's asking for you. I tell him, everyone has to take a few cracks in life, am I right?"

"Well, of course."

"Come on then, don't encourage him to feel sorry for himself. My God, if I'd sat down and cried every time."

Dickie went on playing and whispering the words to himself.

"Can't you do something with him?"

"Let's go and join the others, Dickie," Church said; he drank off the second brandy.

"One thing I've never done is let people down," Mrs. Palmer was saying. "But these kids've got no sense of responsibility. What'd happen without me I don't know."

Dickie spoke. "Well you can have it. You can have the fifty pounds a month and the car. The lot."

"Oh yes, they'd look fine without me, I can tell you. I would have given everything I've built up over to him, that was the idea, once he was married. But they know everything at once, you know, you can't teach them anything."

"Come on Dickie, what the hell—just for an hour."

They jostled him down to the fire-licked faces on the beach. A gramophone was playing and people were dancing barefoot. There were not enough women and men in shorts were drinking and clowning. Dickie was given beer; he made cryptic remarks that nobody listened to. Somebody stopped the gramophone with a screech and Dickie was tugged this way and that in a clamour to have him play the guitar. But the dancers put the record back again. The older men among the bachelors opposed the rhythm of the dancers with a war dance of their own: Hi-zoom-a-zoom-ba, zoom-zoom-zoom. Zelide kept breaking away from her partners to offer a plate of tiny burnt sausages like bird-droppings. HI-ZOOM-A-ZOOM-BA—ZOOM-ZOOM-ZOOM. Light fanned from the fire showed the dancers as figures behind gauze, but where Church was marooned, near the streaming flames, faces were gleaming, gouged with grotesque shadow. Lady Jane had a bottle of gin for the two of them. The heat of the fire seemed to consume the other heat, of the night, so that the spirit going down his gullet snuffed out on the way in a burning evaporation. HI-ZOOM-A-ZOOM-BA. At some point he was dancing with her, and she put a frangipani flower in his ear. Now Dickie, sitting drunk on a box with his long legs at an angle like a beetle's, wanted to play the guitar but nobody would listen. Church could make out

from the shapes Dickie's mouth made that he was singing the
song about the bride and riding away, but the roar of the bachelors drowned it: Hold him down, you Zulu warrior, hold him
DOWN, you Zulu chief-chief-ief. Every now and then a slight
movement through the lake sent a soft, black glittering glance in
reflection of the fire. The lake was not ten feet away but as time
went by Church had the impression that it would not be possible
for him to walk down, through the barrier of jigging firelight
and figures, and let it cover his ankles, his hands. He said to her,
topping up the two glasses where they had made a place in the
sand, "Was there another hotel?"

"There's been talk, but no one else's ever had the initiative,
when it comes to the push."

"But whose was that rather nice building, in the bush?"

"Not *my* idea of a hotel. My husband built it in forty-nine.
Started it in forty-nine, finished it fifty-two or -three. Dickie was
still a kiddie."

"But what happened? It looks as if it's been deliberately pulled
down."

CHIEF-UH-IEF-UH-IEF-IEF-IEF. The chorus was a chanting grunt.
"It was what?"

She was saying, ". . . died, I couldn't even give it away. I always told him, it's no good putting up a bloody palace of a
place, you haven't got the class of person who appreciates it. Too
big, far too big. No atmosphere, whatever you tried to do with
it. People like to feel cosy and free and easy."

He said, "I liked that colonnaded veranda, it must have been
rather beautiful," but she was yanked away to dance with one of
the bachelors. Zelide wandered about anxiously: "You quite
happy?" He took her to dance; she was putting a good face on it.
He said, "Don't worry about them, they're tough. Look at those
eyes."

"If there was somewhere to go," she said. "It's not like a town,
not like at home, you know—you can just disappear. Oh there
she is, for God's sake—"

He said to Mrs. Palmer, "That veranda, before you bulldozed it—" but she took no notice and attacked him at once: "Where's Dickie? I don't see Dickie."

"I don't know where the hell Dickie is."

Clinging to his arm she dragged him through the drinkers, the dancers, the bachelors, round the shadowy human lumps beyond the light that started away from each other, making him give a snuffling laugh because they were like the chickens that first day. She raced him stumbling up the dark terraces to Dickie's cottage, but it was overpoweringly empty with the young man's smell of musky leather and wet wool. She was alarmed as an animal who finds the lair deserted. "I tell you, he'll do something to himself." Ten yards from the bungalows and the main house, the bush was the black end of the world; they walked out into it and stood helplessly. A torch was a pale, blunt, broken stump of light. "He'll do away with himself," she panted. Church was afraid her breathing would turn to hysterics; "Come on, now, come on," he coaxed her back to the lights burning in the empty hotel. She went, but steered towards quarters he had not noticed or visited. There were lamps in pink shades. Photographs of her in the kind of dress she was wearing that night, smiling over the head of an infant Dickie. A flowered sofa they sat down on, and a little table with filigree boxes and a lighter shaped like Aladdin's lamp and gilt-covered matchbooks with *Dorothy* stamped across the corner. "Take some," she said, and began putting them in his pockets, both outer pockets of his jacket and the inner breast pocket. "Take some, I've got hundreds." She dropped her head against him and let the blond curls muffle her face: "Like his father did," she said. "I know it. I tell you I know it."

"He's passed out somewhere, that's all." She smelled of Chanel No 5, the only perfume he could identify, because he had bought it on the black market for various girls in Cairo during the war. Where she leant on him her breasts were warmer than the rest of her.

"I tell you I know he'll do something to himself sooner or later. It runs in families, I know it."

"Don't worry. It's all right." He thought: an act of charity. It was terribly dark outside; the whole night was cupped round the small flickering of flames and figures, figures like flames, reaching upwards in flame, snatched by the dark, on the beach. He knew the lake was there; neither heard nor seen, quite black. The lake. The lake. He felt, inevitably, something resembling desire, but it was more like a desire for the cool mouth of waters that would close over ankles, knees, thighs, sex. He was drunk and not very capable, and felt he would never get there, to the lake. The lake became an unslakable thirst, the night-thirst, the early-morning thirst that cannot stir a hand for the surcease of water.

When he awoke sometime in his chalet, it was because consciousness moved towards a sound that he could identify even before he was awake. Dickie was playing the guitar behind closed doors somewhere, playing again and again the song of the bride and the riding away.

Zelide wore her bikini, drawing up the bill for him in the morning. The demarcation lines at shoulder-straps and thighs had become scarlet weals; the sun was eating into her, poor cheerful adventuring immigrant. She had been taken up by the bachelors and was about to go out with them in their boat. "Maybe we'll bump into each other again," she said.

And of course they might; handed around the world from country to country, minor characters who crop up. There was an air of convalescence about the hotel. On the terrace, empty bottles were coated with ants; down at the beach, boys were burying the ashes of the bonfire and their feet scuffed over the shapes—like resting-places flattened in grass by cattle—where couples had been secreted by the night. He saw Mrs. Palmer in a large sun hat, waving her tough brown arms about in command over a gang who, resting on their implements, accepted her as they did sun, flies, and rain. Two big black pairs of sunglasses—his and hers—flashed back and forth blindly as they stood, with Zelide, amid the building rubble in the garden.

"Don't forget to look us up if ever you're out this way."

"One never knows."

"With journalists, my God, no, you could find yourself at the North Pole! We'll always find a bed for you. Has Dickie said good-bye?"

"Say good-bye to him for me, will you?"

She put out her jingling, gold-flashing hand and he saw (as if it had been a new line on his own face) the fine, shiny tan of her forearm wrinkle with the movement. "Happy landings," she said.

Zelide watched him drive off. "You've not forgotten anything? You'd be surprised at people. I don't know what to do with the stuff, half the time." She smiled and her stomach bulged over the bikini; she had the sort of pioneering spirit, the instincts of self-preservation appropriate to her time and kind.

Past the fowls, water tanks and outhouses, the hot silent arcades of the demolished hotel, the car rocked and swayed over the track. Suddenly he saw the path, the path he had missed the other day, to the graves of Livingstone's companions. It was just where Dickie and Zelide had said. He was beyond it by the time he understood this, but all at once it seemed absurd not even to have gone to have a look, after three days. He stopped the car and walked back. He took the narrow path that was snagged with thorn bushes and led up the hill between trees too low and meagre of foliage to give shade. The earth was picked clean by the dry season. Flies settled at once upon his shoulders. He was annoyed by the sound of his own lack of breath; and then there, where the slope of the hill came up short against a steep rise, the gravestones stood with their backs to rock. The five neat headstones of the monuments commission were surmounted each by an iron cross on a circle. The names, and the dates of birth and death—the deaths all in the last quarter of the nineteenth century—were engraved on the granite. A yard or two away, but in line with the rest, was another gravestone. Carl Church moved over to read the inscription; In Memory of Richard Alastair Macnab, Beloved Husband of Dorothy and Father of Richard and Heather, died 1957. They all looked back, these dead companions, to the lake, the lake that Carl Church (turning to face as they did, now) had had silent behind him all the way up; the lake that, from here, was seen to stretch much farther than one could tell, down there on the shore or at the hotel: stretching still—even from up here—as far as one could see, flat and shining; a long way up Africa.

# A THIRD PRESENCE

$W$HEN ROSE and Naomi, daughters of poor
Rasovsky the tailor, left school in the same year there was no dis-
cussion about what they should do, because there was no question about the necessity to do it. The old Rasovskys had got the
naming of the daughters all wrong. Naomi was everything
"Rose" suggested, Naomi was pretty and must marry the scrap
metal dealer who would give a home to the old Rasovskys and
the girls' brother; Rose, who cruelly bore her name along with
the sad Jewish ugliness of her face, was clever and must get a job
to help support the family. The boys who flocked around Naomi
and with one of whom she might have fallen in love didn't come
into the decision any more than the university scholarship Rose
had won. Certainly, necessity being what it was, Naomi was the
one who came off best: the husband built her a red-brick house
in the new suburb marked out in the veld of the small South African town, she enjoyed the fun of choosing furniture and the
status of being called "Mrs.", and soon she had the importance of
having produced a baby, and a son at that. Rose, on a Sunday af-

ternoon, came to see the baby for the first time and at the bedside, where Naomi was surrounded by frilly jackets, shawls and flowers as by a panoply of a throne, said with wonder, "Was it very painful?" Naomi, full of secret knowledge, said, "Oh no, I wouldn't say painful."

Rose had brought a beautiful little garment for the baby, something exquisite and expensive; she supplemented her salary as a junior typist in a lawyer's office in Johannesburg by doing bookkeeping for a small import agency, at night. She became quite famous for her presents, and Naomi's children used to look forward to the visits of Auntie Rose with special anticipation. These delicate and lovely offerings, unlike anything they saw about them in their own home, were discovered only by Rose; it was she, too, who found that there was a vocational centre to which Raymond, the sisters' younger brother who had had some damage to his brain at birth and had not developed mentally beyond the age of eleven, could go. He should, of course, have been sent to a special school when he was little, but the Rasovskys had been too poor and ignorant to arrange that.

The centre's fees were high and Ben, Naomi's husband, with a growing family to support, could not be expected to be responsible. Rose looked for a better-paid job and hired herself out to a political party as election agent, in addition to her book-keeping. Every month she asked her employer to give her two cheques: one was made payable directly to the vocational centre, the other was hers to live on. She never quite gave up the idea of studying by correspondence for the university degree for which she had forgone the scholarship, but the books lay about in the back room where she lived alone in the city and served only to fill her with sudden realization of time passing and a preoccupation with her many jobs from which she rarely, in the sense of personal liberation, looked up. There would be time next year, perhaps, to study for a Bachelor of Arts degree; and next year . . . And then the time came when she knew: what should she do with a B.A. if she got it? She could not afford to take a junior lecturer's job at a university. And anyway, what a degree had stood for—sharing the world of ideas with other young minds, and so on—she was nearly thirty and surely had by-passed all that. It was too late to splash around in the shallows; so far as the world of ideas was concerned she had had to enter dark water breast-deep.

For there had been Dr. Ferovec, by then, the Hungarian Catholic philosopher who had come to South Africa as a refugee in 1956. His English was too poor for him to be given a professorship, and his temperament too difficult for him to keep a lesser post at a university, so he had ended up teaching in a crammers' "college" in Johannesburg. Because she needed the money, Rose was expected to charge less for her work than others, and she was always being recommended to people like Dr. Ferovec who wanted typing cheaply done. She went to take dictation in his room on Sundays, and there, at last, in this stranger of strangers, talking to himself in an unrecognizable tongue, his grey hair full of bald patches due to a nervous disease, she found her first lover. He lost his job but she believed in him and cooked for him each night before she settled down to type his philosophical treatise, which they had decided they must translate together if he were ever to get the recognition he deserved. He said to her, "You know nothing, nothing" and it was true that the Jewish tailor's daughter had never seen Budapest in the good days, nor the beautiful woman who had been Ferovec's mistress, nor lived through revolution and counter-revolution. All she had were the backroom tasks of petty business—the drawing up of balance sheets, the analysis of some merchant's brand of profit and loss —and the absolutely private and incommunicable matter of her face. But in their distance from one another he and she were nearer than in their distance from others; she was there when he put out his hand for all he had lost.

Rose took him home, once, to Naomi's house, presenting him, with timid assurance, as her "friend". The shrill atmosphere of Sunday lunch among bright children and trite family exchanges repelled his intellectual qualities, antennae-like, into the shell of a beaten, sickly, shabby man. Naomi's husband was not really young, either, but his fleshy chest in a striped towelling shirt as he cavorted round the lawn with the children, and his big face with the cleft chin as he insisted, taking another piece of cake, "So if I put on another pound? So what's the difference, I'll only live once?" looked full-blooded in comparison. If you couldn't *talk* to Ferovec—or rather if he saw he couldn't talk to you —you simply couldn't understand what he was. Rose could see that they felt a family shame and pity for her. She could hear her old mother, when they had gone, taking advantage of her poor sight to say to Naomi, "What sort of a man is that friend of Rose's? What does he do for a living?" And Naomi saying, "Well, Rose lives a life of her own, Ma. She knows all sorts of people. I don't know, perhaps he's someone she works for."

But of course Naomi knew that, at last, her sister had a man, this elderly man with the patches on his head. Out of a need to be kind she would say on the telephone, "And how's your friend, the one who came that day . . . Oh, I'm glad . . ." Face to face with Rose, she did not mention him, and they confined their communication, as usual, to discussions about the welfare of the parents, the problem of Raymond (who was now thought to be capable of taking sheltered employment), and Rose's reception of the exploits of the children, the new curtains, the sun-porch that was being built on, and Naomi's latest dress. Naomi had never looked better than she did at this time. Her three children were all at the indiscriminately charming puppy stage between two and seven, and, seen among them, although no longer the appealing child-mother she had been, her wonderful complexion suggested at once to all sorts of men the simplest desire to sink one's teeth into her, and brought her the simplest pleasure of acknowledging this without ever having the urge to gratify it. Like many sexually-unawakened women, Naomi was a born tease. Rose gave surcease and even joy to Ferovec but no man ever glanced twice at her as she went about her work in her quiet clothes, making the best of herself.

After Ferovec (the translation of his treatise had caught the attention of an Oxford don who had quoted from it extensively in his own paperback popularization of a related subject, and Ferovec was suddenly offered a chair at one of the new English universities) there was Dirk Mosbacher. The family never saw Dirk Mosbacher but no doubt they got to hear about him, remote as they were from the life Rose was living now. They certainly would have heard that poor Rose was being sponged on by another misfit—at least ten years younger than herself, this time, and an Afrikaner, into the bargain. Naomi was not aware of it, but she felt guilty about Rose, and she even tried to bring her together with a distant relative of her husband—shame-facedly, because the man was the owner of a mineral-water factory whose only pretension to interests outside business was Freemasonry, and, after all, Rose was a clever girl. But at least he was a decent Jew. Rose was polite, as always, when she found him in Naomi's house, and, as always, seemed to have no idea how to attract a man. The mineral-water factory owner badly wanted to get married, but it was clear that he couldn't have brought himself to consider a girl like that, unless there happened to be money as well.

Rose had a lot of trouble with herself over Dirk Mosbacher. Through him she fought and discarded once and for all the standards and ambitions by which she had been disqualified, all her life. She had always thought of herself as the one who stood outside the warm-lit house where the faithful husband and the desirable wife created the future in their children. Because she knew no other, in this image she made every private compact she got herself into, however absurdly unsuitable the facts were. When Dirk slept with other women and never thought to conceal this from her, she felt the double affrontation of the wife neither preferred nor sufficiently feared to command deceit. Yet why had Ferovec been "faithful" to her? Because he knew few other women and was not at a stage in his life when he was attractive to them; not because he was a "husband". And why should Dirk, who shared, as she well knew, a number of strange dependencies and loyalties with different people, keep this one form of human intimacy exclusive to her? Would she have expected him to talk to no one but her of his ideas about the relation of man to shelter (he was an architect who had never quite finished his course) or about politics? Yet these were as important to him as sex. There were women and even men, occasionally, with whom, in sex, he had certain things in common, just as there were people with whom he had ideas in common. He was not a "husband" who left his plain, older "wife" for a pretty face; he was a man, free and answerable to the whole world. He lived with her, he told her, because she was the only honest person he knew; and she could believe him, although he took money from her. She threw away the strange structure, semblance of the nest, that she had patiently stuck together again and again out of the torn-up bits and pieces of incongruous instincts.

Often when Rose went home to Naomi's for Sunday lunch it was after one of those Saturday nights that seemed to blow up atmospherically round Dirk. Painter friends, political friends, jazz friends crowded into the flat. They all drank a lot and Rose provided food, though this was not expected. Dirk Mosbacher disliked what he called polite sterility in human contact, and would sit up all night among people who struck sparks off one another, no matter how aggressive the atmosphere might become. His little, yellow face with the thin black beard outlining the mouth perpetually contorted in talk was the curious Mandarin face of many intellectual Afrikaners—a bulky, blue-eyed people in the mass. He was tender to those who did not survive the evening, and would give up his bed and blankets to let them sleep it off until morning. He also gave asylum in Rose's flat to various Africans whose talents or political ideas interested him.

Rose would creep out of the sleeping flat on Sunday morning and take the train home. There was always some occasion in Naomi's house; Naomi was like a child, for whom time is spaced by small personal events. On her tenth wedding anniversary there was her diamond engagement ring, reset, to show on her thrust-out hand. At one time she tinted her hair, and was waiting in the doorway with an air of sensation when Rose appeared, while the old mother looked on indulgently—"*Meshuggah*, what can you do with them today?"—and then brought her eyes to rest

on the other one, a good girl, the image of her father, with her
thick glasses and sad, heavy nose. Rose was the perfect audience.
"It looks fine on you," she would say without a trace of bitterness, of some hat Naomi was displaying. "You put it on, Auntie
Rose, you put it on!" And to please her niece, Rose would con-
sent unembarrassedly to the spectacle of herself, looking back
from the mirror with silk petals pressed down over the face of
some old Talmudic scholar from Eastern Europe. Her family did
not ask her about her life because they feared that it was empty.
She did not speak about it because she did not want them to
know how pathetically limited and meagre the preoccupations of
Naomi's household were.

Dirk Mosbacher was derisive about Rose's former association
with "that posthumous old Popish pundit" Dr. Ferovec, but his
very derision, displayed among friends, partook of the distinction
Johannesburg people feel in anyone who has a connection with
the intellectual centres of Europe. Ferovec had become one of the
popular protagonists in the fashionable newspaper and pamphlet
debates on religion and authority then current in England; even
if the group who frequented the flat were not interested in the
whole business, they still saw in Rose, quiet Rose, the woman
who had been close to one of the "new philosophers" they read
about in the English papers. It gave her the certain quality of an
unknown quantity; one of the painters' girls decided that her
looks were immensely interesting, and that she ought to dress to
match: Rose slowly gave way to severe, strong-coloured, robe-
like dresses in place of the neat suits that had been her protective
colouring for years. With the rigid self-discipline of those who
know they cannot rely on any obvious pleasing qualities to excuse their deficiencies, she had never dared allow the emotional
strains and private trials of her personal life to show in the office,
and—a marvel without sickness or tears—had become the
most invaluable person in a big import agency (she had been with
the boss from the beginning, in the days when he rented a tiny
office and she worked for him in her spare time). The firm had
twice sent her overseas on business. She drove a small car, and

did not have time to visit her family more than once a month, now.

One of the black men with whom Dirk had argued and drunk and for whom Rose had bought shirts and typed letters made his way to England to study, and wrote a book. It was a bitter book, one of the first of its kind, and it created a small stir; the English papers called it a "scathing indictment of white South Africa" and the South African papers called it an "anti-White tirade," but it was prominently dedicated, in flowery language, to two white people, Dirk Mosbacher and Rose Rasovsky, but for whom the author would have "succumbed fatally to the hate in my heart". It was not the sort of book that Naomi's ladies' book circle would buy, but the story of the dedication was the sort of thing that makes news for the Sunday papers. Naomi's eldest daughter, Carolyn, saw it. "Don't read it to granny," said Naomi. She decided not to mention it to Rose, next time they saw her, either; poor Rose, now that Naomi was old enough to look back, what a terrible thing it was to have pushed Rose out into Johannesburg, a little girl of seventeen alone in some miserable room. What sort of chance had Rose been given? What had their parents had to offer them when they were girls? Papa Rasovsky, dead many years now, and the old lady, still going strong although she couldn't see more than blurred shapes—they had a lot to answer for. Naomi felt suddenly sad and heavy; it was true that she had begun to put on flesh and when she sat back in a chair she saw the solid weight of herself.

But Miss Carolyn was a cocky girl, in her first year at the university and full of the superior social status of higher education if not of a love of learning, and she twitted Aunt Rose, "I see you've been getting yourself in the papers, eh? Couldn't they have taken a better picture—honestly, I hardly recognized you!"

Poor Naomi! Rose had lately often seen her face exasperated and bewildered by that girl. The children were so charming when they were little; the boys had grown into louts who looked up from comic books only to growl, "Man, leave me alone."

Naomi complained about them in their presence: a sign of help-lessness. But what could Naomi know of the delicate business, the pain and rebuff, the unexpected acceptance and unexplained rejection of approaching the mystery of the individual? Since she was a child she had known nothing but extensions of herself and her own interest, with her parents and her husband she shared the blood of her children, and the milk the children imbibed from her body was assumed as a guarantee of their identity with her. Naomi had not dreamed of the strange reassurance one could experience, seventeen and alone in the back room of a lodging house in an unfamiliar city, in the daily contact with the black woman who came to clean. Naomi had had no chance to learn that a man who had lived a whole life in another continent, an-other age, another tongue, could be patiently reached through the body. Naomi had no way of knowing the moments of rest in understanding that come, outside sex, outside intellectual compati-bility, outside dependency, between people more than strangers: Rose herself when she was unofficial "teacher," years ago, and Dirk's ambitious, half-literate young black friends.

Dirk Mosbacher left the country and perhaps it was unlikely that he would come back. He had given evidence to the Anti-Apartheid Committee at United Nations and had been offered the opportunity of setting up a cultural centre in one of the new African states. It was exactly the sort of thing that suited him; he would have a jazz group working in one room while a play was being improvised in another, and an adults' summer school was painting in the yard. He wrote long, critical letters to Rose, which she read out to friends at the flat. The flat was as full as ever, though the composition of people was changing somewhat; Rose was living with the correspondent of an overseas newspa-per, now, and he brought along numbers of journalists. She ac-companied him to press dinners and other social events to which a newspaperman of standing was invited. Naomi had seen a pic-ture of him in a group with Rose on the social page. He was a tall, stooping Englishman, with a moustache and an expression of private amusement. No one would have expected Rose to bring him home to the family; what on earth would they have to say to Rose's friends? Yet Rose continued to come home, regularly, dutifully, and as soon as she was there the old relationship of the situation that underlay their lives came into existence in silence between the sisters as if nothing had happened since: they were the two girls of seventeen and eighteen who had not discussed what had to be done.

But when, on her fortieth birthday, Naomi opened the door to her sister Rose there was a difference about their being together. It was as if someone else were also in the room. After Rose had put down the flowers and the box of peaches bought on the road, and they were sitting in the living-room, Naomi looked at Rose gazing out into the garden. The third presence, like a phenomenon of double vision, slid into the single outline of focus: "Something's been done to your nose."

Rose kept her head steady so that it could be looked at, moving only her eyes. "Yes. I was wondering when you would notice."

"As soon as you came in. I didn't know what it was."

Rose still kept her head on display, the habit of obedience of the younger sister, but Naomi was not looking at the nose.

She said, "Was it painful?"

And Rose answered, "No, not at all, really."

Naomi sat with her mouth parted, patting the arm of her chair. The children didn't like the Jacobean style she had chosen for the room when she got married, but it had been the very latest, then; now Ben said they couldn't afford to throw good furniture away.

Rose said, "People think it's a great improvement."

Her sister gave a consenting shrug, as if conscious of the obligation to doubt the need for improvement.

"I hated my nose more than anything" said Rose. But because they had never talked about such things her tone was the one in which, on her visits, she would praise the soup at lunch or remark on the traffic that had delayed her.

"What's it all matter, in the end. It's not the face that counts, it's what's behind it." Naomi's polite platitudes hung in the air, and, confronted with the honesty with which her sister sat before her, she added, "It's nicely done."

Rose mentioned the name of the plastic surgeon: a very expensive one. Rose's little car was new, too. Naomi had never had a car of her own, though it was the fashionable thing in the small town for wives to have their own runabouts; it was the same with the house that had been built for her—what had seemed status and luxury to her then, was now ordinary and almost humble: people going up in the world had left the suburb and gone to a newer one, where they had patios and swimming pools instead of red-brick stoeps.

Fortunately it was a weekday and at lunch there were only Rose, Naomi, the old mother, and their brother, so there was no one to pass remarks. The old lady could not see well enough to distinguish any change in Rose, and Raymond, in the downcast timidity of his slow mind, had always been afraid to look directly at anybody. He had been back living with Naomi for some years, since the only kind of sheltered employment he didn't run away from was being allowed to potter round among the mounds of twisted metal in Ben's scrap yard. Although old Mrs. Rasovsky could scarcely make out Rose's shape, she kept putting out her hand to touch her, with sentimental tears in her eyes that embarrassed her daughters.

"Let Rose have her food, ma," said Naomi.

"You're all right, thank God, you're keeping well?" the old lady kept saying, in Yiddish. It was all she had ever said; it was the formula with which she had disposed of their lives, helpless to ask further or do more.

When Naomi said good-bye to Rose at the car she felt the necessity to make some final reference to the new nose. She wanted to say something nice about it, but she suddenly said: "Now the next thing is contact lenses."

Rose looked terribly uncertain, the smile went out of her eyes though her lips still held it, she had none of the calm self-acceptance with which she used to try on Naomi's pretty hats. She said, with an effort at deprecation, "Do you think so?" And the little car drove away.

Naomi walked back along the gravel path between the yellow privets. She went into the room where the old woman sat, legs apart, in her corner, and said, "The next thing is contact lenses. And then she could have married Ben Sharman instead of me." But the old woman was deaf now, as well as nearly blind.

# THE CREDIBILITY GAP

"You go."

"No, it'll be for you."

The timid ring of the front door bell or the two-syllable call of the telephone produced the same moment of obstinacy: everyone appeared to be going on with what he was doing. The young brother continued to hammer away somewhere. The elder, if it so happened that he was in the house, absolved himself because he now had his own flat with his own front door and telephone. A house-guest—there was usually someone who had nowhere else to live—didn't feel it was his or her place to get up. The mother knew it wouldn't be for her. It was for the daughter, inevitably, since she was in one of the expanding periods of life when one moves through and with the zest and restlessness of the shoal. But often there were reasons why she did not want to respond without an intermediary: the complex social pattern meant that she was supposed to be out when she was in, or in when she was out.

*You go. It'll be for you.*

The schoolboy Rob took no notice, anyway. The cats were
disturbed by anyone leaving a room or entering; they lifted back
their heads from bodies relaxed to tiger-skin flatness before the
fire, and opened their eyes. Pattie's casual, large-footed friends
trod into flowered saucers scummed with disdained milk that
stood about all over the place. Cats and saucers were the
mother's—old-maidish possessions that could be allowed a
woman who, if she had no husband by now, had among other
things the contrary testimony of children grown and half-grown
who were half-brother and -sister. Pattie never thought of her
mother when she was alone with friends her own age, but sometimes when she and the friends and her mother were drinking
beer and arguing in the living-room at home she would have an
impulse the converse of that of the parent to show off its child.
"Don't tease her about her cats. It's her passion for cats that got
her out of solitary confinement when she was in jug. Honestly.
She was supposed to be in solitary for leading a hunger strike
among the political prisoners, but the chief wardress was as dotty
about cats as she is, and they were such buddies discussing their
dear little kitties, the old girl used to let her out secretly to sit in
the prison yard. It's true."

Yes, there once had been a ring at the door in the dark early
hours of the morning that was for Mrs. Doris Aucamp. Years
ago, when the children really were still children, and there still
were real political opposition movements in South Africa. The
two elder children—Andrew and Pattie—at least, remembered something of that time; someone had moved into the house
to take care of them, and they had been set up on the Johannesburg City Hall steps one Saturday among the families of other
political prisoners, wearing placards round their necks: WE WANT
OUR MUMMY BACK. Most of the friends drinking beer in the living-room and discussing the authoritarianism of the university
system or the authenticity of the sense-experience known as getting stoned had heard about the massacre of Sharpeville—if
from no other source, then from references to it that came up in

overseas magazines; one of the boys, studying abroad, had even discovered that in New York there was a commemorative rally at Carnegie Hall on the anniversary of "Sharpeville Day", held by South Africans in exile. It was with quite a momentary thrill of admiring curiosity that they realized that this woman— somebody's mother—had actually served a prison sentence for what she believed (of course, what they *all* believed) about the idiocy of the colour bar. It both added to and detracted from the aura of those among them who now and then were moved to defy minor-sounding laws against marching the streets or assembling for protest: so these "activists" were not the discoverers that danger, in some times and places, is the only form of freedom? They had only dug up, afresh, to offend the docile snouts of the population, what the major punishments of those minor-sounding transgressions had forced people to bury, and forget where.

—This woman wasn't bad, either, in spite of her age, not bad at all. There was at least one of the young men who wouldn't have minded indulging a kind of romantic lust in response to that mature sexuality, confidently lived with for a lifetime, vested in her blunt, nicotine-tanned hands as she stirred her tea, and the turn towards the table of those rather big breasts, sloping away from each other a bit like an African woman's bubs—she was a short, broad woman with nice, nine-pin calves, too wide in the hip ever to wear trousers. Mrs. Doris Aucamp caught the look and was smiling at him, not taking it up but not offended —kindly amused: of course, as well as having been a jail-bird, she was also a writer. He hadn't read her; but it was a well-known name.

*I'll go—it's for me.*
There were times when Pattie leapt up because she had the instinct that some irreparable usurpation would take place if anyone other than herself were to open the door upon the face she expected, or respond with a voice other than hers to the summons of the telephone. A word of criticism of one of her friends

roused a fierce solidarity. "Oh Kip's not what you think at all. People get it all wrong. People just don't understand. He wouldn't trust anyone else. You have to be one of us."

Her mother slapped down a cat who was trying to filch off a plate. "Of course. Every set of friends has private dependencies that make it hang together. Why do I put up with Scoresby? Why does any of his pals?" The man she spoke of was a long-time friend, long-time alcoholic.

Rob was finely paring the wart on the inner side of his third finger, right hand. He looked up a moment, saw that man, who sometimes played chess with him, lying as he had once found him in a lumpy pool of pink vomit in the bathroom. He turned the blade towards his finger once more; everyone told him it was dangerous to cut warts, but he was getting rid of his by persistently slicing them away, right down to the healthy flesh, without squeamishness.

"It's not that so much. I mean, you think it's peculiar because I bring someone home and don't know his surname—even if we don't know each other personally, *we know*—"

"—But you don't really think it's a matter of age? There're people under thirty you couldn't trust as far as I could throw this greedy, shameless cat—mmh?"

"No—I'm sorry—in some ways *you* just can't—"

Her mother nodded her head as if in sympathy for some disability. "You know what Lévi-Strauss says? Something, something . . . 'as man moves forward he takes with him all positions he's occupied in the past and all those he'll occupy in the future.' Wait, I'll get it." They heard her running upstairs; padding down more slowly, probably leafing through the book on the way. She stood behind her daughter, silently following the passage over the girl's shoulder. *As he moves forward within his environment, Man takes with him all the positions that he has occupied in the past, and all those that he will occupy in the future. He is everywhere at the same time, a crowd which, in the act of moving forward, yet recapitulates at every instant every step that it has ever taken in the past.*

The girl put the book down; the two of them looked into each other, but it became purely a moment of physical comprehension: Pattie saw that the skin of her mother's forehead would never have the shine of tautness again, the mother saw that little scars of adolescent turmoil had left their imperfections on the slightly sulky jaw-line that attracted men.

*No—it's all right, I'll go. I'm expecting a friend.*

Some of the girls feared themselves pregnant, one or two had had abortions, and there were even beginning to be a few contemporaries who got married and furnished flats. Pattie knew that if she became pregnant, her mother could deal with the situation; on the other hand, if she got married and bought furniture, well, that was all right, too.

"Isn't there anything else?"

Her mother was putting flea powder on the cats: Liz and Burton, Snorer, and the mother cat of all three, Puss. Snorer's name was really Schnorrer, dubbed for his greedy persistence at table by the Jewish professor who—the girl understood, looking back at things she hadn't known how to interpret then—had been her mother's lover for a time. Dolly, the black servant, had heard the name as Snorer; and so it had become that, just as the professor was now become a family friend, like Scoresby, only less troublesome.

"No. You meet them years later and they tell you their son is married, their daughter's engaged. All smiles, big surprise."

"Except you. You count yourself outside." The girl had trudged the summer through in a pair of Greek sandals whose soles had worn away completely beneath each big toe. She was examining with respect these alien, honest-workmanlike extremities of herself, thickened, ingrained with city dirt round the broken nails, assertive as the mechanic's black-ringed fingernails that can never be scrubbed to deny their toil. After a pause: "People say that story you wrote was about me."

"Which story?"

"The one about the donkey."

"It wasn't about you, it was about me."

"But I saved up for a donkey?"

"Never. It was something I told you about myself."

*You go.*
*No, you.*

Rob did not know that Snorer was not the cat's name any more than he knew that Julius, the professor, had not always been an old family friend. He didn't answer the phone because he was not yet interested in girls, and his boy friends used the kitchen door, coming tramping in past Dolly without knocking. Dolly's man repaired bicycles on the pavement outside the local hardware shop, and she treated the boys like the potential good customers they were, sycophantically addressing them as "My baasie", "Master" Johnny or Dick, although her employer didn't allow her to corrupt the young people of the house in this way into thinking themselves little white lordlings. " 'Master' my eye! Really, Dolly! You should be putting them across your knee and warming their behinds. Nothing's ever going to change for the blacks, here, until people like you understand that nobody's born 'master', never mind white kids in short pants." But Dolly was unresponsive, for another reason. She resented having been given, with equal forthrightness, an ultimatum about closing her back-yard trade in beer.

When the children of the house were small the front door had opened often upon black faces. The children had sat on the knees and laughed at the jokes of black men and women who were their mother's friends and political associates. Pattie remembered some of them quite well; where was so-and-so now, she would sometimes remark; what happened to so-and-so? But all were in exile or prison. She had, tentatively, through her own student set, a different sort of association. The political movements were dead, the university was closed to black students, but there were Africans, usually musicians, with whom was shared the free-for-all of jazz, the suspension from reality in the smoke of the weed —white hangers-on, black hangers-on, there: it depended whose

world you decided it was. She even went once or twice on a
jaunt to one of the black states over the border, and there met
Africans who were not creatures of the night but students, like
herself.

"If I fall for a black one, how would we manage?"

"You must leave the country." Before the mother or anyone
else could answer, Rob had spoken.

He put down the coloured supplement on vintage cars he was
studying. His gaze was hidden under lowered lids, but his head
was slightly inclined to the polarity of his mother as she sat,
a cigarette comfortably between her stained first and third fingers, her square-jawed, sunburned face looking on with a
turned-down neutral smile. They were waiting for her to speak,
but she said nothing. At last she put out her hand and passed it
again and again through the boy's hair, firmly, as the cats loved
to be raked along the fur of their backs.

"There's a nice, God-fearing guardian of the white race growing up." Andrew had dropped in to pick up his allowance; he addressed the room after his younger brother had left it.

Mrs. Doris Aucamp remained serenely in her silence; as her
Professor Julius had once remarked, she could turn bullets to
water. She irritated her elder son by giving him the brief, head-
tilted, warm glance, old childish balm for sibling fears of fa-
voured dispensation granted the last-born.

" 'Sorry, no dice, my little brother doesn't think we should do
it'." Pattie was amused. "Poor kid."

"A man once gave me up because I didn't know the boiling
point of water." But the elder son didn't accept his mother's di-
version of subject; in his turn, did not appear to hear.

"Fahrenheit or centigrade?" A Peace Corps girl from Uganda,
in the house for the time being, was eager to show herself to be
on the family wavelength.

"Neither. —I'm sure that was it. Couldn't get over it.
Thought he'd found a real intellectal to appreciate him, and
then discovers she doesn't even know a thing like that."

"Black or white?" Pattie asked.

There was laughter. "Oh he was white, *very* white."

When the two of them were alone together, the daughter returned to the subject. She did not know, for sure, of anyone since Julius. "When you were young? —The man with the boiling water?"

"Oh no, only a few years ago."

The girl was looking for a number in the telephone directory. She covered her silence by saying kindly, politely, "What is the boiling point of water, anyway? I've forgotten."

"Oh I found out quickly enough. Two-hundred-and-twelve Fahrenheit." Mrs. Doris Aucamp had the smoker's laugh that turns to coughing.

The number Pattie tried was busy. Resting on the receiver fingers wearing as many rings as a Renaissance pope, she said of her little brother, "It's just that he wants God-to-keep-his-hand-over-us."

"Of course." The expression was a family one, derived from a grandmother who mistook superstition for piety.

"Poor little devil." The girl spoke dreamily.

*You go. Go on. It'll never be for me.*

When their mother was out, no one—certainly not Dolly—would answer the bell for Pattie. One afternoon it was a student friend standing there; come to tell her one of their friends had been killed. He and some others had been climbing with the girl the day before on a Sunday picnic, and she had slipped and fallen before their eyes. They picked her up fifteen minutes later at the bottom of a waterfall, her neck broken.

Mrs. Doris Aucamp was waylaid by Dolly as she got out of the car in the garage. She thought for a moment Dolly had been drinking again, but it was not drink that widened her nostrils with drama but the instinct of all servants to enter swiftly into those fearful emotions that they can share with employers, because there, down among death and disaster, there are no privileges or exemptions to be claimed by anyone.

"The friend with the big eyes. The one that always laugh—

that Kathy. She's die. It's true." A big shuddering sigh took the black woman by the throat.

In the doorway of the living-room the mother stood before her daughter and the young man, two faces for which there was no expression to meet the fact of death. They merely looked ashamed. There were tins of beer and cigarettes about. Their eyes were upon her, waiting.

She must have a face for this, of course.

But she stood, with the cats winding themselves about her calves. She said, "Oh *no?*" People said that in books they had all read or films they'd seen. Then she saw the untidy hair and rosy nose of her daughter, alive, and, hand over her open mouth a moment, emotion came for what hadn't happened just as if it had: it could have been this one, mine. There was no face to meet that at the door.

The three of them sat drinking beer, breaking the awkward silences by repeating small certainties left by the girl who had died. "She was here for supper last week. Didn't she forget a raincoat?"

"It's behind the door in my room. I noticed it this morning, it smells of her—"

"She always looked just like that when she was asleep. Honestly, it was just the same. Limp. Soft." The young man himself looked afraid; sleeping with her, making love to her, then, he had been holding death in his arms?

He was a witty young man whose instincts were always to puncture the hot air of a distrusted solemnity. As the talk drifted away from the dead girl, tugged back to her, away again, he dashed off one of his wry mimicries of someone, and they found themselves laughing a little, slightly drunk by now, anyway. There was a closeness between them, a complicity of generations.

It had grown dark. Mrs. Doris Aucamp got up to pull the curtains and wandered off upstairs by way of the kitchen, telling Dolly there would be an extra mouth at dinner. And then she met her younger son; he was repairing Dolly's radio. "I wish my darned sister would leave my things alone. I look all over the

house for my small pliers, and where are they? Lying around in
the mess in her room, of course."

"Well, don't make a fuss now. You see, darling, Kathy—"

"I heard about it."

"It isn't the time. She's upset."

There were shiny patches on his thin, dirty fingers where the
warts had been pared away. The patches were watermarked, like
moiré, in a design of whorls unique to him out of all the millions
of human beings in the world. He was carefully, exasperatedly
scraping the insulation tape from wire. He lifted his face and the
preoccupation fell away. He said, "She wasn't crying at all. She
and Davy were yapping in there, quite ordinary. And then when
one of her girl friends phoned she started to make herself cry
over the phone, she put it on." His faced was without malice,
clear, open, waiting.

His mother said, "I wanted to cry—for a moment."

He asked, "Did you believe in it?"

"What?"

He gave a little jerk to his shoulder. "*It*. I mean, you didn't see
that girl lying dead."

"Davy did." She searched his eyes to see if the explanation was
one.

He said nothing.

She said, hesitantly, "Davy says she was the same as when she
was asleep. It didn't seem she was dead."

He nodded his head: *you see*—in the manner of one who ac-
cepts that no one will have an explanation for him.

This time she did not put out her hand to touch him. She wandered back into the dark hall of the house, her bent head making
a double chin; the followers of those African prophets who
claimed bullets could be turned to water had, after all, fallen everywhere on battlefields, from the Cape to Madagascar.

# ABROAD

Manie Swemmer talked for years about going up to Northern Rhodesia for a look around. His two boys, Thys and Willie, were there, and besides, he'd worked up there himself in the old days, the early thirties.

He knew the world a bit although he was born in Bontebokspruit. His grandmother had been a Scots woman, Agnes Swan, and there was a pack of relatives in Scotland; he hadn't got that far, but in a sergeants' mess in Alex just before Sidi Rezegh, when he was with the South African First Division, he had met a Douglas Swan who must have been a cousin—there was quite a resemblance about the eyes.

Yes, he thought of going up, when he could get away. He had been working for the Barends brothers, the last five years, he had put up the Volkskas Bank and the extensions to the mill as well as the new waiting rooms for Europeans and non-Europeans at the station. The town was going ahead. Before that, he worked for the Provincial Public Works Department, and had even had a spell in Pretoria, at the steel works. That was after the motor business went bust; when he came back from the war he had sold his share of the family land to his uncle, and gone into the motor business with the money. Fortunately—as Manie Swemmer said to the people he had known all his life, in the bar of Buks Jacobs' hotel on Saturdays after work—although he'd had no real training there wasn't much in the practical field he couldn't do. If he'd had certificates, he wouldn't have been working for a salary from Abel and Johnnie Barends, today, that was for sure; but there you are. People still depended on him; if he wanted to take his car and drive up North, he needed three weeks, and who could Abel find to take his place and manage his gang of boys on the site?

He often said he'd like to drive up. It was a long way but he didn't mind the open road and he'd done it years ago when it was strip roads if you were lucky, and plain murder the rest of the way. His old '57 Studebaker would make it; he looked after her himself, and there were many people in the town— including Buks Jacobs from the hotel with his new Volkswagen combi —who wouldn't have anybody else touch their cars. Manie spent most of his Saturday afternoons under somebody's; he had no one at home (the boys' mother, born Helena Thys, had died of a diseased kidney, leaving him to bring up the two little chaps, all alone) and he did it more out of friendship than for anything else.

On Sundays, when he was always expected at the Gysbert Swemmers', he had remarked that he'd like to go up and have a look around. And there were his boys, of course. His cousin Gysbert said, "Let them come down and visit you." But they were busy making their way; Thys was on the mines, but didn't like it, Willie had left the brewery and was looking for an opening down in the capital. After the British Government gave the natives the country and the name was changed to Zambia, Gysbert said, "Man, you don't want to go there now. What for? After you waited so long."

But he had moved around the world a bit: Gysbert might run three hundred head of cattle, and was making a good thing out of tobacco and chillies as well as mealies on the old Swemmer farm where they had all grown up, but Gysbert had never been farther than a holiday in Cape Town. Gysbert had not joined up during the war. Gysbert sat in their grandfather's chair at Sunday dinner and served roast mutton and sweet potatoes and rice to his wife and family, including Manie, and Gysbert's mother, Tante Adela. Tante Adela had her little plot on the farm where she grew cotton, and after lunch she sat in the dark *voorkamer*, beside the big radio and record player combination, and stuffed her cotton into the cushion-covers she cut from sheets of plastic foam. There was coffee on the stoep, handed round by pregnant daughters and daughters-in-law, and there were grandchildren whose mouths exploded huge bubbles of gum before Oom Manie and made him laugh. Gysbert even still drank *mampoer*, home-made peach brandy sent from the Cape, but Manie couldn't stand the stuff and never drank any spirits but Senator Brandy—Buks Jacobs, at the hotel, would set it up without asking.

At the end of the Sunday Manie Swemmer would drive home from the old family farm that was all Gysbert knew, past the fields shuffling and spreading a hand of mealies, then tobacco, and then chilli bushes blended by distance, like roof-tiles, into red-rose-yellows. Past the tractor and the thresher with its beard of torn husks, and down into the dip over the dried-up river bed, where they used to try and catch leguaans, as youngsters. Past the cattle nibbling among the thorn bushes and wild willow. Through the gates opened by picannins running with the kaffir dogs, from the kraal. Past the boys and their women squatting around paraffin tins of beer and pap, and the Indian store, old Y. S. Mia's, boarded up for Sunday, and all the hundred-and-one relations those people have, collected on the stoep of the bright pink house next to the store. At that time in the late afternoon the shadow of the hilly range had taken up the dam; Manie looked, always, for the glittering circles belched by fish. He fished there, in summer, still; the thorn trees they used to play under were dead, but stood around the water.

The town did not really leave the lands behind. His house in

Pretorius Street was the same as the farm-houses, a tin roof, a polished stoep on stumpy cement pillars darkening the rooms round two sides, paint the colour of the muddy river half-way up the outside walls and on the woodwork. Inside there was flowered linoleum and a swordfern in a painted kaffir pot that rocked a little on its uneven base as he walked in. The dining-table and six chairs he and Helena had bought when they got married, and Tante Adela's plastic foam cushions, covering the places on the sofa where the kids had bounced the springs almost through. He had a good old boy, Jeremiah, looking after him. The plot was quite big and was laid out in rows of beetroot, onions and cabbage behind a quince hedge. Jeremiah had his mealie patch down at his *khaya*. There were half-a-dozen Rhode Island Reds in the *hok*, and as for the tomatoes, half the town ate presents of Manie Swemmer's tomatoes.

He'd never really cleared out his sons' room, though once there'd been a young chappie from the railways looking for somewhere to rent. But Willie was only sixteen when he went up North to have a look round—that's how kids are, his brother Thys had gone up and it was natural—he might want to come back home again sometime. The beds were there, and Willie's collection of bottle-tops. On the netted-in stoep round the back there was his motorbike, minus wheels. Manie Swemmer often thought of writing to ask Willie what he ought to do with the bike; but the boys didn't answer letters often. In fact, Willie was better than Thys; Thys hadn't written for about eighteen months, by the time the place had gone and changed its name from Northern Rhodesia to Zambia. Not that the change would frighten Manie Swemmer if he decided to make the trip. After all, it wasn't as if he were going to drag a woman up there. And it might be different for people with young daughters. But for someone like him, well, what did he have to worry about except himself?

One September, when the new abattoir was just about off his hands, he told the Barends brothers that he was taking leave. "No, not down to Durban—I'm pushing off up there for a couple of weeks—" His rising eyebrows and backward jerk of the head indicated the back of the hotel bar, the mountain range, the border.

"Gambia, Zambia! These fancy names. With the new kaffir government. Doctor or Professor or whatever-he-calls-himself Kaunda," said Carel Janse van Vuuren, the local solicitor, who had been articled in Johannesburg, making it clear by his amusement that he, too, knew something of the world.

"Tell your sons to come home here, man. *Hulle is ons mense*." Dawie Mulder was hoping to be nominated as a candidate for the next provincial elections and liked to put a patriotic edge on his remarks.

"Oh they know their home, all right, don't you worry," Manie Swemmer said, in English, because some of the regulars on the commercial travellers' run, old Joe Zeff and Edgar Bloch, two nice Jewish chappies, had set up the beers for the group. "They'll settle down when they've had their fling, I'm not worried."

"Up in this, uh, Northern Rhodesia—I hear the natives don't bother the white people on the mines, eh?" said Zeff. "I mean you don't have to worry, they won't walk into your house or anything—after all, it's not a joke, you have a big kaffir coming and sitting down next to us here? It's all you're short of."

Sampie Jacobs, the proprietor's wife and a business woman who could buy and sell any man in Bontebokspruit, if it came to money matters, said, "Willie was a bea-utiful child. When he was a little toddler! Eyes like saucers, and blue!" She hung the fly-swatter on its hook, and mentally catching somebody out, scratched at some fragment of food dried fast to a glass. "If Helena could have seen him"—she reminded Manie Swemmer of the pimple-eroded youth who had bought an electric guitar on credit and gone away leaving his father to meet the instalments.

"They'll settle down! Thys is earning good money up there now, though, man. You couldn't earn money like that here! Not a youngster."

"Twenty-six—no, twenty-seven by now," said Sampie Jacobs.

"But Willie. Willie's not twenty-one."

Buks Jacobs said, "Well, you can have it for me, Oom Manie."

"Man, I nearly died of malaria up there in thirty-two," Manie Swemmer said, putting a fist on the counter. "Good Lord, I knew the place when it was nothing but a railhead and a couple of mine shafts in the bush. There was an Irish doctor, that time, Fitzgerald was his name, he got my boss-boy to sponge me down every hour . . ."

On the third day of the journey, in the evening, the train drew into the capital, Lusaka. Manie Swemmer had taken the train, after all; it would have been different if there had been someone to drive up with him. But the train was more restful and, with this trip in the back of his mind all the time, it was some years since he'd taken a holiday. He was alone in the second-class compartment until the Bechuanaland border, wondering if Abel Barends wouldn't make a mess, now, of that gang of boys it had taken years to get into shape, a decent gang of boys but they had to know where they were with you, the native doesn't like to be messed around, either. He mouthed aloud to himself what he had meant to say to Abel, "Don't let me come back and find you've taken on a lot of black scum from the location." But then the train stopped at a small station and he got up to lean on the let-down window; and slowly the last villages of the Transvaal were paused at and passed, and as he looked out at them with his pipe in his mouth and the steam letting fly from beneath the carriage, Barends and the building gang sank to the bottom of his mind. Once or twice, when the train moved on again, he checked his post office savings book (he had transferred money to Lusaka) and the indigestion pills he had put in with his shaving things. He had his bedding ticket (everything under control, he had joked, smiling to show how easy it was if you knew how, to Gysbert and his wife and Sampie Jacobs, who had seen him onto the train) and a respectful coloured boy made up a nice bunk for him and was grateful for his five-cent tip. By the time the train reached Mafeking after dinner, he felt something from the past that he had forgotten entirely, although he talked about it often: the jubilant lightness of moving on, not a stranger among strangers, but a new person discovered among new faces. He felt as if he had been travelling forever and could go on forever. Through Rhodesia the hills, the bush, the smell of a certain shrub came back to him across thirty years. It was like the veld at home, only different. The balancing rocks, the white-barked figs that split them and held them in tightspread roots, the flat-topped trees turning red with spring—yes, he remembered that—the bush becoming tangled forest down over the rivers, the old baobabs and the kaffir-orange trees with their green billiard-balls sticking out all over, the huge vleis with, far off, a couple of palms craning up looking at you. Two more days slid past the windows. He bought a set of table mats from a picannin at a siding; nicely made, the reeds dyed pink and black—he saw Sampie Jacobs putting them under her flower arrangements in the hotel lounge, far, far away, far, far ahead. When the train reached the Rhodesian-Zambian border there was a slight nervous bracing of his manner; he laid out his open passport—HERMANUS STEFANUS SWEMMER, national of the Republic of South Africa. The young Englishman and the black man dressed exactly like him, white socks, gold shoulder tabs, smart cap, the lot, said, "Thank you Sir"; the black one scribbled and stamped.

Well, he was in.

As the train neared Lusaka he began to get anxious. About Willie. About what he would say to Willie. After all, five years. Willie's twenty-first was coming up in December. He forgot that he was drawing into Lusaka through the dark, he forgot that he was travelling, he thought: Willie, Willie. There were no outskirts to Lusaka, even now. A few lights at a level crossing or two, bicycles, native women with bundles—and they were in the station. The huge black sky let down a trail of rough bright stars as close as the lights of a city. Bells rang and the train, standing behind Manie Swemmer, stamped backwards. People sauntered and yelled past him; white people, Indians, natives in moulded plastic shoes.

Willie said, "Hell, where were you?"

Tall. Sideburns. A black leather jacket zipped up to where the button was missing at the neck of the shirt. The same; and Manie Swemmer had forgotten. Never sent a snap of himself, and naturally you'd expect him to have changed in five years.

They spoke in English. "I was just beginning to wonder did the letter get lost. I was just going to take a taxi. Well how's it! Quite a trip, eh? Since Wednesday, man!" Manie knew how to behave; he had his hands on the kid's biceps, he was pushing him and shaking him. Willie was grinning down the side of his mouth. He stood there while his father talked about the train, and why he hadn't driven up, and what Gysbert said, that backvelder tied to Tante Adela's apron, and the good dinner the dining car had put up. "Give us your things," Willie said. "What's this?" The mats were tied up in a bit of newspaper. 'Presents, man. I can't go back empty-handed." "Just hang on here a minute, ay, Dad, I'mna get some smokes." Held his shoulders too high when he ran; that was always his fault, when he did athletics at Bontebokspruit High. Willie. Couldn't believe it. Suddenly, Mannie Swemmer landed in Lusaka, knew he was there, and exhilaration spread through his breast like some pleasurable form of heartburn.

Willie opened the pack and shook out a cigarette, tenting his hands round the match. "Where were you gunna take the taxi?"

"Straight to your place, man. I've got the letter on me."

"I've pushed off from there."

"But what happened, son, I thought it was so near for work and everything?"

Willie took a deep draw at his cigarette, put his head back as if swallowing an injury and then blew smoke at it, with narrowed eyes; there was a line between them, already, his father noticed. "Didn't work out at Twyford's Electric. So I had to find a cheaper room until I get fixed up."

"But I thought they told you there was prospects, son?"

"I'm going to see someone at the cement works Monday.

Friend of mine says he'll fix me up. And there's a job going at a
motor spares firm, too. I don't want to jump at anything."

"For Pete's sake, no. You must think of your future. Fancy
about Twyford's, eh, they started up in the thirties, one of the
first. But I suppose the old boy's dead now. Watch out for the
motor spares outfit—I don't trust that game."

They were still standing on the platform; Willie was leaning
against one of the struts that held up the roof, smoking and feeling a place near his left sideburn where he had nicked himself.
That poor kid would never be able to get a clean shave—his
skin had never come right. He seemed to have forgotten about
the luggage.

"So where you staying now, Willie?" Everyone from the train
had left.

"I'm at another chap's place. There's a bed on the stoep.
There's five people in the house, only three rooms. They can't
put you up."

"What's wrong with a hotel?" Manie Swemmer consoled,
chivvying, cheerful. "Come let's take this lot and get into town.
I'll get a room at the Lusaka Hotel, good Lord, do I remember
that place. I know all about the posh new one out on the Ridge-
way, too. But I don't have to splash it. The Lusaka'll do me fine."

Willie was shaking his head, hang-dog.

"You'll never get *in*, man, Dad. You don't know—you won't
get a room in this place. It's the independence anniversary next
week—"

"When? The anniversary, eh—" He was pleased to have arrived for a festival.

"I dunno. Monday. I think. You haven't a hope."

"Wait a minute, wait a minute." They were gathering the luggage. Manie Swemmer had put on his hat to emerge into the
town, although he had suddenly realized that the night was very
hot. He looked at his son.

"I thought maybe it's the best thing if you go straight on to
the Copper Belt," said Willie. "To Thys."

"To Thys?" He lifted the hat to let the air in upon his head.

"I dunno about a train, but it's easy to thumb a lift on the road."

"The Regent!" Manie Swemmer said. "Is there still a Regent Hotel? Did you try there?"

"What you mean try, Dad, I told you, it's no use to *try*, you'll never get *in*—"

"Well, never mind, son, let's go and have a beer there, anyway. Okay?" Manie Swemmer felt confused, as if the station itself were throwing back and forth all sorts of echoes. He wanted to get out of it, never mind where. There was only one clear thought; silly. He must put new buttons on the kid's shirt. A man who has brought up two youngsters and lived alone a long time secretly knows how to do these things.

Lusaka was a row of Indian stores and the railway station, facing each other. In the old days.

Manie Swemmer was a heavy man but he sat delicately balanced, forward, in the taxi, looking out under the roof at the new public buildings and shopping centres lit up round paved courts in Cairo Road, the lights of cars travelling over supermarkets and milk bars. "The post office? Ne-ver!" And he could not stop marvelling at it, all steel and glass, and a wide parking lot paved beside it. Here and there was a dim landmark—one of the Indian stores whose cracked veranda had been a quay above the dust of the road—with a new shopfront but the old tin roof. No more sewing machines going under the hands of old natives on the verandas; even just in passing, you could see the stuff in the smart window displays was factory-made. Fishing tackle and golf clubs: shiny sets of drums and electric guitars; a grubby-looking little bar with kaffir music coming out. "Looks as if it should be down in the location, eh?" He laughed, pointing it out to Willie. There were quite a few nicely-dressed natives about, behaving themselves, with white shirts and ties. The women in bright cotton dresses, the latest styles and high-heeled shoes. And everywhere, Europeans in cars. "Ah, but the old trees are still going strong!" he said to Willie. Along the middle of the Cairo

Road there was the same broad island with red-flowering trees, he recognized the shape of the blooms although he couldn't see their colour. Willie was sitting back, smoking. He said, "They don't leave you alone, with their potatoes and I don't know what." He wasn't looking, but was speaking of the natives who hung around even after dark under the trees—venders, young out-of-works.

The way to the Regent was too short for Manie Swemmer's liking. He could have done with driving around a bit; this kind of confusion was different—exciting, like being blindfolded, whirled around, and then left to feel your way about a room you knew well. But in no time they were at the hotel, and that had changed and hadn't changed, too. The old rows of rooms in the garden had been connected with a new main building, but the "garden" was still swept earth with a few hibiscus and snake plants.

They found themselves in what had been the veranda and was now closed in with glass louvres and called the terrace lounge. Willie made no suggestions, and his father, chatting and commenting in the husky undertone he used among other people, was misled by the layout of the hotel as he remembered it. "Never mind, never mind! What's the odds. We'll have a drink before we start any talking, man, why not? This'll do all right." With his big behind in its neat grey flannels rising apologetically towards the room, he supervised the stowing of his two suit cases and newspaper parcel beside the small table where he urged Willie to sit. He ordered a couple of beers, and looked around. The place was filling up with the sort of crowd you get on hot evenings; one or two families with kids climbing about the chairs, young men buying their girls a drink, married couples who hadn't gone home after the office—men alone would be in the pub itself. There was only one coloured couple—not blacks, more like Cape Coloureds. You'd hardly notice them. Willie didn't know anyone. They went, once again, over the questions and answers they had exchanged over Willie's prospects of a new job. But it had always been hard to know what Willie was thinking, even when he was quite a little kid; and Manie Swemmer's attention kept getting out of range, around the room, to the bursts of noise that kept coming, perhaps when some inner door connected with the bar was opened—to the strange familiar town outside, and the million-and-one bugs going full blast for the night with the sound of sizzling, of clocks being wound, and ratchets jerking. "What a machine shop, eh?" he said; but of course, living there five years, Willie wouldn't even be hearing it any more.

"Who's running the place these days?" he suggested to Willie confidentially, when the beer was drunk. "You know the chap at all?"

"Well, I mean I know who he is. Mr. Davidson. We come here sometimes. There's a dance, first Saturday of the month."

"Do you think he'd know you?"

"Don't know if he knows me," said Willie.

"Well, come on, let's see what we can do." Manie Swemmer asked the Indian waiter to keep an eye on the luggage for a moment, and was directed to the reception desk. Willie came along behind him. A redhead with a skin that would dent blue if you touched it said, "Full up, sir, I'm sorry, sir—" almost before Manie Swemmer began speaking. He put his big, half-open fist on the counter, and smiled at her with his head cocked: "Now listen here, young miss, I come all the way from a place you never heard of, Bontebokspruit, and I'm sure you can find me just a bed. Anywhere. I've travelled a lot and I'm not fussy." She smiled sympathetically, but there it was—nothing to offer. She even ran her ballpoint down the list of bookings once again, eyebrows lifted and the pretty beginnings of a double chin showing.

"Look, I lived in this town while you were still a twinkle in your father's eye—I'd like to say hello to Mr. Davidson, anyway. D'you mind, eh?"

She called somewhere behind a stand of artificial roses and tulips, "Friend of Mr. Davidson's here. Can he come a minute?"

He was a little fellow with a recognizable way of hitching his arms forward at the elbow to ease his shirt cuffs up his wrists as he approached: ex-barman. He had a neat, patient face, used to dealing with trouble.

"Youngster like you wouldn't remember, but I lived in this hotel thirty years ago—I helped build this town, put up the first reservoir. Now they tell me I'll have to sleep in the street to-night."

"That's about it," the manager said.

"I can hear you're a Jock, like me, too!" Manie Swemmer seized delightedly upon the hint of a Scots accent. "Yes, you may not believe it but my grandmother was a Miss Swan. From the Clyde. Agnes Swan. I used to wear the kilt when I was a kiddie. Yes, I did! An old Boer like me."

The little man and the receptionist conferred over the list of bookings; she knew she was right, there was nothing. But the man said, "Tell you what I'll do. There's this fellow from Delhi. He h's a biggish single I could m'be put another bed in. I promised him he'd have it to himself, but still an' all. He can't object to someone like yourself, I mean."

"There you are! The good old Regent! Didn't I say to you, Willie?" Willie was leaning on the reception desk smoking and looking dazedly at the high heel of his Chelsea boot; he smiled down the side of his mouth again.

"I'll apologize for barging in on this chap, don't you worry, I'll make it all right. You say from Delhi—India?" Manie Swemmer added suddenly. "You mean an Indian chappie?"

"But he's not one of your locals," said the manager. "Not one of these fellows down here. A businessman, flown in this morning on the VC10."

"Oh, he's well-dressed, a real gentleman," the receptionist reassured in the wide-eyed recommendation of something she wouldn't care to try for herself.

"That's the way it is," the manager said, in confidence.

"Okay, okay, I'll buy. I'm not saying a word!" said Manie Swemmer. "Ay, Willie? Somewhere to lay my head, that's all I ask."

The redhead took a key out of the nesting boxes numbered on

the wall: "Fifty-four, Mr. Davidson? The boy'll bring your luggage, sir."

"Good Lord, you've got to have a bit of a nerve or you don't get anywhere, eh?" Manie walked gaily close beside his son along the corridors with their path of flowered runner and buckets of sand filled with cigarette stubs, stepping round beer bottles and tea-trays that people had put outside their doors. In the room the servant opened for him, he at once assumed snug possession. "I hope the Oriental gentleman's only going to stay one night. This'll do me fine." A divan, ready made-up with bedding and folded in the middle like a wallet, was wheeled in. He squeaked cupboards open, forced up the screeching steel fly-screens and pushed the windows wide—"Air, air, that's what we need." Willie sat on the other bed, whose cover had already been neatly turned back to allow a head to rest on the pillow; the dent was still there. The chap's things were on the dressing table. Willie fingered a pair of cufflinks with red stones in them. There was a tissue-paper airmail edition of some London newspaper, an open tin of cough lozenges, and a gold-tooled leather notebook. Rows of exquisitely neat figures, and then writing like something off a fancy carpet: "Hell, look at this, eh?" said Willie.

"Willie, I always taught you to respect other people's belongings no matter who they are."

Willie dropped the notebook finickily. "Okay, okay."

Manie Swemmer washed, combed his moustache and the back of his head where there was still some hair, put back on again the tropical-weight jacket he had bought especially for the trip. "I never used to look sloppy, not even when the heat was at its height," he remarked to Willie. Willie nodded whether he had been listening to what you said or not.

When they had returned the key to the reception desk Willie said, "We gunna eat now, Dad," but there wasn't a soul in the dining-room but a young woman finishing supper with her kiddies, and if there was one thing that depressed Manie Swemmer it was an empty hotel dining-room.

In fact, he was attracted to the bar with a mixture of curiosity and shyness, as if Manie Swemmer, twenty-three years old, in bush-jacket and well-pressed shorts, might be found drinking there. He strolled through the garden, Willie behind him, listening to the tree-frogs chinking away at the night. In spite of the town, you could still smell woodsmoke from the natives' fires. But youngsters don't notice these things. The street entrance to the bar was through a beer garden now, screened by lattice. Coloured bulbs poked red and blue light through the pattern of slats and dark blotches of creeper. There were loud voices in the local native lingo and the coughs of small children. "It's for them, let's go this way," Willie said, and he and his father went back into the hotel and entered the bar from the inside door.

It was full, all right. Manie Swemmer had never been what you would call a drinker, but for a man who lives alone there is no place where he feels at home the way he does among men in a bar. And yet there were blacks. Oh yes, that was something. Blacks sitting at the tables, and some of them not too clean or well-dressed, either. Looked like boys from the roads, labourers. Up at the bar were the white men, the wide backs and red necks almost solidly together; a black face or two above white shirts at the far end. The backs parted for father and son: they might have been expected. "Well, what's the latest from Thys, man?" Manie Swemmer was at ease at last, wedged between the shoulder of a man telling a story with large gestures, and the bar counter ringed shinily, like the dark water at Gysbert's dam.

"Nothing. Oh this girl. He's got himself engaged to this doll Lynda Thompson."

"Good grief, so he must have written! The letter's missed me. Getting engaged! Well, I've picked the right time, eh, independence anniversary and my son's engagement! We've got something to drink to, all right. When's the engagement going to be?"

"Oh it was about ten days ago. A party at her people's place in Kitwe. I couldn't get a lift up to the Copper Belt that weekend."

"But if I'd known! Why'n't Thys send me a telegram, man! I'd have taken my leave sooner!"

Willie said nothing, only looked sideways at the men beside him.

Manie Swemmer took a deep drink of his beer. "If he'd sent a telegram, man! Why'n't he let me know? I told him I was coming up the middle of the month. Why not just send a telegram at least?"

Willie had no answer. Manie Swemmer drank off his beer and ordered another round. Now he said softly, in Afrikaans, "Just go to the post office and write out a telegram, eh?"

Willie shrugged. They drank. The swell of other people's spirits, the talk and laughter around them lifted Manie Swemmer from the private place where he was beached. "Well, I'll go up and look at Miss Lynda Thompson for myself in a few days. Kitwe's a beautiful town, eh? What's the matter with the girl, is he ashamed of her or what? Is she bowlegged and squint?" He laughed. "Trust old Thys for that!"

At some point the shoulder pressing against his had gone without his noticing. A native's voice said in good English, "Excuse me, did you lose this?" The black hand with one of those expensive calendar watches at the wrist held out a South African two-rand note.

Manie Swemmer began struggling to get at his pockets. "Hang on a tick, just let me . . . yes, must be mine, I pulled it out by mistake to pay with . . . thanks very much."

"A pleasure."

One of the educated kind, some of them have studied at universities in America, even. And England was just pouring money into the hands of these people, they could go over and get the best education going, better than whites could afford. Manie Swemmer said to Willie, but in a voice to be overheard, because after all, you didn't expect such honesty of a native, it was really something to be encouraged: "I thought I'd put away all my money from home when I took out my Zambian currency in the train. Two rand! Well, that would have been the price of a few beers down the drain!"

The black said, "The price of a good bottle of brandy down there." He wore a spotless bush jacket and longs; spotless.

"You've been to South Africa?" said Manie Swemmer.

"You ever heard of Fort Hare College? I was there four years. And I used to spend my holidays with some people in Germiston. I know Johannesburg well."

"Well, let me buy you a South African brandy. Come on, man, why not?" The black man smiled and indicated casually that his bottle of beer had already been put before him. "No, no, man, that'll do for a chaser; you're going to have a brandy with me, eh?" Manie Swemmer's big body curved over the bar as he agitated for the attention of the barman. He jolted the black man's arm and almost threw Willie's glass over. "Sorry—come on, there—two brandies—wait a minute, have you got Senator? D'you want another beer, Willie?" The kid might drink brandy on his own but he wasn't going to get it from his father.

"You'll get a shock when you have to pay." The black chap was amused. He had taken a newspaper out of his briefcase and was glancing over the headlines.

"Brandy's expensive here, eh? The duty and that. When I was up on the Copper Belt as a youngster we had to drink it to keep going. Brandy and quinine. It was a few bob a bottle. That's how I learnt to drink brandy."

"Is that so?" The black man spoke kindly. "So you know this country quite a long time."

Manie Swemmer moved his elbow within half-an-inch of a nudge—"I'll bet I knew it before you did—before you were born!"

"I'm sure, I'm sure." They laughed. Manie Swemmer looked excitedly from the man to his son, but Willie was mooning over his beer, as usual. The black man—he told his name but who could catch their names—was something in the Ministry of Local Government, and he was very interested in what Manie Swemmer could tell him of the old days; he listened with those continual nods of the chin that showed he was following carefully; a proper respect—if not for a white man, then for a man as old as his father might be. He could still speak Afrikaans, Manie Swemmer discovered. He said a few sentences in a low voice but Manie Swemmer was pretty sure he could have carried on a whole conversation if he'd wanted to. "You'll excuse me if I don't join you, but you'll have another brandy?" the black man offered. "I have a meeting in"—he looked at the watch— "less than half-an-hour, and I must keep a clear head."

"Of course! You've got responsibility, now. I always say, any fool can learn to do what he's told, but when it comes to making the decisions, when you got to shift for yourself, that's the time you've either got it up here, or . . . It doesn't matter who or what you are . . ."

The man had slipped off the bar stool, briefcase between chest and arm. "Enjoy your holiday . . ."

"Everything of the best!" Manie Swemmer called after him. "I'll tell you something, Willie, he may be black as the ace of spades, but that's a gentleman. Eh? You got to be open-minded, otherwise you can't move about in these countries. But that's a gentleman!"

"Some of them put on an act," said Willie. "You get them wanting to show how educated they are. The best thing is don't take any notice."

"What's the name of that feller was talking to me?" Manie Swemmer asked the white barman. He wanted to write it down so he'd be able to remember when he told the story back home.

"You know who that is? That's Thompson Gwebo, that's one of the Under Minister's brothers," the barman said. "When he married last November they had their roast oxen and all that at his village, but the wedding reception for the government people and white people and so on was here. Five tiers to the cake. Over three hundred people. Mrs. Davidson did the snacks herself."

They began to chat, between interruptions when the barman was called away to dispense drinks. Two or three beers had their effect on Willie, too; he was beginning to talk, in reluctant spates

that started with one of his mumbled remarks, half-understood by
his father, and then developed, through his father's eager questions, into the bits and pieces of a life that Manie Swemmer
pieced together. "This feller said . . ." "Which one was that, the
manager or your mate?" "No, the one I told you . . . the one
who was supposed to turn up at the track . . ." "What track?"
"Stock car racing . . . there was this feller asked me to change the
plugs . . ."

In a way, it was just like the old days up there. Nobody
thought about going home. Not like Buks Jacobs' place, the pub
empty over dinner-time. This one was packed. The white men
were solid at the bar again, but the blacks at the tables—the
labourers—were getting rowdy. They were joined by a crowd
of black ducktails in jeans who behaved just like the white ones
you saw in the streets of Johannesburg and Pretoria. They surged
up and down between the tables and were angrily hit off, like
flies, by the labourers heavily drunk over their beer: one lifted his
bottle and brought it down on the back of one of the hooligans'
hands; there was a roar. A black lout in a shirt with 007 printed
across it kept jolting against Manie Swemmer's shoulder in the
brand-new tropical jacket. Manie Swemmer went on talking and
ignored him, but the hooligan taunted in English—"Sorry!"
He did it again: "Sorry!" The drunken black face with a fleck of
white matter at the corner of each eye breathed over him. If it'd
been a white man Manie Swemmer wouldn't have stood for
it, he'd have punched him in the nose. And at home if a native
—but at home it couldn't happen; here he was, come up to have
a look, and he'd been in some tough spots before—Good Lord,
those gyppos in Egypt, they didn't all smell of roses, either. He
knew how to hold himself in if he had to.

Then another native—one in a decent shirt and tie—came
over and said something angrily, in their own language, to the
hooligans. He said to the barman in English, "Can't you see these
men are making a nuisance of themselves? Why don't you have
them thrown out?"

The barman was quick to take the support. "These people

should be outside in the beer garden!'" he said to the company at large. "Go on, I don't want trouble in here." The hooligans drifted away from the bar counter but would not go out. Manie Swemmer had not noticed the decently-dressed native leave, but suddenly he appeared, quiet and business-like, with two black policemen in white gloves. "What's the complaint?" One shouldered past Willie to ask the barman. "Making a nuisance of themselves, those over there." There was a brief uproar; of course natives are great ones for shouting. But the black hooligans were carted away by their own policemen like a bunch of scruffy dogs; no nonsense.

"No nonsense!" said Manie Swemmer, laughing and putting his hand over Willie's forearm. "D'you see that? Good Lord, they've got marvellous physiques, that pair. Talk about smart! That's something worth seeing!" Willie giggled; his dad was talking very loud; he was talking to everyone in the place, joking with everyone. At last they found themselves at dinner, after half-past nine it must have been. There were shouts of laughter from other late diners, telling stories. Manie Swemmer began to think very clearly and seriously, and to talk very seriously to Willie, about the possibility of moving up here, himself. "I've still a lot of my life ahead of me. Must I see out my time making money for Abel Barends? In Bontebokspruit? Why shouldn't I start out on my own again? The place is going ahead!"

The jolly party left the dining-room and all at once he was terribly tired: the journey, the arrival, the first look around—it left him winded, like too hearty a slap on the back. "Let's call it a day, son," he said, and Willie saw him to the room.

But the key would not open the door. Willie investigated by the flare of a match. "S'bolted on the inside." They rapped softly, then hammered. "Well I'm damned," said Manie Swemmer. "The Indian." He had been going to tell him about how many years Y. S. Mia had had a store near the farm.

They went down to the reception desk. The redhead thrust her tongue in a bulge between lower lip and teeth, in consternation. "Have you knocked?" "The blooming door down!" said Manie Swemmer. "Mind you, I thought as much," the girl said. "He was on his high horse when he came back and saw your bed and things. I mean I don't know what the fuss was about—as I said to him, it isn't as if we've put an African in with you, it's a white man. And him Indian himself."

"Well, what're you going to do about my dad?" Willie said suddenly.

"What can I do?" She made a peaked face. "Mr. Davidson's gone off to Kapiri Mposhi, his mother's broken her hip at eighty-one. I can't depend on anyone else here to throw that chap out. And if he won't even answer the door."

Manie Swemmer said nothing. Willie waited, but all he could hear was his father's slow breathing, with little gasps on the intake. "But what about my dad?"

She had her booking list out again. They waited. "Tell you what. No.—There's a room with four beds out in the old wing, we keep it, you know—sometimes now, these people come in and you daren't say no. They don't want to pay for more than one room for the lot. It was booked, I mean, but it's after eleven now and no one's showed up, so I should think you could count on it being all right. . . ."

Manie Swemmer put his big forearm and curled hand on the reception desk like a dead thing. "Look," he said. "The coolie, all right, I didn't say anything. But don't put me in with an African, now, man! I mean, I've only just got here, give me a bit of time. You can't expect to put me in with a native, right away, first thing."

"Oh I should think it would be all right," she said in her soothing, effusive way, something to do with some English accent she had. "I wouldn't worry if I was you. It's late now. Very unlikely anyone'd turn up. Don't you think?"

She directed him to the room. Willie went with him again. Across the garden; the old block, the way it was in the old days. There was no carpet in the passage; their footsteps tottered over the unevennesses of cracked granolithic. When Willie had left him, he pulled down the bedding of the best-looking bed to have a good look at the sheets, opened the window, and then, working away at it with a grunt that was almost a giggle, managed to drive the rusty bolt home across the door.

# AN INTRUDER

SOMEONE had brought her along; she sat looking out of the rest of the noisy party in the nightclub like a bush-baby between trees. He was one of them, there was no party without him, but under the cross-fire of private jokes, the anecdotes and the drinking he cornered her, from the beginning, with the hush of an even more private gentleness and tenderness: "The smoke will brown those ears like gardenia petals." She drank anything, so long as it was soft. He touched her warm hand on the glass of lemonade; "Pass the water," he called, and dipping his folded handkerchief in among the ice cubes, wrung it out and drew the damp cloth like cool lips across the inside of her wrists. She was not a giggler, despite her extreme youth, and she smiled the small slow smile that men brought to her face without her knowing why. When one of the others took her to dance, he said seriously, "For God's sake don't breathe your damned brandy on her, Carl, she'll wilt." He himself led her to the dark crowded circle in shelter, his arms folded round her and his handsome face pressed back at the chin, so that his eyes

looked down on her in reassurance even while the din of bouzouki and drum stomped out speech, stomped through bones and
flesh in one beat pumped by a single bursting heart.

He was between marriages, then (the second or third had just
broken up—nobody really knew which), and this was always a
high time, for him. They said, Seago's back in circulation; it
meant that he was discovering his same old world anew, as good
as new. But while he was setting off the parties, the weekend
dashes here and there, the pub-crawls, he was already saying to
her mother as he sat in the garden drinking coffee, "Look at the
mother and see what you're getting in the daughter. Lucky man
that I am."

Marie and her mother couldn't help laughing and at the same
time being made to feel a little excited and worldly. His frail little marmoset—as he called her—was an only child, they
were mother-and-daughter, the sort of pair with whom a father
couldn't be imagined, even if he hadn't happened to have been
dispensed with before he could cast the reminder of a male embrace between them in the form of a likeness or gesture they
didn't share. Mrs. Clegg had earned a living for them both, doing
very pale pastels of the children of the horsy set, and very dark
pastels of African women for the tourist shops. She was an artist
and therefore must not be too conventional: she knew James
Seago had been married before, but he was so attractive—so
charming, so considerate of Marie and her and such a contrast to
the boys of Marie's own age who didn't even bother to open a
car door for a woman—there was something touching about
this man, whose place was in a dinner-jacket among the smart set,
appreciating the delicacy of the girl. "You don't mind if I take
her out with my ruffian friends? You'll let me look after her?"
—In the face of this almost wistful candour and understanding,
who could find any reality in his "reputation" with women? He
came for Marie night after night in his old black Lancia. His
ruddy, clear-skinned face and lively eyes blotted out the man her
mother heard talked about, the creation of gossip. He was—no,
not like a son to her, but an equal. When he said something nice,

he was not just being kind to an older woman. And his photograph was often on the social page.

In the nightclubs and restaurants he liked to go to he drank
bottle after bottle of wine with friends and told his mimicking
stories, all the time caressing Marie like a kitten. Sometimes he insisted that she literally sit on his knees. She spoke little, and when
she did it was to utter small, slow, sensible things that com-
manded a few seconds' polite attention before the voices broke
out at one another again. But on his knees she did not speak at
all, for while he was gesturing, talking, in response to the whole
cave of voices and music and movement, she felt his voice
through his chest rather than heard him and was filled, like a
child bottling up tears, with appalling sexual desire. He never
knew this and when he made love to her—in his bed, in the afternoons, because he kept the evenings for his friends—she was
as timid and rigid as if she had never been warmed by lust. He
had to coax her: "My little marmoset, my rabbit-nose, little teenage-doll, you will learn to like this, really you will. . . ." And in
time, always using the simple words with which some shy pet is
persuaded to drink a saucer of milk, he taught her to do all the
strange things she would not have guessed were love-making at
all, and that he seemed to enjoy so much. Afterwards, they
would go home and have tea with her mother in the garden.

With his usual upper-class candour, he constantly remarked
that he hadn't a bean; but this, like his reputation with women,
didn't match the facts of his life as Marie and her mother knew
them. He had enough money for the luxuries of bachelor life, if
not for necessities. There was the old but elegant Lancia and
there were always notes in the expensive crocodile-skin wallet (an
inscription on a silver plate, from a former wife, inside) to pay
the hotel managers and *restaurateurs* he was so friendly with,
though he lived in a shabby room in an abandoned-looking old
house rented by a couple who were his close friends. His Eng-
lish-public-school accent got him a number of vague jobs on the
periphery of influential business groups, where the crude-speak-
ing experts felt themselves hampered in public relations by their

South African inarticulateness; these jobs never lasted long. Wifeless and jobless after many wives and jobs, he still appeared to be one of those desirable men who can take anything they want of life if they think it worth the bother.

Marie, gravely fluffing out her dark hair in the ladies' rooms of nightclubs where old attendants watched from their saucers of small change, wondered what she would say when her mother found out about the afternoons in James' room. But before this could happen, one day in the garden when she was out of earshot, he said to her mother, "You know, I've been making love to her, I know one shouldn't . . . ? But we'll be able to get married very soon. Perhaps next year."

He was looking after Marie, as she walked into the house, with the rueful, affectionate gaze with which one marks a child growing up. Mrs. Clegg was irresistibly tempted to fit the assumption that she took sexual freedom for granted: after all, she was an artist, not a bourgeois housewife. She decided, again, his frankness was endearingly admirable; he was human, Marie was beautiful, what else could you expect?

The marriage was put off several times—there was some business of his trying to get back his furniture from his divorced wife, and then there was a job connected with an Angolan diamond-mining company that didn't come off. At last he simply walked in one morning with the licence and they were married without Marie or her mother going to the hairdresser or any friends being told. That night there was a surprise for his bride: apparently two of his best friends were arriving on a visit from England, and all their old friends were to meet them at the airport and go straight to their favourite nightclub, the place where, incidentally, he and Marie had met. The bouzouki player was persuaded to carry on until nearly five in the morning, and then they went to someone's house where champagne was produced as the sky pinkened and the houseboy came in with his dust-pan and brush. Marie did not drink and she repaired her perfect makeup every hour; though pale, she was as fresh and circumspect among their puffy faces and burning eyes at the end of the night as she was at the beginning. He slept all next day and she lay contentedly beside him in the room in the old house, watching the sun behind the curtains try first this window and then the next. But no one could get in; he and she were alone together.

They found a flat, not a very pleasant one, but it was only temporary. It was also cheap. He was so amusing about its disadvantages, and it was such fun to bob in and out of each other's way in the high dark cell of a bathroom every morning, that after the dismay of her first look at the place, she really ceased to see the things she disliked about it so much—the fake marble fireplace and the thick mesh burglar-proofing over all the windows. "What are these people afraid of?" Her tiny nostrils stiffened in disdain.

"Angel . . . your world is so pink and white and sweet-smelling . . . there are stale women with mildew between their breasts who daren't open doors."

She put up white gauzy curtains everywhere, and she went about in short cotton dressing-gowns that smelt of the warm iron. She got a part-time job and saved to buy a scrubbed white wood dining-table and chairs, and a rose silk sari to make up as a divan cover. "Damned lawyers twiddling their thumbs. When'll I see my furniture from that freckled bitch," he said. The wife-before-the-last, a Catholic, was referred to as "Bloody-minded Mary, Our Lady of the Plastic Peonies" because, looking back on it, what he really couldn't stand about her was the habit she had of putting artificial flowers on the table among real leaves. He seemed to have parted from these women on the worst of terms and to dismiss his association with them—a large part of his life—as a series of grotesque jokes.

"What do you think you'd call me if we were divorced?"

"You . . ." He took Marie's head between his hands and smoothed back the hair from her temples, kissing her as if trying with his lips the feel of a piece of velvet. "What could anyone say about you." When he released her she said, going deep pink from the ledges of her small collar-bones to her black eyes, all pupil: "That sugar-tit tart." The vocabulary was his all right, coming out in her soft, slow voice. He was enchanted, picked her up, carried her round the room. "Teenage-doll! Marmoset-angel! I'll have to wash your mouth out with soap and water!"

They continued to spend a lot of time at nightclubs and drinking places. Sometimes at eleven o'clock on a weekday night, when lights were going out in bedrooms all over the suburb, he would take the old Lancia scrunching over the dark drive of someone's house, and while Marie waited in the car, stand throwing gravel at a window until his friends appeared and could be persuaded to get dressed and come out. He and his friends were well known in the places they went to and they stayed until they were swept out. Manolis or Giovanni, the Greek or Italian owner, would sit deep in the shadows, his gaze far back in fatigue that ringed his eyes like a natural marking, and watch these people who were good business and would not go to bed: these South Africans who did not know any better. Sometimes she and the proprietor in whose blood the memory of Dionysiac pleasures ran were the only spectators left. James, her husband, did not appear drunk during these sessions, but next day he would remember nothing of what he had said or done the night before. She realized that she, too, sitting on his lap while he murmured loving things into her ear under the talk, was blacked out along with the rest. But she had seen envy behind the expressions of other women that suggested they wouldn't care for such an exhibition of affection.

There were people who seemed to know him whom he didn't remember at all, either; a man who came up to them as they were getting out of the car in town one day and laid a hand on his shoulder—"James . . ."

He had looked round at the man, casual, edgy, with the patient smile of someone accosted by a stranger.

"James . . . What's the matter? Colin—"

"Look, old man, I'm sorry, but I'm afraid—"

"Colin. Colin. The Golden Horn Inn, Basutoland."

He continued to look into the man's face as if at an amiable lu-

natic, while the man's expression slowly changed to a strange, co-
quettish smile. "Oh I see. Well, that's all right, James."

She supposed they must have been drinking together once.

Sometimes she wondered if perhaps he had been as crazy about
those other women, his wives, as he was about her, and did not
remember: had forgotten other wild nights in the wine that
washed them all out. But that was not possible; she enjoyed the
slight twinge of jealousy she induced in herself with the thought.
She was going to have a baby, and he had never had a child with
anyone else. She said, "You haven't a child somewhere?"

"Breed from those gorgons? Are you mad?"

But coarse words were not for her; he said to her mother, "Do
you think I should have given her a child? She's a little girl herself." He kissed and petted her more than ever; the signs of her
womanhood saddened and delighted him, like precocity. She did
not talk to him about after the baby was born, about a bigger
flat—a little house, perhaps, with a garden?—and where to
dry napkins and not being able to leave a baby at night. In the
meantime, they had a good time, just as before.

And then one night—or rather one early morning—
something awful happened that made it suddenly possible for
her to speak up for a move, napkins, the baby as a creature with
needs rather than as a miraculous function of her body. They had
been at Giovanni's until the small hours; as usual, there had been
some occasion for celebration. She drove home and they had
gone to bed and into a sleep like a death—his, from drink, hers
from exhaustion. Pregnancy made her hungry and she woke at
eight o'clock to the church bells of Sunday morning and slid out
of bed to go to the kitchen. She bumped into a chair askew in the
passage, but in her sleepy state it was nothing more significant
than an obstacle, and when she reached the kitchen she stood
there deeply puzzled as if she had arrived somewhere in sleep and
would wake in the presence of familiar order in a moment.

For the kitchen was wrecked; flour had been strewn, syrup had
been thrown at the walls, soap powder, milk, cocoa, salad oil

were upset over everything. The white muslin curtains were ripped to shreds. She began to shake; and suddenly ran stumbling back to the bedroom.

He lay fast asleep, as she had lain, as they both had lain while this—Thing—happened. While Someone. Something. In the flat with them.

"James," she screamed hoarsely whispering, and flung herself on him. His head came up from under his arm, the beard strong-textured in the pink firm skin; he frowned at her a moment, and then he was holding her in a kind of terror of tenderness. "Marmoset. Rabbit." She buried her head in the sleep-heat between his shoulder and neck and gestured fiercely back at the door.

"Christ almighty! What's wrong?"

"The kitchen! The kitchen!"

He struggled to get up.

"Don't go there."

"Sweetling, tell me, what happened?"

She wouldn't let him leave her. He put his two hands round her stone-hard belly while she controlled shuddering breaths. Then they went together into the other rooms of the flat, the kitchen, the living-room, and the dark hole of a bathroom, her bare feet twitching distastefully like a cat's at each step. "Just look at it." They stood at the kitchen door. But in the living-room she said, "*What is it?*" Neither of them spoke. On each of the three divisions of the sofa cushions there was a little pile, an offering. One was a slime of contraceptive jelly with hair-combings—hers—that must have been taken from the waste-paper basket in the bedroom; the other was toothpaste and razor blades; the third was a mucous of half-rotted vegetable matter—peelings, tea leaves, dregs—the intestines of the dustbin.

In the bathroom there were more horrors; cosmetics were spilt, and the underwear she had left there was arranged in an obscene collage with intimate objects of toilet. Two of her pretty cotton gowns lay in the bath with a bottle of liqueur emptied on them. They went again from room to room in silence. But the mess spoke secretly, in the chaos there was a jeering pattern, a logic outside sense that was at the same time *recognizable*, as a familiar object turned inside-out draws a blank and yet signals. There was something related only to them in this arrangement without values of disrelated objects and substances; it was, after all, the components of their daily existence and its symbols. It was all horrible: horribly familiar, even while they were puzzled and aghast.

"This flat. The light has to be on in the bathroom all day. There's no balcony for the baby to sleep on. The washing will never dry. I've never been able to get rid of the black beetles in the kitchen, whatever I put down."

"All right, angel, poor angel."

"We can't live here. It's not a place for a baby."

He wanted to phone for the police but it did not seem to occur to her that there could be a rational explanation for what had happened, a malicious and wicked intruder who had scrawled contempt on the passionate rites of their intimacy, smeared filth on the cosy contemporary home-making of the living-room, and made rags of the rose silk cover and the white muslin curtains. To her, evil had come out of the walls, as the black beetles did in the kitchen.

It was not until some days had passed and she had calmed down—they found another flat—that the extraordinariness of the whole business began to mean something to her: she and James had gone round the flat together, that morning, and there wasn't a door or window by which anyone could have got in. Not a pane was broken and there was that ugly burglar-proofing, anyway. There was only one outer door to the flat, and she had locked it when they came home and put the key, as usual, on the bedside table; if someone had somehow managed to steal the key, how could they have put it back on the table after leaving the flat, and how could the door have been left bolted on the inside? But more amazing than how the intruder got in, why had he done so? Not a penny or a piece of clothing had been stolen.

They discussed it over and over again; as he kept saying, "There must be an explanation, something so simple we've missed it. Poltergeists won't do. Are you sure there couldn't have been someone hiding in the flat when we came home, marmoset-baby? Did either of us go into the living-room before we went to bed?" —For of course he didn't remember a thing until he woke and found she had flung herself on him terrified.

"No, I told you, I went into the living-room to get a bottle of lime juice, I went into all the rooms," she repeated in her soft, slow, reasonable voice; and this time, while she was speaking, she began to know what else he would never remember, something so simple that she had missed it.

She stood there wan, almost ugly, really like some wretched pet monkey shivering in a cold climate. But she was going to have a child, and—yes, looking at him, she was grown-up, now, suddenly, as some people are said to turn white-haired over-night.

# INKALAMU'S PLACE

Inkalamu Williamson's house is sinking and I
don't suppose it will last out the next few rainy seasons. The red
lilies still bloom as if there were somebody there. The house was
one of the wonders of our childhood and when I went back to
the territory last month for the independence celebrations I
thought that on my way to the bauxite mines I'd turn off the
main road to look for it. Like our farm, it was miles from anywhere when I was a child, but now it's only an hour or two
away from the new capital. I was a member of a United Nations
demographic commission (chosen to accompany them, I suppose,
because of my old connection with the territory) and I left the
big hotel in the capital after breakfast. The Peking delegation, who
never spoke to any of us and never went out singly, came down
with me in the lift. You could stare at them minutely, each in
turn, neither they nor you were embarrassed. I walked through
the cocktail terrace where the tiny flags of the nations stood
on the tables from last night's reception, and drove myself out

along the all-weather road where you can safely do eighty and drive straight on, no doubt, until you come out at the top of the continent—I only think of these things this way now; when I grew up here, this road didn't go anywhere else but home.

I had expected that a lot of the forest would have been cut down, but once outside the municipal boundary of the capital, it was just the same as always. There were no animals and few people. How secretly Africa is populated; when I got out of the car to drink coffee from my flask, I wanted to shout: Anybody there? The earth was neatly spaded back from the margins of the tar. I walked a few steps into the sunny forest, and my shoes exploded twigs and dry leaves like a plunderer. You must not start watching the big, egg-timer-bodied ants: whole afternoons used to go, like that.

The new tarred road cuts off some of the bends of the old one, and when I got near the river I began to think I'd overshot the turn-off to Inkalamu's place. But no. There it was, the long avenue of jacarandas plunging into the hilly valley, made unfamiliar because of a clearing beside the main road and a cottage and little store that never used to be there. A store built of concrete blocks, with iron bars on the windows, and a veranda: the kind of thing that the Africans, who used to have to do their buying from Indians and white people, are beginning to go in for in the territory, now. The big mango tree was still there—a home-made sign was nailed to it: KWACHA BEER ALL BRANDS CIGARETTES. There were hens, and someone whose bicycle seemed to have collapsed on its side in the heat. I said to him, "Can I go up to the house?"

He came over holding his head to one shoulder, squinting against the flies.

"Is it all right?"

He shook his head.

"Does someone live in the house, the big house?"

"Is nobody."

"I can go up and look?"

"You can go."

Most of the gravel was gone off the drive. There was just a hump in the middle that scraped along the underside of the low American car. The jacarandas were enormous; it was not their blooming time. It was said that Inkalamu Williamson had made this mile-and-a-half-long avenue to his house after the style of the carriage-way in his family estate in England; but it was more likely that, in the elevation of their social status that used to go on in people's minds when they came out to the colonies, his memory of that road to the great house was the village boy's game of imagining himself the owner as he trudged up on an errand. Inkalamu's style was that of the poor boy who has found himself the situation in which he can play at being the lordly eccentric, far from aristocrats who wouldn't so much as know he existed, and the jeers of his own kind.

I saw this now; I saw everything, now, as it had always been, and not as it had seemed to us in the time when we were children. As I came in sight of the shrubbery in front of the house, I saw that the red amaryllis, because they were indigenous anyway, continued to bloom without care or cultivation. Everything else was blurred with overgrowth. And there was the house itself; sagging under its own weight, the thatch over the dormer windows sliding towards the long grass it came from. I felt no nostalgia, only recognition.

It was a red mud house, as all our houses were then, in the early thirties, but Inkalamu had rather grandly defied the limitations of mud by building it three stories tall, a sandcastle reproduction of a large, calendar-picture English country house, with steep thatch curving and a wide chimney at either end, and a flight of steps up to a portico. Everyone had said it would fall down on his head; it had lasted thirty years. His mango and orange trees crowded in upon it from the sides of the valley. There was the profound silence of a deserted man-made place—the silence of absence.

I tried to walk a little way into the mango grove, but year after year the crop must have been left to fall and rot, and between the rows of old trees hundreds of spindly saplings had grown up from seed, making a dark wood. I hadn't thought of going into the house, but walked round it to look for the view down the valley to the mountains that was on the other side; the rains had washed a moat at the foot of the eroded walls and I had to steady myself by holding on to the rusty elbows of plumbing that stuck out. The house was intimately close to me, like a body. The lop-sided wooden windows on the ground floor with their tin panes, the windows of the second floor with their panes of wire mesh, hung half-open like the mouths of old people asleep. I found I could not get all the way round because the bush on the valley side had grown right to the walls, and instead I tried to pull myself up and look inside. Both the mud and wattle gave way under my feet, the earth mixture crumbling and the supporting structure—branches of trees neither straightened nor dressed—that it had plastered, collapsing, hollowed by ants. The house had not fallen on Inkalamu and his black children (as the settlers had predicted) but I felt I might pull it down upon myself. Wasps hovered at my mouth and eyes, as if they, too, wanted to look inside: me. Inkalamu's house, that could have housed at least ten people, was not enough for them.

At the front again, I went up the steps where we used to sit scratching noughts and crosses while my father was in the house. Not that our families had been friends; only the children, which didn't count—my father and mother were white, my father a member of the Legislative Assembly, and Inkalamu's wives were native women. Sometimes my father would pay a call on Inkalamu, in the way of business (Inkalamu, as well as being a trader and hunter—the Africans had given him the name Inkalamu, "the lion"—was a big land-owner, once) but my mother never accompanied him. When my brothers and I came by ourselves, Inkalamu's children never took us to the house; it didn't seem to be *their* home in the way that our small farm-house was our home, and perhaps their father didn't know that we came occasionally, on our own, to play, any more than our mother and father knew we secretly went there. But when we were with my father—there was a special attraction about going to that house openly, with him—we were always called in, after business was concluded, by Inkalamu Williamson, their white father, with his long yellow curly hair on to his shoulders, like Jesus, and his sun-red chest and belly folded one upon the other and visible through his unbuttoned shirt. He gave us sweets while those of his own children who had slipped inside stood in the background. We did not feel awkward, eating in front of them, for they were all shades of brown and yellow-brown, quite different from Inkalamu and my father and us.

Someone had tied the two handles of the double front door with a piece of dirty rag to prevent it from swinging open, but I looped the rag off with a stick, and it was easy to push the door and go in. The place was not quite empty. A carpenter's bench with a vice stood in the hall, some shelves had been wrenched from the wall and stood on the floor, through the archway into the sitting-room I saw a chair and papers. At first I thought someone might still be living there. It was dim inside and smelled of earth, as always. But when my eyes got accustomed to the dark I saw that the parts of the vice were welded together in rust and a frayed strip was all that was left on the rexine upholstery of the chair. Bat and mouse droppings carpeted the floor. Piles of books looked as if they had been dumped temporarily during a spring-cleaning; when I opened one the pages were webbed together by mould and the fine granules of red earth brought by the ants.

*The Tale of a Tub. Mr. Perrin and Mr. Traill. Twenty Thousand Leagues Under the Sea.* Little old red Everymans, mixed up with numbers of *The Farmer's Weekly* and *Titbits.* This room with its crooked alcoves moulded out of mud and painted pink and green, and its pillars worm-tracked with mauve and blue by someone who had never seen marble to suggest marble to people who did not know what it was—it had never looked habitable. Inkalamu's roll-top desk, stuffed like a pigeon-loft with accounts ready to take off in any draught, used to stand on one of the uneven-boarded landings that took up more space than the dingy coops of rooms. Here in the sitting-room he would perform for-

malities like the distribution of sweets to us children. I don't
think anyone had ever actually sat between the potted ferns and
read before a real fire in that fireplace. The whole house, inside,
had been curiously uninhabitable; it looked almost the real thing,
but within it was not the Englishman's castle but a naïve artifact,
an African mud-and-wattle dream—like the VC10 made of
mealie stalks that a small African boy was hawking round the airport when I arrived the previous week.

A grille of light gleamed through the boards over my head.
When Inkalamu went upstairs to fetch something, his big boots
would send red sand down those spaces between the boards. He
was always dressed in character, with leather leggings, and the
cloudy-faced old watch on his huge round wrist held by a strap
made of snakeskin. I went back into the hall and had a look at
the stairs. They seemed all right, except for a few missing steps.
The banisters made of the handrails of an old tram-car were still
there, and as I climbed, flakes of the aluminium paint that had once
covered them stuck to my palms. I had forgotten how ugly
the house was upstairs, but I suppose I hadn't been up very often;
it was never clear whether Inkalamu's children actually lived in
the house with him or slept down at the kraal with their mothers. I think his favourite daughters lived with him sometimes—anyway, they wore shoes, and used to have ribbons for
their hair, rather pretty hair, reddish-dun and curly as bubbles;
I hadn't understood when I was about six and my brothers
rolled on the floor giggling when I remarked that I wished I had
hair like the Williamson girls. But I soon grew old enough to
understand, and I used to recount the story and giggle, too.

The upstairs rooms were murmurous with wasps and the little
windows were high as those of a prison-cell. How good that it
was all being taken apart by insects, washed away by the rain,
disappearing into the earth, carried away and digested, frag-
mented to compost. I was glad that Inkalamu's children were free
of it, that none of them was left here in this house of that "character" of the territory, the old Africa hand whose pioneering
spirit had kept their mothers down in the compound and allowed

the children into the house like pets. I was glad that the school where they weren't admitted when *we* were going to school was open to their children, and our settlers' club that they could never have joined was closed, and that if I met them now they would understand as I did that when I was the child who stood and ate sweets under their eyes, both they and I were what our fathers, theirs and mine, had made of us. . . . And here I was in Inkalamu Williamson's famous bathroom, the mark of his civilization, and the marvel of the district because those very pipes sticking out of the outside walls that I had clung to represented a feat of plumbing. The lavatory pan had been taken away but the little tank with its tail of chain was still on the wall, bearing green tears of verdigris. No one had bothered to throw his medicines away. He must have had a year or two of decline before he died, there must have been an end to the swaggering and the toughness and the hunting trips and the strength of ten men: medicines had been dispensed from afar, they bore the mouldering labels of pharmacists in towns thousands of miles away—Mr. Williamson, the mixture; the pills, three times a day; when necessary; for pain. I was glad that the Williamsons were rid of their white father, and could live. Suddenly, I beat on one of the swollen windows with my fist and it flung open.

The sight there, the silence of it, smoking heat, was a hand laid to quiet me. Right up to the house the bush had come, the thorn trees furry with yellow blossom, the overlapping umbrellas of rose, plum and green *msasa*, the shouldering mahogany with castanet pods, and far up on either side, withdrawn, moon-mountainous, the granite peaks, lichen-spattered as if the roc perched there and left its droppings. The exaltation of emptiness was taken into my lungs. I opened my mouth and received it. Good God, that valley!

And yet I did not stand there long. I went down the broken stairs and out of the house, leaving the window hanging like the page of an open book, adding my destruction to all the others just as careless, that were bringing the house to the ground; more rain would come in, more swifts and bats to nest. But it is the

ants who bring the grave to the house, in the end. As I pushed
the swollen front doors roughly closed behind me I saw them, in
their moving chain from life to death, carrying in the grains of
red earth that will cover it.

They were black, with bodies the shapes of egg-timers. I
looked up from them, guilty at waste of time, when I felt someone watching me. In the drive there was a young man without
shoes, his hands arranged as if he had an imaginary hat in them. I
said good morning in the language of the country—it suddenly
came to my mouth—and he asked me for work. Standing on
the steps before the Williamsons' house, I laughed: "I don't live
here. It's empty."

"I have been one years without a work," he said mouthingly in
English, perhaps as a demonstration of an additional qualification.

I said, "I'm sorry. I live very far from here."

"I am cooking and garden too," he said.

Then we did not know what to say to each other. I went to
the car and gave him two shillings out of my bag and he did
what I hadn't seen since I was a child, and one of Inkalamu's servants used to take something from him—he went on his knees,
clapped once, and made a bowl of his hands to receive the
money.

I bumped and rocked down the drive from that house that I
should never see again, whose instant in time was already forgotten, renamed, like the public buildings and streets of the
territory—it didn't matter how they did it. I only hoped that
the old man had left plenty of money for those children of his,
Joyce, Bessie—what were the other ones' names?—to enjoy
now that they were citizens of their mothers' country. At the
junction with the main road the bicycle on its side and the man
were still there, and a woman was standing on the veranda of the
store with a little girl. I thought she might have something to do
with the people who owned the land, now, and that I ought to
make some sort of acknowledgment for having entered the prop-

erty, so I greeted her through the car window, and she said, "Was the road very bad?"

"Thank you, no. Thank you very much."

"Usually people walks up when they come, now. I'm afraid to let them take the cars. And when it's been raining!"

She had come down to the car with the smile of someone for whom the historic ruin is simply a place to hang the washing. She was young, Portuguese, or perhaps Indian, with piled curls of dull hair and large black eyes, inflamed and watering. She wore tarnished gilt earrings and a peacock brooch, but her feet swished across the sand in felt slippers. The child had sore eyes, too; the flies were at her.

"Did you buy the place, then?" I said.

"It's my father's," she said. "He died about seven years ago."

"Joyce," I said. "It's Joyce!"

She laughed like a child made to stand up in class. "I'm Nonny, the baby. Joyce is the next one, the one before."

Nonny. I used to push her round on my bicycle, her little legs hanging from the knee over the handlebars. I told her who I was, ready to exchange family news. But of course our families had never been friends. She had never been in our house. So I said, "I couldn't go past without going to see if Inkalamu Williamson's house was still there."

"Oh yes," she said. "Quite often people comes to look at the house. But it's in a terrible mess."

"And the others? Joyce, and Bessie, and Roger—?"

They were in this town or that; she was not even sure which, in the case of some of them.

"Well, that's good," I said. "It's different here now, there's so much to do, in the territory." I told her I had been at the independence celebrations; I was conscious, with a stab of satisfaction at the past, that we could share now as we had never been able to.

"That's nice," she said.

"—And you're still here. The only one of us still here! Is it a long time since it was lived in?" The house was present, out of sight, behind us.

"My mother and I was there till—how long now—five years ago,"—she was smiling and holding up her hand to keep the light from hurting her eyes—"but what can a person do there, it's so far from the road. So I started this little place." Her smile took me into the confidence of the empty road, the hot morning, the single customer with his bicycle. "Well, I must try. What can you do?"

I asked, "And the other farms, I remember the big tobacco farm on the other side of the river?"

"Oh that, that was gone long before he died. I don't know what happened to the farms. We found out he didn't have them any more, he must have sold them, I don't know . . . or what. He left the brothers a tobacco farm—you know, the two elder brothers, not from my mother, from the second mother—but it came out the bank had it already. I don't know. My father never talk to us about these business things, you know."

"But you've got this farm." We were of the new generation, she and I. "You could sell it, I'm sure. Land values are going to rise again. They're prospecting all over this area between the bauxite mines and the capital. Sell it, and—well, do—you could go where you like."

"It's just the house. From the house to the road. Just this little bit," she said, and laughed. "The rest was sold before he died. It's just the house, that he left to my mother. But you got to live, I mean."

I said warmly, "The same with my father! Our ranch was ten thousand acres. And there was more up at Lebishe. If he'd have hung on to Lebishe alone we'd have made a fortune when the platinum deposits were found."

But of course it was not quite the same. She said sympathetically, "Really!" to me with my university-modulated voice. We were smiling at each other, one on either side of the window of the big American car. The child, with bows in its hair, hung on to her hand; the flies bothered its small face.

"You couldn't make some sort of hotel, I suppose."

"It's in a mess," she said, assuming the tone of a flighty, apologetic housewife. "I built this little place here for us and we just left it. It's so much rubbish there still."

"Yes, and the books. All those books. The ants are eating them." I smiled at the little girl as people without children of their own do. Behind, there was the store, and the cottage like the backyard quarters provided for servants in white houses. "Doesn't anyone want the books?"

"We don't know what to do with them. We just left them. Such a lot of books my father collected up." After all, I knew her father's eccentricities.

"And the mission school at Balondi's been taken over and made into a pretty good place?" I seemed to remember that Joyce and one of the brothers had been there; probably all Inkalamu's children. It was no longer a school meant for black children, as it had been in our time. But she seemed to have only a polite general interest: "Yes, somebody said something the other day."

"You went to school there, didn't you, in the old days?"

She giggled at herself and moved the child's arm. "I never been away from here."

"Really? Never!"

"My father taught me a bit. You'll even see the schoolbooks among that lot up there. Really."

"Well, I suppose the shop might become quite a nice thing," I said.

She said, "If I could get a licence for brandy, though. It's only beer, you see. If I could get a licence for brandy. . . . I'm telling you, I'd get the men coming." She giggled.

"Well, if I'm to reach the mines by three, I'd better move," I said.

She kept smiling to please me; I began to think she didn't remember me at all; why should she, she had been no bigger than her little daughter when I used to take her on the handlebars of my bicycle. But she said, "I'll bring my mother. She's inside." She turned and the child turned with her and they went into the shade of the veranda and into the store. In a moment they came out with a thin black woman bent either by age or in greeting —I was not sure. She wore a head-cloth and a full long skirt of the minutely-patterned blue-and-white cotton that used to be in bales on the counter of every store, in my childhood. I got out of the car and shook hands with her. She clapped and made an obeisance, never looking at me. She was very thin with a narrow breast under a shrunken yellow blouse pulled together by a flower with gaps like those of missing teeth in its coloured glass corolla. Before the three of them, I turned to the child rubbing at her eyes with hands tangled in the tendrils of her hair. "So you've a daughter of your own now, Nonny."

She giggled and swung her forward.

I said to the little girl, "What's hurting you, dear?— Something wrong with her eyes?"

"Yes. It's all red and sore. Now I've got it too, but not so bad."

"It's conjunctivitis," I said. "She's infected you. You must go to the doctor."

She smiled and said, "I don't know what it is. She had it two weeks now."

Then we shook hands and I thought: I mustn't touch my face until I can wash them.

"You're going to Kalondwe, to the mine." The engine was running. She stood with her arms across her breasts, the attitude of one who is left behind.

"Yes, I believe old Doctor Madley's back in the territory, he's at the W.H.O. centre there." Dr. Madley had been the only doctor in the district when we were all children.

"Oh yes," she said in her exaggeratedly interested, conversational manner. "He didn't know my father was dead, you know, he came to see him!"

"I'll tell him I've seen you, then."

"Yes, tell him." She made the little girl's limp fat hand wave good-bye, pulling it away from her eyes—"Naughty, naughty." I suddenly remembered—"What's your name now, by the way?"; the times were gone when nobody ever bothered to know the married names of women who weren't white. And I didn't want to refer to her as Inkalamu's daughter. Thank God she was free of him, and the place he and his kind had made for her. All that was dead, Inkalamu was dead.

She stood twiddling her ear-rings, bridling, smiling, her face not embarrassed but warmly bashful with open culpability, "Oh, just Miss Williamson. Tell him Nonny."

I turned carefully on to the tar, I didn't want to leave with my dust in their faces. As I gathered speed I saw in the mirror that she still had the child by the wrist, waving its hand to me.

# THE LIFE OF THE IMAGINATION

As a child she did not inhabit their world, a place where whether the so-and-sos would fit in at dinner, and whose business it was to see that the plumber was called, and whether the car should be traded in or overhauled were the daily entries in a ledger of living. The sum of it was the comfortable, orderly house, beds with turned-down sheets from which nightmares and dreams never overstepped the threshold of morning, good-night kisses as routine as the cleaning of teeth, a woman stating her truth, "Charles would never eat a warmed-over meal," a man defining his creed, "One thing I was taught young, the value of money".

From the beginning, for her, it was the mystery and not the carefully-knotted net with which they covered it, as the high-wire performer is protected from the fall. Instead of dust under the beds there was (for her) that hand that Malte Laurids Brigge saw reaching out towards him in the dark beneath his mother's table. Only she was not afraid, as she read, later, he was; she recognized, and grasped it.

And she never let go.

She did not make the mistake of thinking that because of this she must inevitably be able to write or paint; that was just another of the axioms that did for them (Barbara has such a vivid imagination, she is so artistic). She knew it was one thing to have entry to the other world, and another entirely to bring something of it back with you. She studied biology at the university for a while (the subject, incising soft fur and skin to get at the complexities beneath, lured her, and they heard there were good positions going for girls with a BSc. degree) but then left and took a job in a municipal art gallery. She began by sorting sepia postcards and went on to dust Chinese ceramic roof tiles and to learn how to clean paintings. The smell of turpentine, size, and coffee in the room where she and the director worked was her first intimacy. They wondered how she could be so happy there, cut off from the company of young people, and once her father remarked half-meaningfully that he hoped the director wouldn't get any ideas.

The director had many ideas, including the only one her father thought of. He was an oldish man—to her, at the time, anyway—with the proboscis-face that often goes with an enquiring mind, and a sudden nakedness of tortoise-shell-coloured eyes when he took off his huge glasses. His wife said, "It's wonderful for Dan to have you working for him. He's always been one of those men who are at their best mentally only when they are more or less in love." He told his assistant the story of Wu Ch'eng-ên's characters, the monkey, the pilgrim Tripitaka, Sandy, Pigsy and the two horses she had dusted, as well as giving her a masterly analysis of the breakdown of feudalism in relation to the success of the Long March. He had a collection of photographs he had taken of intricate machinery and microphotography of the cells of plants, and together, using her skill in dissecting rats and frogs and grasshoppers, they added blow-ups of animal tissue. He kissed her occasionally, but rather as if that were simply part of the order of the cosmos; his lips were thin, now, and he knew it. It was through him that she met and fell in love with the young architect whom she married, and with whom she went to Japan, where he had won a scholarship to the University of Tokyo. They wandered about the East and Europe together for a year or two (it was just as her parents expected; she had no proper home) and then came back to South Africa where he became a very successful architect indeed and made an excellent living.

It was as simple and confounding as that. Government administration as well as the great mining and industrial companies employed him to design one public building after another. He and Barbara had a serene, self-effacing house on a *kopje* outside Pretoria—the garden demonstrated how well the spare, indigenous thorn trees of the Middle Veld followed the Japanese architectural idiom. They had children. Barbara remained, in her late thirties, a thin, tall creature with a bony face darkened by freckles, good-looking and much given to her own company. Money changed her dress little, and her tastes not at all; she was able to indulge them rather more. She had a *pondokkie* down in the Low Veld, on the Crocodile River, where she went sometimes in the winter to stay for a week or two on her own. Marriage was not possible, of course. Certainly not of true minds, because if one is ever going to find release from the mesmerism of appearances one is condemned to make the effort by oneself. And daily intimacy was an inevitable attempt to avoid this that left one sharing bed, bathroom, and table, solitary as in any crowd. She and Arthur, her husband, knew it; they got on almost wordlessly well, now and then turned instinctively to each other, and were alone, he with his work and she with her books and her *pondokkie*. They made their children happy. The school headmaster said they were the most "creative" children that had ever passed through his hands (Barbara's children are so artistic, Barbara's children are so imaginative).

They got measles and ran sudden fevers at awkward times, just like other children, and one evening when Barbara and Arthur were about to go out to dinner, Pete was discovered to have a high temperature. The dinner was for a visiting Danish architect who had particularly requested to meet Arthur, so he went on ahead while Barbara stayed to see what the doctor would say. She had not been particularly pleased to hear that the family doctor was away on holiday in Europe, and his locum tenens would be coming instead. He was perhaps a little surprised to be met at the door by a woman in evening dress—the house itself was something that made unexpected demands on the attention of people who had not seen anything like it before. She felt the necessity to explain her appearance, partly to disguise the slight hostility she felt towards him for being a substitute for a reassuring face—"We were just going out when I noticed my son looked like a beetroot."

He smiled. "It's a change from curlers and dressing-gowns." And they stood there, she in her long dress, he with coat and brown bag, as if for a split second the situation of their confrontation was not clear; had they bumped into one another, stupidly both dodging in the same direction to avoid colliding in the street? Then the lapse closed and they proceeded to the bedroom where Pete and Bruce sat up in their beds expectantly. Pete said, "That's not our doctor."

"No, I know, this is Doctor Asher, he's looking after everybody while Doctor Dickson's away."

"You won't give me an injection?" said Pete.

"I don't think you've got the sort of sickness that's going to need an injection," the man said. "Anyway, I give injections so fast you don't even know they've happened. Really."

The little one, Bruce, giggled, flopped back in bed and pulled the sheet over his mouth.

The doctor said, "You mustn't laugh at me. You can ask my children. One, two—before you can count three—it's done."

Bruce said to him, "It's not nice to swank."

The doctor looked up over his open bag and appeared to flinch at this grown-up dictum. "I'm sorry. I won't do it any more."

When he had examined Pete he prescribed a mixture that Dr. Dickson had often given the children; Barbara went to look in the medicine chest, and there was an almost full bottle there. Pete had swollen glands at the base of his skull and under the jawline.

THE LIFE OF THE IMAGINATION

"We'll watch it," the doctor said, as Barbara preceded him down the passage. "I've seen several cases of glandular fever since I've been here. Ring me in the morning if you're worried." Again they stood in the entrance, she with her hands hanging at the sides of her long skirt, he getting into his coat. He was no taller than she, and probably about the same age, but tired, with the travel-worn look of general practitioners, perpetually lugging a bag around with them. His hair was a modified version of the sort of Julius Caesar cut affected by architects, journalists and advertising men; doctors usually stuck to short back and sides. She thanked him, using his name, and he remarked, pausing at the door, "By the way, it's Usher—with a U."

"Oh, I'm sorry—I misheard, over the phone. Usher."

He was looking up and around the house. "Japanese style, isn't it? They grow those miniature trees—amazing. There was an article about them the other day, I can't remember where I . . . What d'you call it?"

She had kept from childhood an awkward gesture of jerking her chin when embarrassed. One look at the house and people racked their brains for something apposite to say and up came those horrible little stunted trees. "Oh yes. Bonsai. Thank you very much. Good night."

When he had gone she went at once to give Pete his medicine and the nanny the telephone number of the hotel where the dinner was being held. Afterwards, she remembered with a detached clarity those few minutes before she left the house, when she was in and out of her sons' room: the light that seemed reddish, with the stuffy warmth of childhood colouring it, the stained rugs, the nursery-school daubs stuck on the walls, Dora's cheerfully scornful African voice and the hoist of her big rump as she bent about tidying up, the smell of fever on Pete's lips as she kissed him and the encounter, under the hand she leaned on, with the comforting midden of a child's bed—bits of raw potato he had been using as ammunition in a pea-shooter, the hard shape of a piece of jigsaw puzzle, the wooden spatula the doctor had used to flatten his tongue. And it seemed to her that even at the time, she had

had a rare momentary vision of herself (she was not a woman given to awareness of creating effects). She had thought— moving between the small beds slowly because of the long dress, perfumed and painted—this is the image of the mother that men have often chosen to perpetuate, the autobiographers, the Prousts. This is what I may be for one of these little boys when I have become an old woman with bristles on her chin, dead.

Pete was better next day. The doctor came at about half-past one, when the child was asleep and she was eating her lunch off a tray in the sun. The servant led the doctor out onto the terrace. He didn't want to disturb her; but she was simply having a snack, as he could see. He sat down while she told him about the child. She had a glass of white wine beside her plate of left-over fish salad—the wine was a left-over, too, but still, what interest could that be to him, whether or not she habitually bibbed wine alone at lunch? The man looked with real pleasure round the calm and sunny terrace and she felt sorry for him because he thought bonsai trees were wonderful. "Have a glass of wine— it's lovely and cold." Her bony feet were bare in the winter sun. He refused; of course, a doctor can't do as he likes. But he took out a pipe, and smoked that. "The sun's so pleasant. I must say Pretoria has its points." They were both looking at her toes, on each foot the second one was crooked; it was because the child was asleep, of course, that he sat there. He told her that he came from Cape Town, where it rained all winter. They went upstairs to look at the child; he was breathing evenly and soundlessly. "Leave him," the doctor said. Downstairs he added, "Another day or two in bed, I'd say. I'd like to check those glands again."

He came just before two the following day. This time he ac- cepted a cup of coffee. It was just as it had been yesterday; it might have been yesterday. It was almost the same time of day. The sun had exactly the same strength. They sat on the broad brick seat with its thick cushion. His pipe smoke hung a little haze before their eyes. She was telling him the child was so much better that it really was impossible to keep him in bed, when he looked at her amusedly, as if he had found them both out—

himself and her—and his arm, with the hand curved to bring her to him, drew her in. They kissed and without thinking at all whether she wanted to kiss him or not, she found herself anxious to be skilful. She seemed to manage very well because the kissing went on for minutes, their heads turning this way and that as their mouths slowly detached and met.

And so it began. When they drew back from each other the words flew to her: why this man, for heaven's sake—why you? And because she was ashamed of the thought, she said aloud instead, "Why me?"

He found this apparent unawareness of her own attractions so moving that he kissed her fiercely, answering, for her, both questions, the spoken and unspoken.

While they were kissing she became aware of the slightest, quickest sideways movement of the one slate-coloured eye she could see, a second before she herself heard the squeak of the servant's sandshoes approaching from within the house. They drew apart, she in jerky haste, he with composed swiftness so that the intimacy between them held good even while he put his pipe in his pocket, took out a prescription pad and was remarking, when the servant picked up the coffee tray, "It mightn't be a bad idea to keep some sort of mild anti-pyretic in the house, not as strong as that mixture he's been having, I mean, but . . ."

So it began. The love-making, the absurdities of concealment; even the acceptance of the knowledge that this hard-working doctor with the sickle-line of a smile cut down either side of his mouth, and the brown, coarse-grained forehead, had gone through it all before, perhaps many times. So it began, exactly as it was to be.

They made love the first time in the flat he was living in temporarily. It was a ravishing experience for both of them and when it was over—for the moment—they knew that they must turn their attention urgently and at once to the intensely practical business of how, when and where they were to continue to be together. After a month his wife came up from Cape Town and things were more difficult. He had taken a house for his family; the sublet flat with other people's books and sheets and bric-à-brac, in which he and Barbara were the only objects familiar to each other, became a paradise lost. They drove then, separately, all the way to Johannesburg to spend an afternoon together in an hotel (Pretoria was too small a place for one to expect to go unrecognized). He was tied to his endless working hours; they had nowhere to go. Their problem was passion but they could hope for only the most down-to-earth, realistic solutions. One could not flinch from them. After the last patient left the consulting rooms in the evening the building was deserted—an office block. He made little popping noises on his pipe as he decided they would be quite safe there. Deaf and blind with anticipation of the meeting, she would come from the side street where her car was parked, through the dark foyer, past the mops and bucket of the African cleaner, up in the lift with its glowing eye showing as it rose through successive levels, then along the corridors of closed doors and commercial name-plates until she was there: Dr. J. McDow Dickson, M.B.B.Ch. Edin. Consulting Hours, Mornings 11–1, Afternoons 4–6. On the old day-bed in Dr. Dickson's anteroom they made love, among the medical insurance calendars and the desk accessories advertising antibiotics. Once the cleaner was heard turning his pass-key in the waiting-room door; once someone (a patient, no doubt) hammered at it for a while, and then went away. She had always been sure, without censure, that shabby love-affairs would be useless, for her. She learnt that shabbiness is the judgment of the outsider, the one left in the cold; there are no shabby love affairs for those who are the lovers.

They met wherever and however and for whatever length of time they could, but still by far the greater part of their time was spent apart. Communications, movements, meeting-places—all this had to be settled as between two secret agents whom the world must not suspect to be in contact. In order to plan strategy, each had to brief the other about the normal pattern of his life: this was how they got to know, bit by bit, that yawning area of each other's lives that existed outside one another's arms. "On

Thursday nights I'm always alone because Arthur takes a seminar at the university." "You can safely ring me any Sunday morning between eight and nine because Yvonne goes to Mass."

So his wife was a Catholic. Well, yes; but he was not. Of course that meant that his children were being brought up as Catholics. One evening when he and Barbara were putting on their clothes again in the consulting rooms she had seen the picture of the three little girls, under the transparent plastic slot in his wallet. White-blond hair, short and straight as a nylon toothbrush, threaded ribbon, net petticoats, white socks held by elastic—the children of one of those nice, neat pretty women, who look after them just as carefully as they used to take care of their dolls. Barbara never met her. He said that the local doctors' wives were being very kind—she was playing tennis regularly at the house of one, and another had little girls the same age who had become inseparable from his girls. If he and Barbara met at the consulting rooms on Friday evenings, he had to keep an eye on his watch—"Bridge night," he said, doggedly, resignedly. Sometimes he said, "Blast bridge night."

Between embraces, confessions, questions came easily, up to a point. "You lead a very different life," he said.

He meant "from mine." Or from hers, perhaps—his wife's.

Lying there, Barbara pulled a dismissing face.

"Oh yes." He did not want to be excepted, indulged, out of love; he had his own regard for the truth. "What was wrong about the Japanese trees, that time—that first night I came to your house—what did I say? There was such a look on your face."

"Oh that. The bonsai business." The reproach was for herself; he didn't understand the shrinking in repugnance from "good taste"—well, wasn't the shrinking as daintily fastidious, in its way, as the "good taste" itself? You went whoring after one concept or the other of your own sensibility. "Not different at all," —she returned to his original remark; she had this quality, he noticed, of keeping a series of remarks you had passed laid out before her, and then unhesitatingly turning to pick up this one or that— "It's like putting a net into the sea. You bring up small fish or big fish, weeds, muck, little bright bits of things. But the water, the element that's living—that's drained away."

"—So tonight it's bridge," she added, putting out her hand to caress his chest.

He took the pipe out of his mouth. "When you're down at the Crocodile," he said—they called her *pondokkie* that because it was on the Crocodile River— "What are you doing there, when you're alone?"

She lay under his gaze; she felt the quality she had for him, awkwardly, as if he had stuck a jewel on her forehead. She didn't answer.

"Reading, eh? Reading and thinking your own thoughts." For years he had barely had time to get through the medical journals.

She was seeing the still, dry stretch to the horizon, each thorn bush like every other thorn bush, the narrow cattle paths leading back on themselves through the clean, dry grass, the silence into which one seemed to fall, at midday, as if into an airpocket; the silence there would be one day when one's heart stopped, while everything went on as it did in that veld silence, the hard trees waiting for sap to rise, the dead grass waiting to be sloughed off the new under rain, the boulders cracking into new forms under frost and sun.

But alive under her hand was the hair of his breast, still damp and soft from contact with her body, and she said, keeping her teeth together, "I wish we could go there. I wish we were in bed there now."

That winter she did not go once to the shack. It had become nothing but a shelter where they could have made love, whole nights and days. There were so many hours when they could not see each other. Could not even telephone; he was at home with his family, she with hers. Such slow stretches of mornings, thawing in the sun; such long afternoons when the interruption of her children was a monstrous breaking-in upon—what? She was doing nothing. She saw him as she had once watched him without his being aware of her, crossing a street and walking the length of a block to their meeting-place: a slight man with a pipe held between his teeth in a rather brutal way, a smiling curve of the mouth denied by the downward, inward lines of brow and eyelids as his head bobbed. In his hand the elegant pigskin bag she had given him because it was easy to explain away as the gift of some grateful patient. He sees nobody, only where he is going. Sitting at dinner parties or reading at night, she saw him like this in broad daylight, crossing the street, bag in hand. It seemed she could follow him through all the hill-cupped small city, make out his back among all others, crossing the square past Dr. Dolittle in his top hat (that was what her little boys thought the statue of President Kruger was), doing the rounds in the suburbs, the car full of pipe-smoke and empty phials with their necks snapped off, the smile a grim habit, greeting no one.

Sometimes he materialized at her own door—he'd had a call in the neighbourhood, or told the nurse so, anyway. It would be in the morning, when the boys were at school and Arthur was at the town studio. He always went straight to the telephone and rang up the consulting rooms, so that he'd be covered if his car happened to be seen: "Oh Birdie, I'm around Muckleneuk—if there's anyone I ought to drop in on out this way? My next call will be the Wilson child, Waterkloof Road, so—" Then they would sit on the terrace again and have coffee. And he would give his expert glance round doors and windows before kissing her; he smelt of the hospital theatre he had been in, or the soap he had washed his hands with in other people's houses. He wore a pullover his mother had sent him, he had pigskin gloves Yvonne had bought him—he smiled, telling it—because she thought the smart new bag made his old ones look so shabby. For Barbara there was the bloom on him of the times when he was not with her.

She had never been in his house, of course, and she did not know the disposition of the rooms, or the sound of voices calling through it in the early morning rush to get to school and hospital rounds (she knew he got up very early, before she would even be awake), or the kind of conversation that came to life over drinks when friends were there; or the atmosphere, so strongly personal in every house, of the hour late at night when outsiders have gone and doors are being locked and lights switched off, one by one.

She had never been with him in the company of other people (unless one counted Pete and Bruce) and she did not know how he would appear in their eyes, or what his manner would be. She listened with careful detachment when he telephoned the nurse; he had a tired, humorous way with her—but that was just professional camaraderie, with a touch of the flirtatiousness that pleases old ladies. Once or twice he had had to phone his wife in Barbara's presence: it was the anonymous telecommunication of long marriage—"Yvonne? I'm on my way. Oh, twenty minutes or so. Well, if he does, say I'll be in any time after nine. Yes. No, I won't. See you."

When they were together after love-making they talked about their past lives and discussed his future. He intended, within the next year, to go to America to do what he had always wanted —biological research. They discussed in great detail the planning of his finances: he had sold his practice in Cape Town in order to be able to keep his family while studying on a grant he'd been promised. The six months' locum-tenency was a stop-gap between selling the practice and taking up the grant in Boston. He had moments of deep uncertainty: he should have gone ten years ago, young and single-minded—but, helplessly, even then there was a girl, marriage, babies. From the depths of his uncertainty he and Barbara looked at each other like two prisoners who wake up and find themselves on the floor of the same cell. He said, as if for what it was worth, "I love you." They became absorbed again in the questions of how he should best use his opportunities in America, and under whom he should try to get the chance to work. And then it was time to get dressed, time up, time to go, time to be home to change for his bridge evening, time to be home to receive Arthur's friends. Standing in the lift together they were silent, weary, at one. They left the consulting room building separately; as she walked away he became again that figure crossing streets, going in and out of houses and car, pigskin doctor's bag in hand, seeing nobody, only where he was going.

Her mind constructed snatches of dialogue, like remembered fragments of a play. She was following him home to the bridge table (she had never played card games) or the dinner table—there was a roast, that would be the sort of thing, a brown leg of pork with apple sauce, and he was carving, knowing what cut each member of the little family liked best. The white-haired, white-socked little girls had washed their hands. The bridge players talked with the ease of colleagues, the wives were saying, "John wouldn't touch it," "I must say the only thing he always does remember is when to pay the insurance," "I can't get anyone to do shirt collars properly." She had the feeling his wife bought his clothes for him; but the haircut—that he chose for himself. As he chose her, Barbara, and other women. On Sundays she lay with an unread book on the terrace or laughed and talked without listening among Arthur's friends (they all seemed to be Arthur's friends, now) and he was running about some clean, hard tennis court, red in the face, agile, happy perhaps, in the mindless happiness of physical exercise. She was not jealous, only slightly excited by the thought of him with her completely out of mind. Or perhaps this Sunday they had taken the children on some outing. Once when she had visualized him all afternoon on that tennis court, he had happened to mention that Sunday afternoon had been swallowed up in a family outing—the children had heard about a game park in Krugersdorp. The plain, white-haired little girl clambered over him to see better; was he irritated? Or was he smoothing the hair behind the child's ears with that lover's gesture of his, also, perhaps, a father's gesture? She read over again a paragraph in the book lying between her elbows on the grass: ". . . the word *lolo* means both 'soul' and 'butterfly' . . . the dual meaning is due to the fact that the chrysalis resembles a shrouded corpse and that the butterfly emerges from it like the soul from the body of a sleeping man." But the idea had no meaning for her. The words floated on her mind; no, a moth, quite an ordinary-looking, protectively-coloured moth, not noticed going about the streets, quickly crossing the square in the early evening, coming softly along the corridor, touching softly. Fierily, making quick the sleeping body.

One night when she had the good luck to be alone for a few days (Arthur was in the Cape), he was able to slip away and come to her at home. This rare opportunity required careful planning, like every other arrangement between them. He said he was going to a meeting of the medical association; she had an early dinner, to be sure the servants would be out of the way. She saw to it that all the windows of the house except those of her bedroom should be in darkness, so that any unexpected caller would presume she had gone to bed and not disturb her. In fact she did lie on her bed, fully dressed, waiting for him. She had given him the key of the side door, off the terrace, that afternoon. He came with a quiet, determined hesitancy through another man's house. He had never been into the bedroom before but he knew where the children's rooms were. When she heard him reach the passage where a turn divided the parents' quarters from the children's, she got up and went softly to meet him. But the little boys were asleep, long ago. She took his two clean hands, dryly cold from the winter night, in hers, and then they crept along together. In the bedroom, when she had shut the door behind them, she was cold and trembling, as if she too had just found shelter.

He had to leave not long after the time the meeting would end; now, because this was her own bed, in her own home, she lay there naked, flung back under the disarray of bedclothes, and watched him dress alone. He took her brush and put it through his hair before the mirror, with a quick, knowing look at himself. He sat on the bed, like a doctor, to embrace her a last time. She watched him softly release the handle of the door, almost without a click, as he closed it on her, heard him going evenly, quietly down the corridor, listened to the faint creak and stir of him

making his way through the big living-room, and then, after a
pause, heard the clip of his footsteps dying away across the terrace. The engine of the car started up; shadows from its lights
flew across the bedroom windows.

She put up her hand to switch off the bed lamp but did not
move her head or body. She lay in the dark for a long time just
as he had left her; perhaps she slept. There seemed to be a dark
wind blowing through her hollow mind; she was awake, and
there was a night wind come up, the cold gale of the winter veld,
pressing against the walls and windows like pressure in one's ears.
A thorn branch scrabbled on the terrace wall. She heard dry
leaves swirl and trail across the flagstones. And irregularly, at
long intervals, a door banged without engaging its latch. She
tried to sleep or to return to sleep, but some part of her mind
waited for the impact of the door in the wind. And it came,
again and again. Slowly, reasoned thought cohered round the
sound: she identified the direction from which it came, her mind
travelled through the house the way he had gone, and arrived at
the terrace door. The door banged, with a swinging shudder,
again.

He's left the door open. She saw it; saw the gaping door, and
the wind bellying the long curtains and sending papers skimming
about the room, the leaves sailing in and slithering across the
floors. The whole house was filling up with the wind. There had
been burglaries in the suburb lately. This was one of the few
houses without an alarm system—she and Arthur had refused
to imprison themselves in the white man's fear of attack on himself and his possessions. Yet now the door was open like the door
of a deserted house and she found herself believing, like any other
suburban matron, that someone must enter. They would come in
unheard, with that wind, and approach through the house, black
men with their knives in their hands. She, who had never submit-
ted to this sort of fear ever in her life, could hear them coming,
hear them breathe under their dirty rag masks and their *tsotsi*
caps. They had killed an old man on a farm outside Pretoria last
week; someone described in the papers as a mother of two had

held them off, at her bedside, with a golf club. Multiple wounds, the old man had received, multiple wounds.

She was empty, unable to summon anything but this stale fantasy, shared with the whole town, the whole white population. She lay there possessed by it, and she thought, she violently longed —they will come straight into the room and stick a knife in me. No time to cry out. Quick. Deep. Over.

The light came instead. Her sons began to play the noisy whispering games of children, about the house in the very early morning.

# A MEETING IN SPACE

EVERY MORNING he was sent to the baker
and the French children slid out of dark walls like the village cats
and walked in his footsteps. He couldn't understand what they
said to each other, but he thought he understood their laughter:
he was a stranger. He looked forward to the half-fearful, disdain-
ful feeling their presence at his back gave him, and as he left the
house expected at each alley, hole and doorway the start of dread
with which he would see them. They didn't follow him into the
baker's shop. Perhaps the baker wouldn't have them—they
looked poor, and the boy knew, from the piccanins at home, that
poor kids steal. He had never been into a bakery at home in
South Africa; the baker-boy, a black man who rode a tricycle
with a rattling bin on the front, came through the yard holding
the loaves out of the way of the barking dogs, and put two white
and one brown on the kitchen table. It was the same with fruit
and vegetables; at home the old Indian, Vallabhbhai, stopped his
greengrocer's lorry at the back gate, and his piccanin carried into
the kitchen whatever you bought.

But here, the family said, part of the fun was doing your own shopping in the little shops that were hidden away by the switch-back of narrow streets. They made him repeat over and over again the words for asking for bread, in French, but once in the baker's shop he never said them, only pointed at the loaf he wanted and held out his hand with money in it. He felt that he was someone else, a dumb man perhaps. After a few days, if he were given change he would point again, this time at a bun with a glazing of jam. He had established himself as a customer. The woman who served chattered at him, smiled with her head on one side while she picked the money out of his palm; but he gave no sign of response.

There was another child who sometimes turned up with the usual group. He would hail them loudly, from across a street, in their own language, and stalk along with them for a bit, talking away, but he looked different. The boy thought it was just be-cause this one was richer. Although he wore the usual canvas shoes and cotton shorts, he was hung about with all sorts of equipment—a camera and two other leather cases. He began to appear in the bakery each morning. He stood right near, as if the dumb person were also invisible, and peering up experiencedly under a thick, shiny fringe of brown hair, looked along the cakes on top of the counter while apparently discussing them in a jok-ing, familiar way with the woman. He also appeared unexpect-edly in other places, without the group. Once he was leaning against the damp archway to the tunnel that smelled like a school lavatory—it was the quick way from the upper level of streets to the lower. Another time he came out of the door of the streaky-pink-painted house with the Ali Baba pots, as if he must have been watching at the window. Then he was balancing along the top of the wall that overlooked the pitch where in the afternoons the baker and other men played a bowling game with a heavy ball. Suddenly, he was outside the gate of the villa that the family were living in; he squatted on the doorstep of the house opposite, doing something to the inside of his camera. He spoke: "You English?"

"Yes—not really—no. I mean, I speak English, but I come from South Africa."

"Africa? You come from *Africa?* That's a heck of a way!"

"Fifteen hours or so. We came in a jet. We actually took a little longer because, you see, something went wrong with the one engine and we had to wait three hours in the middle of the night in Kano. Boy, was it hot, and there was a live camel wandering around." The anecdote cut itself off abruptly; the family often said long-winded stories were a bore.

"I've had some pretty interesting experiences myself. My parents are travelling round the world and I'm going with them. Most of the time. I'll go back home to school for a while in the Fall. Africa. Fan-tastic. We may get out there sometime. D'you know anything about these darned Polaroids? It's stuck. I've got a couple of pictures of you I must show you. I take candid shots. All over the place. I've got another camera, a Minox, but I mostly use this one here because it develops the prints right in the box and you can give them to people right off. It's good for a laugh. I've got some pretty interesting pictures, too."

"Where was I—in the street?"

"Oh I'm taking shots all the time. All over the place."

"What's the other case?"

"Tape-recorder. I'll get you on tape, too. I tape people at Zizi's Bar and in the *Place*, they don't know I'm doing it, I've got this mi-nute little mike, you see. It's fan-tastic."

"And what's in here?"

The aerial was pulled out like a silver wand. "My transistor, of course, my beloved transistor. D'you know what I just heard? —'Help!' Are the Beatles popular down in Africa?"

"We saw them in London—alive. My brother and sister and me. She bought the record of 'Help!' but we haven't got anything to play it on, here."

"Good God, some guys get all the breaks! You *saw* them. You notice how I've grown my hair? Say, look, I can bring down my portable player and your sister can hear her record."

"What time can you come?"

"Any time you say. I'm easy. I've got to go for this darned French lesson now, and I *have* to be in at noon so that old Madame Blanche can give me my lunch before she quits, but I'll be around in-definitely after that."

"Straight after lunch. About two. I'll wait for you here. Could you bring the pictures, as well—of me?"

Clive came racing through the tiny courtyard and charged the flyscreen door, letting it bang behind him. "Hey! There's a boy who can speak English! He just talked to me! He's a real Amur-r-rican—just wait till you hear him. And you should see what he's got, a Polaroid camera—he's taken some pictures of me and I didn't even know him—and he's got a tiny little tape-recorder, you can get people on it when they don't know—and the smallest transistor I've ever seen."

His mother said, "So you've found a pal. Thank goodness." She was cutting up green peppers for salad, and she offered him a slice on the point of her knife, but he didn't see it.

"He's going round the world, but he goes back to America to school sometimes."

"Oh, where? Does he come from New York?"

"I don't know, he said something about Fall, I think that's where the school is. The Fall, he said."

"That's not a place, silly—it's what they call autumn."

The shower was in a kind of cupboard in the kitchen-dining room, and its sliding door was shaken in the frame, from inside. The impatient occupant got it to jerk open: she was his sister. "You've found what?" The enormous expectancy with which she had invested this holiday, for herself, opened her shining face under its plastic mob-cap.

"We can hear the record, Jen, he's bringing his player. He's from America."

"How old?"

"Same as me. About."

She pulled off the cap and her straight hair fell down, covering her head to the shoulders and her face to her eyelashes. "Fine," she said soberly.

His father sat reading *Nice-Matin* on one of the dining-table chairs, which was dressed, like a person, in a yellow skirt and a cover that fitted over its hard back. He had—unsuccessfully —put out a friendly foot to trip up the boy as he burst in, and now felt he ought to make another gesture of interest. As if to claim that he had been listening to every word, he said, "What's your friend's name?"

"Oh, I don't know. He's American, he's the boy with the three leather cases—"

"Yes, all right—"

"You'll see him this afternoon. He's got a Beatle cut." This last was addressed to the young girl, who turned, halfway up the stone stairs with a train of wet footprints behind her.

But of course Jenny, who was old enough to introduce people as adults do, at once asked the American boy who he was. She got a very full reply. "Well, I'm usually called Matt, but that's short for my second name, really—my real names are Nicholas Matthew Rootes Keller."

"Junior?" she teased, "The Third?"

"No, why should I be? My father's name is Donald Rootes Keller. I'm named for my grandfather on my mother's side. She has one hell of a big family. Her brothers won five decorations between them, in the war. I mean, three in the war against the Germans, and two in the Korean War. My youngest uncle, that's Rod, he's got a hole in his back—it's where the ribs were— you can put your hand in. My hand, I mean"—he made a fist with a small, thin, tanned hand—"not an adult person's. How much more would you say my hand had t'grow, I mean— would you say half as much again, as much as that?—to be a full-size, man's hand—" He measured it against Clive's; the two ten-year-old fists matched eagerly.

"Yours and Clive's put together—one full-size, king-size,

man-size paw. Clip the coupon now. Enclose only one box-top or reasonable facsimile."

But the elder brother's baiting went ignored or misunderstood by the two small boys. Clive might react with a faint grin of embarrassed pleasure and reflected glory at the reference to the magazine ad culture with which his friend was associated by his brother Mark. Matt went on talking in the innocence of one whose background is still as naturally accepted as once his mother's lap was.

He came to the villa often after that afternoon when the new Beatle record was heard for the first time on his player. The young people had nothing to do but wait while the parents slept after lunch (the *Place*, where Jenny liked to stroll, in the evenings, inviting mute glances from boys who couldn't speak her language, was dull at that time of day) and they listened to the record again and again in the courtyard summer-house that had been a pig-sty before the peasant cottage became a villa. When the record palled, Matt taped their voices—"Say something African!"—and Mark made up a jumble of the one or two Zulu words he knew, with cheer-leaders' cries, words of abuse, and phrases from familiar road signs, in Afrikaans. "*Sakabona! Voetsak hambakahle hou links malingi mushle—Vrystaat!*" The brothers and sister rocked their rickety chairs back ecstatically on two legs when it was played, but Matt listened with eyes narrowed and tongue turned up to touch his teeth, like an ornithologist who is bringing back alive the song of rare birds. "Boy, thanks. Fan-tastic. That'll go into the documentary I'm going to make. Partly with my father's movie camera, I hope, and partly with my candid stills. I'm working on the script now. It's in the family, you see." He had already explained that his father was writing a book (several books, one about each country they visited, in fact) and his mother was helping. "They keep to a strict schedule. They start work around noon and carry on until about one a.m. That's why I've got to be out of the house very early in the morning and I'm not supposed to come back in till they wake up for lunch. And that's why I've got to keep out of the house in the afternoons, too; they got to have peace *and* quiet. For sleep *and* for work."

Jenny said, "Did you see his shorts—that Madras stuff you read about? The colours run when it's washed. I wish you could buy it here."

"That's a marvellous transistor, Dad." Mark sat with his big bare feet flat on the courtyard flagstones and his head hung back in the sun—as if he didn't live in it all the year round, at home; but this was France he basked in, not sunlight.

"W-e-ll, they spoil their children terribly. Here's a perfect example. A fifty-pound camera's a toy. What's there left for them to want when they grow up."

Clive would have liked them to talk about Matt all the time. He said, "They've got a Maserati at home in America, at least, they did have, they've sold it now they're going round the world."

The mother said, "Poor little devil, shut out in the streets with all that rubbish strung around his neck."

"Ho, rubbish, I'm sure!" said Clive, shrugging and turning up his palms exaggeratedly. "Of course, hundreds of dollars of equipment are worth nothing, you know, nothing at all."

"And how much is one dollar, may I ask, mister?" Jenny had learned by heart, on the plane, the conversion tables supplied by the travel agency.

"I don't know how much it is in our money—I'm talking about America—"

"You're not to go down out of the village with him, Clive, ay, only in the village," his father said every day.

He didn't go out of the village with the family, either. He didn't go to see the museum at Antibes or the potteries at Vallauris or even the palace, casino, and aquarium at Monte Carlo. The ancient hill village inside its walls, whose disorder of streets had been as confusing as the dates and monuments of Europe's overlaid and overlapping past, became the intimate map of their domain—his and Matt's. The alley cats shared it but the people, talking their unintelligible tongue, provided a babble beneath which, while performed openly in the streets, his activities with Matt acquired secrecy: as they went about, they were hidden even more than by the usual self-preoccupation of adults. They moved from morning till night with intense purpose; you had to be quick around corners, you mustn't be seen crossing the street, you must appear as if from nowhere among the late afternoon crowd in the *Place* and move among them quite unobtrusively. One of the things they were compelled to do was to get from the church—very old, with chicken-wire where the stained glass must have been, and a faint mosaic, like a flaking transfer—to under the school windows without attracting the attention of the children. This had to be done in the morning, when school was in session; it was just one of the stone houses, really, without playgrounds: the dragging chorus of voices coming from it reminded him of the schools for black children at home. At other times the village children tailed them, jeering and mimicking, or in obstinate silence, impossible to shake off. There were fights and soon he learned to make with his fingers effective insulting signs he didn't understand, and to shout his one word of French, their bad word—*merde!*

And Matt talked all the time. His low, confidential English lifted to the cheerful rising cadence of French as his voice bounced out to greet people and rebounded from the close walls back to the privacy of English and their head-lowered conclave again. Yet even when his voice had dropped to a whisper, his round dark eyes, slightly depressed at the outer corners by the beginning of an intelligent frown above his dainty nose, moved, parenthetically alert, over everyone within orbit. He greeted people he had never seen before just as he greeted local inhabitants. He would stop beside a couple of sightseers or a plumber lifting a manhole and converse animatedly. To his companion standing by, his French sounded much more French than when the village children spoke it. Matt shrugged his shoulders and thrust out his lower lip while he talked, and if some of the people he accosted were uncomfortable or astonished at being addressed volubly, for no particular reason, by someone they didn't know, he asked them questions (Clive could hear they were questions) in the jolly tone of voice that grown-ups use to kid children out of their shyness.

Sometimes one of the inhabitants, sitting outside his or her doorway on a hard chair, would walk inside and close the door when Matt called out conversationally. "The people in this town are really psychotic, I can tell you," he would say with enthusiasm, dropping back to English. "I know them all, every one of them, and I'm not kidding." The old women in wrinkled black stockings, long aprons and wide black hats who sat on the *Place* stringing beans for Chez Riane, the open-air restaurant, turned walnut-meat faces and hissed toothlessly like geese when Matt approached. Riane ("She topped the popularity poll in Paris, can you believe it? It was just about the time of the Flood, my father says"), a woman the size of a prize fighter who bore to the displayed posters of herself the kinship of a petrified trunk to a twig in new leaf, growled something at Matt from the corner of her vivid mouth. "I've got some great pictures of *her*. Of course, she's a bit *passé*."

They got chased when Matt took a picture of a man and a girl kissing down in the parking area below the château. Clive carried his box camera about with him, now, but he only took pictures of the cats. Matt promised that Clive would get a shot of the dwarf—a real man, not in a circus—who turned the spit in the restaurant that served lamb cooked the special way they did it here, but, as Matt said, Clive didn't have the temperament for a great photographer. He was embarrassed, ashamed, and frightened when the dwarf's enormous head with its Spanish dancer's sideburns reddened with a temper too big for him. But Matt had caught him on the Polaroid; they went off to sit in someone's doorway hung with strips of coloured plastic to keep out flies, and had a look. There was the dwarf's head, held up waggling on his little body like the head of a finger-puppet. "Fan-tastic." Matt was not boastful but professional in his satisfaction. "I didn't have a good one of him before, just my luck, we hadn't been here a week when he went crazy and was taken off to some hospital. He's only just come back into circulation, it's a good thing you didn't miss him. You might've gone back to Africa and not seen him."

The family, who had admired the boy's Madras shorts or his transistor radio, enjoyed the use of his elegant little record player, or welcomed a friend for Clive, began to find him too talkative, too often present, and too much on the streets. Clive was told that he *must* come along with the family on some of their outings. They drove twenty miles to eat some fish made into soup. They took up a whole afternoon looking at pictures. "What time'll we be back?" he would rush in from the street to ask. "I don't know—sometime in the afternoon." "Can't we be back by two?" "Why on earth should we tie ourselves down to a time? We're on holiday." He would rush back to the street to relay the unsatisfactory information.

When the family came home, the slim little figure with its trappings would be ready to wave at them from the bottom of their street. Once in the dark they made him out under the street-light that streaked and flattened his face and that of the village half-wit and his dog; he looked up from conversation as if he had been waiting for a train that would come in on time. Another day there was a message laid out in the courtyard with matches end-to-end: WILL SEE YOU LATER MATT.

"What's the matter with those people, they don't even take the child down to the beach for a swim," said the mother. Clive heard, but was not interested. He had never been in the pink house with the Ali Baba pots. Matt emerged like one of the cats, and he usually had money. They found a place that sold bubble-gum and occasionally they had pancakes—Clive didn't know that that was what they were going to be when Matt said he was going to buy some *crêpes* and what kind of jam did Clive like? Matt paid; there was his documentary film, and he was also writing a book—"There's a lot of money in kids' books actually written by a kid," he explained to the family. It was a spy story

—"Really exotic." He expected to do well out of it, and he might sell some of his candid shots to *Time* and *Life* as well.

But one particularly lovely morning Clive's mother said as if she couldn't prevent herself, perhaps Matt would like to come with the family to the airport? The boys could watch the jets land while the grownups had business with the reservation office. "Order yourselves a lemonade if you want it," said the father; he meant that he would pay when he came back. They drank a lemonade-and-ice cream each and then Matt said he'd like a black coffee to wash it down, so they ordered two coffees, and the father was annoyed when he got the bill—coffee was nothing at home, but in France they seemed to charge you for the glass of water you got with it.

"I can drink five or six coffees a day, it doesn't bother my liver," Matt told everyone. And in Nice, afterwards, trailing round the Place Masséna behind Jenny, who wanted to buy a polo shirt like the ones all the French girls were wearing, the boys were not even allowed to go and look at the fountain alone, in case they got lost. Matt's voice fell to a whisper in Clive's ear but Clive hardly heard and did not answer: here, Matt was just an appendage of the family, like any other little boy.

It was Saturday and when they drove home up the steep road (the half-wit and his dog sat at the newly-installed traffic light and Matt, finding his voice, called out of the window a greeting in French) the village was already beginning to choke with weekend visitors. Directly lunch was down the boys raced to meet beneath the plaque that commemorated the birth in this street of Xavier Duval, Resistance fighter, killed on the 20th October, 1944. Clive was there first and faithfully carrying out the technique and example of his friend, delightedly managed to take a candid shot of Matt before Matt realized that he was observed. It was one of the best afternoons they'd had. "Saturdays are always good," said Matt. "All these psychotic people around. Just keep your eyes open, brother. I wrote Chapter Fourteen of my book at lunch. Oh, it was on a tray in my room—they were out until about four this morning and they didn't get up. It's set in this airport, you see—remember how you could just see my mouth moving and you couldn't hear a thing in the racket with that jet taking off?—well, someone gets murdered right there drinking coffee and no one hears the scream."

They were walking through the car-park, running their hands over the nacre-sleek hoods of sports models, and half-attentive to a poodle-fight near the *petanque* pitch and a human one that seemed about to break out at the busy entrance to the men's lavatories that tunnelled under the *Place*. "Ah, I've got enough shots of delinquents to last me," Matt said. In accord they went on past the old girl in flowered trousers who was weeping over her unharmed, struggling poodle, and up the steps to the *Place*, where most of the local inhabitants and all the visitors, whose cars jammed the park and stopped up the narrow streets, were let loose together, herded by Arab music coming from the boutique run by the French Algerians, on the château side, and the recorded voice, passionately hoarse, of Riane in her prime, from the direction of Chez Riane. The dwarf was there, talking between set teeth to a beautiful blonde American as if he were about to tear her apart with them; her friends were ready to die laughing, but looked kindly in order not to show it. The old women with their big black hats and apron-covered stomachs took up space on the benches. There were more poodles and an Italian greyhound like a piece of wire jewellery. Women who loved each other sat at the little tables outside Riane's, men who loved each other sat in identical mauve jeans and pink shirts, smoking, outside Zizi's Bar. Men and women in beach clothes held hands, looking into the doorways of the little shops and bars, and pulling each other along as the dogs pulled along their owners on fancy leashes. At the *Crêperie*, later, Matt pointed out Clive's family, probably eating their favourite liqueur pancakes, but Clive jerked him away.

They watched *petanque* for a while; the butcher, a local champion, was playing to the gallery, all right. He was pink and wore a tourist's fish-net vest through which wisps of reddish chest-hair twined like a creeper. A man with a long black cape and a huge cat's whisker moustache caused quite a stir. "My God, I've been trying to get him for weeks—" Matt ducked, Clive quickly following, and they zigzagged off through the *petanque* spectators. The man had somehow managed to drive a small English sports car right up onto the *Place;* it was forbidden, but although the part-time policeman who got into uniform for Saturday afternoons was shouting at him, the man couldn't be forced to take it down again because whatever gap it had found its way through was closed by a fresh influx of people. "He's a painter," Matt said. "He lives above the shoemaker's, you know that little hole. He doesn't ever come out except Saturdays and Sundays. I've got to get a couple of good shots of him. He looks to me the type that gets famous. Really psychotic, eh?" The painter had with him a lovely, haughty girl dressed like Sherlock Holmes in a man's tweeds and deerstalker. "The car must be hers," said Matt. "He hasn't made it, yet; but I can wait." He used up almost a whole film: "With a modern artist, you want a few new angles."

Matt was particularly talkative, even going right into Zizi's Bar to say hello to her husband, Emile. The family were still sitting at the *Crêperie;* the father signed to Clive to come over and at first he took no notice. Then he stalked up between the tables. "Yes?"

"Don't you want some money?"

Before he could answer, Matt began jerking a thumb frantically. He ran. His father's voice barred him: "Clive!" But Matt had come flying: "Over there—a woman's just fainted or died or something. We got to go—"

"What *for?*" said the mother.

"God almighty," said Jenny.

He was gone with Matt. They fought and wriggled their way into the space that had been cleared, near the steps, round a heavy woman lying on the ground. Her clothes were twisted; her mouth bubbled. People argued and darted irresistibly out of the crowd to do things to her; those who wanted to try and lift her up were pulled away by those who thought she ought to be left. Someone took off her shoes. Someone ran for water from Chez

Riane but the woman couldn't drink it. One day the boys had found a workman in his blue outfit and cement-crusted boots lying snoring near the old pump outside the Bar Tabac, where the men drank. Matt got him, too; you could always use a shot like that for a dead body, if the worst came to the worst. But this was the best ever. Matt finished up what was left of the film with the painter on it and had time to put in a new one, while the woman still lay there, and behind the noise of the crowd and the music the see-saw hoot of the ambulance could be heard, coming up the road to the village walls from the port below. The ambulance couldn't get onto the *Place*, but the men in their uniforms carried a stretcher over people's heads and then lifted the woman aboard. Her face was purplish as cold hands on a winter morning and her legs stuck out. The boys were part of the entourage that followed her to the ambulance, Matt progressing with sweeping hops, on bended knee, like a Russian dancer, in order to get the supine body in focus at an upward angle.

When it was all over, they went back to the *Crêperie* to relate the sensational story to the family; but they had not been even interested enough to stay, and had gone home to the villa. "It'll be really *something* for you to show them down in Africa!" said Matt. He was using his Minox that afternoon, and he promised that when the films were developed, he would have copies made for Clive. "Darn it, we'll have to wait until my parents take the films to Nice—you can't get them developed up here. And they only go in on Wednesdays."

"But I'll be gone by then," said Clive suddenly.

"Gone? Back to Africa?" All the distance fell between them as they stood head-to-head jostled by the people in the village street, all the distance of the centuries when the continent was a blank outline on the maps, as well as the distance of miles. "You mean you'll be back in *Africa?*"

Clive's box camera went into his cupboard along with the other souvenirs of Europe that seemed to have shed their evocation when they were unpacked amid the fresh, powerful familiarity of home. He boasted a little, the first day of the new term at school, about the places he had been to; but within a few weeks, when cities and palaces that he had seen for himself were spoken of in history or geography classes, he did not mention that he had visited them and, in fact, the textbook illustrations and descriptions did not seem to be those of anything he knew. One day he searched for his camera to take to a sports meeting, and found an exposed film in it. When it was developed, there were the pictures of the cats. He turned them this way up and that, to make out the thin, feral shapes on cobblestones and the disappearing blurs round the blackness of archways. There was also the picture of the American boy, Matt, a slim boy with knees made big out of focus, looking—at once suspicious and bright—from under his uncut hair.

The family crowded round to see, smiling, filled with pangs for what the holiday was and was not, while it lasted. "The *Time-Life* man himself!" "Poor old Matt—what was his other name?" "You ought to send it to him," said the mother. "You've got the address? Aren't you going to keep in touch?"

But there was no address. The boy Matt had no street, house, house in a street, room in a house like the one they were in. "America," Clive said, "he's in America."

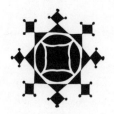

# OPEN HOUSE

FRANCES TAVER was on the secret circuit for
people who wanted to find out the truth about South Africa.
These visiting journalists, politicians, and churchmen all had an
itinerary arranged for them by their consular representatives
and overseas information services, or were steered around by a
"foundation" of South African business interests eager to improve
the country's image, or even carted about to the model black
townships, universities and beerhalls by the South African State
Information service itself. But all had, carefully hidden among the
most private of private papers (the nervous ones went so far as to
keep it in code), the short list that would really take the lid off
the place: the people one must see. A few were names that had
got into the newspapers of the world as particularly vigorous op-
ponents or victims of *apartheid;* a writer or two, a newspaper ed-
itor or an outspoken bishop. Others were known only within the
country itself, and were known about by foreign visitors only
through people like themselves who had carried the short list before. Most of the names on it were white names—which was

rather frustrating, when one was after the real thing; but it was said in London and New York that there *were* still ways of getting to meet Africans, provided you could get hold of the right white people.

Frances Taver was one of them. Had been for years. From the forties when she had been a trade union organizer and run a mixed union of garment workers while this was legally possible, in the fifties, after her marriage, when she was manager of a black-and-white theatre group before that was disbanded by new legislation, to the early sixties, when she hid friends on the run from the police—Africans who were members of the newly-banned political organizations—before the claims of that sort of friendship had to be weighed against the risk of the long spells of detention without trial introduced to betray it.

Frances Taver had few friends left now, and she was always slightly embarrassed when she heard an eager American or English voice over the telephone, announcing an arrival, a too-brief stay (of course), and the inevitable fond message of greetings to be conveyed from so-and-so—whoever it was who happened to have supplied the short list. A few years ago it had been fun and easy to make these visitors an excuse for a gathering that quite likely would turn into a party. The visitor would have a high old time learning to dance the *kwela* with black girls; he would sit fascinated, trying to keep sober enough to take it all in, listening to the fluent and fervent harangue of African, white, and Indian politicals, drinking and arguing together in a paradox of personal freedom that, curiously, he couldn't remember finding where there were *no* laws against the mixing of races. And no one enjoyed his fascination more than the objects of it themselves; Frances Taver and her friends were amused, in those days, in a friendly way, to knock the "right" ideas slightly askew. In those days: that was how she thought of it; it seemed very long ago. She saw the faces, sometimes, a flash in an absence filled with newspaper accounts of trials, hearsay about activities in exile, chance remarks from someone who knew someone else who had talked over the fence with one who was under house arrest. Another, an African friend banned for his activities with the African National Congress, who had gone "underground," came to see her at long intervals, in the afternoons when he could be sure the house would be empty. Although she was still youngish, she had come to think of "those days" as her youth; and he was a vision strayed from it.

The voice on the telephone, this time, was American—soft, cautious—no doubt the man thought the line was tapped. Robert Greenman Ceretti, from Washington; while they were talking, she remembered that this was the political columnist who had somehow been connected with the Kennedy administration. Hadn't he written a book about the Bay of Pigs? Anyway, she had certainly seen him quoted.

"And how are the Brauns—I haven't heard for ages—" She made the usual enquiries about the well-being of the mutual acquaintance whose greetings he brought, and he made the usual speech about how much he was hoping he'd be able to meet her? She was about to say, as always, come to dinner, but an absurd recoil within her, a moment of dull panic, almost, made her settle for an invitation to drop in for a drink two days later. "If I can be of any help to you, in the meantime?" she had to add; he sounded modest and intelligent.

"Well, I do appreciate it. I'll look forward to Wednesday."

At the last minute she invited a few white friends to meet him, a doctor and his wife who ran a tuberculosis hospital in an African reserve, and a young journalist who had been to America on a leadership exchange programme. But she knew what the foreign visitor wanted of her and she had an absurd—again, that was the word—compulsion to put him in the position where, alas, he could ask it. He was a small, cosy, red-headed man with a chipmunk smile, and she liked him. She drove him back to his hotel after the other guests had left, and they chatted about the articles he was going to write and the people he was seeing— had he been able to interview any important Nationalists, for example? Well, not yet, but he hoped to have something lined up for the following week, in Pretoria. Another thing he was worried about (here it came), he'd hardly been able to exchange a word with any black man except the one who cleaned his room at the hotel. She heard her voice saying casually, "Well, perhaps I might be able to help you, there," and he took it up at once, gravely, gratefully, sincerely, smiling at her—"I hoped you just might. If I could only get to talk with a few ordinary, articulate people. I mean, I think I've been put pretty much in the picture by the courageous white people I've been lucky enough to meet —people like you and your husband—but I'd like to know a little at first hand about what Africans themselves are thinking. If you could fix it, it'd be wonderful."

Now it was done, at once she withdrew, from herself rather than him. "I don't know. People don't want to talk any more. If they're doing anything, it's not something that can be talked about. Those that are left. Black and white. The ones you ought to see are shut away."

They were sitting in the car, outside the hotel. She could see in his encouraging, admiring, intent face how he had been told that she, if anyone, could introduce him to black people, hers, if anyone's, was the house to meet them.

There was a twinge of vanity: "I'll let you know. I'll ring you, then, Bob." Of course they were already on first-name terms; lonely affinity overleapt acquaintance in South Africa when likeminded whites met.

"You don't have to say more than when and where. I didn't like to talk, that first day, over the phone," he said.

They always had fantasies of danger. "What can happen to you?" she said. Her smile was not altogether pleasant. They always protested, too, that their fear was not for themselves, it was on your behalf, etc. "You've got your passport. You don't live here."

She did not see Jason Madela from one month's end to the next but when she telephoned him at the building where she remembered him once having had an office on the fringe of the white town, he accepted the invitation to lunch just as if he had been one of the intimates who used to drop in any time. And then there was Edgar, Edgar Xixo the attorney, successor to her old friend Samson Dumile's practice; one could always get him. And after that? She could have asked Jason to bring someone along, perhaps one of the boxing promoters or gamblers it amused him to produce where the drinks were free—but that would have been too obvious, even for the blind eye that she and Jason Madela were able to turn to the nature of the invitation. In the end she invited little Spuds Butelezi, the reporter. What did it matter? He was black, anyway. There was no getting out of the whole business, now.

She set herself to cook a good lunch, just as good as she had ever cooked, and she put out the drinks and the ice in the shelter of the glassed-in end of the big veranda, so that the small company should not feel lost. Her fading hair had been dyed to something approximating its original blonde and then streaked with grey, the day before, and she felt the appearance to be pleasingly artificial; she wore a bright, thick linen dress that showed off sunburned shoulders like the knobs of well-polished furniture, and she was aware that her blue eyes were striking in contrast with her tough brown face. She felt Robert Greenman Ceretti's eyes on her, a moment, as he stood in the sunny doorway; yes, she was also a woman, queening it alone among men at lunch. "You mix the martinis, there's a dear," she said. "It's such a treat to have a real American one." And while he bent about over bottles with the neatness of a small man, she was in and out of the veranda, shepherding the arrival of the other guests. "This is Bob—Bob Ceretti, here on a visit from the States—Edgar Xixo."

"Jason, this is Bob Ceretti, the man who has the ear of presidents—"

Laughter and protests mingled with the handing round of the drinks. Jason Madela, going to fat around the nape but still handsome in a frowning, Clark Gable way, stood about glass in hand as if in the habit acquired at cocktail parties. With his air of being distracted from more important things by irresistibly amus-

ing asides, he was correcting a matter of terminology for Robert
Ceretti—"No, no, but you must understand that in the townships, a 'situation' is a different thing entirely—well, *I'm* a situation, f'rinstance—" He cocked his smile, for confirmation, to
Xixo, whose eyes turned from one face to another in obedient
glee—"Oh, you're the *muti* man!" "No, wait, but I'm trying to
give Bob an obvious example"—more laughter, all round—
"—a man who wears a suit every day, like a white man. Who
goes to the office and prefers to talk English."

"You think it derives from the use of the word as a genteelism
for 'job'? Would you say? You know—the Situations Vacant
column in the newspapers?" The visitor sat forward on the edge
of his chair, smiling up closely. "But what's this *'muti'* you mentioned, now—maybe I ought to have been taking notes instead
of shaking Frances' martini pitcher."

"He's a medicine man," Xixo was explaining, while Jason
laughed—"Oh for God's sake!" and tossed off the rest of his
gin, and Frances went forward to bring the late arrival, Spuds
Butelezi, in his lattice-knit gold shirt and pale blue jeans, into the
circle. When the American had exchanged names and had Spuds
by the hand, he said, "And what's Spuds, then?"

The young man had a dough-shaped, light-coloured face with
tiny features stuck in it in a perpetual expression of suspicious
surprise. The martinis had turned up the volume of voices that
met him. "I'll have a beer," he said to Frances; and they laughed
again.

Jason Madela rescued him, a giant flicking a fly from a glass of
water. "He's one of the egg-heads," he said. "That's another cate-
gory altogether."

"Didn't you used to be one yourself, Jason?" Frances pre-
tended a reproof: Jason Madela would want a way of letting Ceretti know that although he was a successful businessman in the
townships, he was also a man with a university degree.

"Don't let's talk about my youthful misdemeanours, my dear
Frances," he said, with the accepted light touch of a man hiding
a wound. "I thought the men were supposed to be doing the

work around here—I can cope with that" and he helped her chip apart the ice-cubes that had welded together as they melted. "Get your servant to bring us a little hot water, that'll do it easily—"

"Oh I'm really falling down on the job!" Ceretti was listening carefully, putting in a low "Go on" or "You mean?" to keep the flow of Xixo's long explanation of problems over a travel document, and he looked up at Frances and Jason Madela offering a fresh round of drinks.

"You go ahead and talk, that's the idea," Frances said.

He gave her the trusting grin of some intelligent small pet. "Well, you two are a great combination behind the bar. Real team-work of long association, I guess."

"How long is it?" Frances asked, drily but gaily, meaning how many years had she and Jason Madela been acquaintances, and, playfully making as if to anticipate a blow, he said, "Must be ten years and you were a grown-up girl even then"—although both knew that they had seen each other only across various rooms perhaps a dozen times in five years, and got into conversation perhaps half as often.

At lunch Edgar Xixo was still fully launched on the story of his difficulties in travelling back and forth to one of the former British Protectorates, now small, newly independent states surrounded by South African territory. It wasn't, he explained, as if he were asking for a passport: it was just a travel document he wanted, that's all, just a piece of paper from the Bantu Affairs Department that would allow him to go to Lesotho on business and come back.

"Now have I got this straight—you'd been there sometime?" Ceretti hung over the wisp of steam rising from his soup like a seer over a crystal ball.

"Yes, yes, you see, I had a travel document—"

"But these things are good for one exit and re-entry only." Jason dispatched it with the good-humoured impatience of the quick-witted. "We blacks aren't supposed to want to go wandering about the place. Tell them you want to take a holiday in Lour-

enço Marques—they'll laugh in your face. If they don't kick
you downstairs. Oppenheimer and Charlie Engelhard can go off
in their yachts to the South of France, but Jason Madela?"

He got the laugh he wanted, and, on the side, the style of his
reference to rich and important white industrialists as decent
enough fellows, if one happened to know them, suggested that *he*
might. Perhaps he did, for all Frances Taver knew; Jason would
be just the kind of man the white establishment would find if
they should happen to decide they ought to make a token gesture
of being in touch with the African masses. He was curiously reassuring to white people; his dark suits, white shirts, urbane conversation and sense of humour, all indistinguishable from their
own and apparently snatched out of thin air, made it possible for
them to forget the unpleasant facts of the life imposed on him
and his kind. How tactful, how clever he was, too. She, just as
well as any millionaire, would have done to illustrate his point;
she was culpable: white, and free to go where she pleased. The
flattery of being spared passed invisibly from her to him, like a
promissory note beneath the table.

Edgar Xixo had even been summoned to The Greys, Special
Branch headquarters, for questioning, he said—"And I've never
belonged to any political organization, they know there've never
been any charges against me. I don't know any political refugees
in Lesotho, I don't want to *see* anybody—I have to go up and
down simply because of business, I've got this agency selling
equipment to the people at the diamond diggings, it could be a
good thing if. . . ."

"A little palm-grease, maybe," said Jason Madela, taking some
salad.

Xixo appealed to them all, dismayed. "But if you offer it to the
wrong one, that's the . . . ? In my position, an attorney!"

"Instinct," said Madela. "One can't learn it."

"Tell me," Ceretti signalled an appreciative refusal of a second
helping of duck, while turning from his hostess to Madela.
"Would you say that bribery plays a big part in daily relations
between Africans and officials? I don't mean the political police,

of course—the white administration? Is that your experience?"

Madela sipped his wine and then turned the bottle so that he could read the label, saying meanwhile, "Oh not what you'd call graft, not by your standards. Small stuff. When I ran a transport business I used to make use of it. Licences for the drivers and so on. You get some of these young Afrikaner clerks, they don't earn much and they don't mind who they pick up a few bob from. They can be quite reasonable. I was thinking there might be someone up at the Bantu Affairs offices. But you have to have a feeling for the right man"—he put down the bottle and smiled at Frances Taver—"Thank heaven I'm out of it, now. Unless I should decide to submit some of my concoctions to the Bureau of Standards, eh?" and she laughed.

"Jason has broken the white monopoly of the hair-straightener and blood-purifier business," Frances said gracefully, "and the nice thing about him is that he has no illusions about his products."

"But plenty of confidence," he said. "I'm looking into the possibilities of exporting my pills for men, to the States. I think the time's just ripe for American Negroes to feel they can buy back a bit of old Africa in a bottle, eh?"

Xixo picked about his leg of duck as if his problem itself were laid cold before them on the table. "I mean, I've said again and again, show me anything on my record—"

The young journalist, Spuds Butelezi, said in his heavy way, "It might be because you took over Samson Dumile's show."

Every time a new name was mentioned the corners of Ceretti's eyes flickered narrow in attention.

"Well, that's the whole thing!" Xixo complained to Ceretti. "The fellow I was working for, Dumile, was mixed up in a political trial and he got six years—I took over the *bona fide* clients, that's all, my office isn't in the same building, nothing to do with it—but that's the whole thing!"

Frances suddenly thought of Sam Dumile, in this room of hers, three—two?—years ago, describing a police raid on his house the night before and roaring with laughter as he told how his little daughter said to the policeman, "My father gets very cross if you play with his papers."

Jason picked up the wine bottle, making to pass it round— "Yes, please do, please do—what happened to the children?" she said. Jason knew whose she meant; made a polite attempt. "Where are Sam's kids?"

But Edgar Xixo was nodding in satisfied confirmation as Ceretti said, "It's a pretty awful story. My God. Seems you can never hope to be in the clear, no matter how careful you are. My God."

Jason remarked, aside, "They must be around somewhere with relatives. He's got a sister in Bloemfontein."

The dessert was a compound of fresh mangoes and cream, an invention of the house: "*Mangoes Frances*" said the American. "This is one of the African experiences I'd recommend." But Jason Madela told them he was allergic to mangoes and began on the cheese which was standing by. Another bottle of wine was opened to go with the cheese and there was laughter—which Robert Ceretti immediately turned on himself—when it emerged out of the cross-talk that Spuds Butelezi thought Ceretti had something to do with an American foundation. In the sympathetic atmosphere of food, drink, and sunshine marbled with cigarette smoke, the others listened as if they had not heard it all before while Butelezi, reluctant to waste the speech he had primed himself with, pressed Ceretti with his claim to a study grant that would enable him to finish his play. They heard him again outlining the plot and inspiration of the play—"right out of township life" as he always said, blinking with finality, convinced that this was the only necessary qualification for successful authorship. He had patiently put together and taken apart, many times, in his play, ingredients faithfully lifted from the work of African writers who got published, and he was himself African: what else could be needed but someone to take it up?

Foundation or no foundation, Robert Ceretti showed great interest. "Do you know the play at all, Frances? I mean" (he turned back to the round, wine-open face of the young man) "is it far enough along to show to anybody?" And she said, finding herself smiling encouragingly, "Oh yes—an early draft, he's worked on it a lot since then haven't you—and there's been a reading . . . ?"

"I'll certainly get it to you," Butelezi said, writing down the name of Ceretti's hotel.

They moved back to the veranda for the coffee and brandy. It was well after three o'clock by the time they stood about, making their good-byes. Ceretti's face was gleaming. "Jason Madela's offered to drop me back in town, so don't you worry, Frances. I was just saying, people in America'll find it difficult to believe it was possible for me to have a lunch like this, here. It's been so very pleasant—pleasant indeed. We all had a good time. He was telling me that a few years ago a gathering like this would be quite common, but now there aren't many white people who would want to risk asking Africans and there aren't many Africans who would risk coming. I certainly enjoyed myself. . . . I hope we haven't put you out, lingering so long . . . it's been a wonderful opportunity. . . ." Frances saw them to the garden gate, talking and laughing; last remarks and good-byes were called from under the trees of the suburban street.

When she came back alone the quiet veranda rang tense with vanished voices, like a bell tower after the hour has struck. She gave the cat the milk left over from coffee. Someone had left a half-empty packet of cigarettes; who was it who broke matches into little tents? As she carried the tray into the deserted kitchen, she saw a note written on the back of a bill taken from the spike. HOPE YOUR PARTY WENT WELL.

It was not signed, and was written with the kitchen ball-point which hung on a string. But she knew who had written it; the vision from the past had come and gone again.

The servants Amos and Bettie had rooms behind a granadilla vine at the bottom of the yard. She called, and asked Bettie whether anyone had asked for her? No, no one at all.

He must have heard the voices in the quiet of the afternoon, or perhaps simply seen the cars outside, and gone away. She wondered if he knew who was there. Had he gone away out of consideration for her safety? They never spoke of it, of course, but he must know that the risks she took were carefully calculated, very carefully calculated. There was no way of disguising that from someone like *him*. Then she saw him smiling to himself at the sight of the collection of guests: Jason Madela, Edgar Xixo, and Spuds Butelezi—Spuds Butelezi, as well. But probably she was wrong, and he would have come out among them without those feelings of reproach or contempt that she read into the idea of his gait, his face. HOPE YOUR PARTY WENT WELL. He may have meant just that.

Frances Taver knew Robert Ceretti was leaving soon, but she wasn't quite sure when. Every day she thought; I'll phone and say good-bye. Yet she had already taken leave of him, that afternoon of the lunch. Just telephone and say good-bye. On the Friday morning, when she was sure he would be gone, she rang up the hotel, and there it was, the soft, cautious American voice. The first few moments were awkward; he protested his pleasure at hearing from her, she kept repeating, "I thought you'd be gone. . . ." Then she said, "I just wanted to say—about that lunch. You mustn't be taken in—" He was saying, "I've been so indebted to you, Frances, really you've been great."

"—not phonies, no, that's not what I mean, on the contrary, they're very real, you understand?"

"Oh, your big good-looking friend, he's been marvellous. Saturday night we were out on the town, you know." He was proud of the adventure but didn't want to use the word *"shebeen"* over the telephone.

She said, "You must understand. Because the corruption's real. Even they've become what they are because things are the way they are. Being phony is being corrupted by the situation . . . and that's real enough. We're made out of *that*."

He thought maybe he was finding it difficult to follow her over the telephone, and seized upon the word: "Yes, the 'situation'—he was able to slip me into what I gather is one of the livelier places."

Frances Taver said, "I don't want you to be taken in—"

The urgency of her voice stopped his mouth, was communicated to him even if what she said was not.

"—by anyone," the woman was saying.

He understood, indeed, that something complicated was wrong, but he knew, too, that he wouldn't be there long enough to find out, that perhaps you needed to live and die there, to find out. All she heard over the telephone was the voice assuring her, "Everyone's been marvellous . . . really marvellous. I just hope I can get back here some day—that is, if they ever let me in again. . . ."

# RAIN-QUEEN

WE WERE LIVING in the Congo at the time; I was nineteen. It must have been my twentieth birthday we had at the *Au Relais*, with the Gattis, M. Niewenhuys, and my father's site manager. My father was building a road from Elisabethville to Tshombe's residence, a road for processions and motorcades. It's Lubumbashi now, and Tshombe's dead in exile. But at that time there was plenty of money around and my father was brought from South Africa with a free hand to recruit engineers from anywhere he liked; the Gattis were Italian, and then there was a young Swede. I didn't want to leave Johannesburg because of my boy friend, Alan, but my mother didn't like the idea of leaving me behind, because of him. She said to me, "Quite honestly, I think it's putting too much temptation in a young girl's way. I'd have no one to blame but myself." I was very young for my age, then, and I gave in. There wasn't much for me to do in E'ville. I was taken up by some young Belgian married women who were only a few years older than I was. I had coffee with them in town in the mornings, and played with their babies. My mother begged them to speak French to me; she didn't want the six months there to be a complete waste. One of them taught me how to make a chocolate mousse, and I made myself a dress under the supervision of another; we giggled together as I had done a few years before with the girls at school.

Everyone turned up at the *Au Relais* in the evenings and in the afternoons when it had cooled off a bit we played squash—the younger ones in our crowd, I mean. I used to play every day with the Swede, and Marco Gatti. They came straight from the site. Eleanora Gatti was one of those Mediterranean women who not only belong to a different sex, but seem to be a species entirely different from the male. You could never imagine her running or even bending to pick something up; her white bosom in square-necked dresses, her soft hands with rings and jewel-lidded watch, her pile of dark hair tinted a strange tarnished marmalade-colour that showed up the pallor of her skin—all was arranged like a still-life. The Swede wasn't married.

After the game Marco Gatti used to put a towel round his neck tennis-star fashion and his dark face was gilded with sweat. The Swede went red and blotchy. When Marco panted it was a grin, showing white teeth and one that was repaired with gold. It seemed to me that all adults were flawed in some way; it set them apart. Marco used to give me a lift home and often came in to have a drink with my father and discuss problems about the road. When he was outlining a difficulty he had a habit of smiling and putting a hand inside his shirt to scratch his breast. In the open neck of his shirt some sort of amulet on a chain rested on the dark hair between his strong pectoral muscles. My father said proudly, "He may look like a tenor at the opera, but he knows how to get things done."

I had never been to the opera; it wasn't my generation. But when Marco began to kiss me every afternoon on the way home, and then to come in to talk to my father over beer as usual, I put it down to the foreignness in him. I said, "It seems so funny to walk into the room where Daddy is." Marco said, "My poor little girl, you can't help it if you are pretty, can you?"

It rains every afternoon there, at that time of year. A sudden wind would buffet the heat aside, flattening paper against fences in the dust. Fifteen minutes later—you could have timed it by the clock—the rain came down so hard and noisy we could scarcely see out of the windscreen and had to talk as loudly as if we were in an echoing hall. The rain usually lasted only about an hour. One afternoon we went to the site instead of to my parents' house—to the caravan that was meant to be occupied by one of the engineers but never had been, because everyone lived in town. Marco shouted against the downpour, "You know what the Congolese say? 'When the rain comes, quickly find a girl to take home with you until it's over.' " The caravan was just like a little flat, with everything you needed. Marco showed me— there was even a bath. Marco wasn't tall (at home the girls all agreed we couldn't look at any boy under six foot) but he had the fine, strong legs of a sportsman, covered with straight black hairs, and he stroked my leg with his hard yet furry one. That was a caress we wouldn't have thought of, either. I had an inkling we really didn't know anything.

The next afternoon Marco seemed to be taking the way directly home, and I said in agony, "Aren't we going to the caravan?" It was out, before I could think. "Oh my poor darling, were you disappointed?" He laughed and stopped the car there and then and kissed me deep in both ears as well as the mouth. "All right, the caravan." We went there every weekday afternoon—he didn't work on Saturdays, and the wives came along to the squash club. Soon the old Congolese watchman used to trot over from the labourers' camp to greet us when he saw the car draw up at the caravan; he knew I was my father's daughter. Marco chatted with him for a few minutes, and every few days gave him a tip. At the beginning, I used to stand by as if waiting to be told what to do next, but Marco had what I came to realize must be adult confidence. "Don't look so worried. He's a nice old man. He's my friend."

Marco taught me how to make love, in the caravan, and everything that I had thought of as "life" was put away, as I had at other times folded the doll's clothes, packed the Monopoly set and the sample collection, and given them to the servant. I stopped writing to my girl friends; it took me weeks to get down to replying to Alan's regular letters, and yet when I did so it was with a kind of professional pride that I turned out a letter of the most skilful ambiguity—should it be taken as a love-letter, or should it not? I felt it would be beyond his powers—powers of experience—to decide. I alternately pitied him and underwent an intense tingling of betrayal—actually cringing away from myself in the flesh. Before my parents and in the company of friends, Marco's absolutely unchanged behaviour mesmerized me: I acted as if nothing had happened because for him it was really as if nothing had happened. He was not pretending to be natural with my father and mother—he *was* natural. And the same applied to our behaviour in the presence of his wife. After the first time he made love to me I had looked forward with terror and panic to the moment when I should have to see Eleanora again; when she might squeeze my hand or even kiss me on the cheek as she sometimes did in her affectionate, feminine way. But when I walked into our house that Sunday and met her perfume and then all at once saw her beside my mother talking about her family in Genoa, with Marco, my father, and another couple, sitting there—I moved through the whirling impression without falter. Someone said, "Ah here she is at last, our Jillie!" And my mother was saying (I had been riding with the Swede), "I don't know how she keeps up with Per, they were out dancing until three o'clock this morning—" and Marco, who was twenty-nine (1st December, Sagittarius, domicile of Jupiter), was saying, "What it is to be young, eh?", and my father said, "What time did you finally get to bed, after last night, anyway, Marco—" and Eleanora, sitting back with her plump smooth knees crossed, tugged my hand gently so that we should exchange a woman's kiss on the cheek.

I took in the smell of Eleanora's skin, felt the brush of her hair on my nose; and it was done, forever. We sat talking about some shoes her sister-in-law had sent from Milan. It was something I could never have imagined: Marco and I, as we really were, didn't exist here; there was no embarrassment. The Gattis, as always on Sunday mornings, were straight from eleven o'clock Mass at the Catholic cathedral, and smartly dressed.

As in most of these African places there was a shortage of white women in Katanga and my mother felt much happier to see me spending my time with the young married people than she would have been to see me taken up by the mercenaries who came in and out of E'ville that summer. "They're experienced men," she said—as opposed to boys and married men, "and of course they're out for what they can get. They've got nothing to lose; next week they're in another province, or they've left the country. I don't blame them. I believe a girl has to know what the world's like, and if she is fool enough to get involved with that crowd, she must take the consequences." She seemed to have forgotten that she had not wanted to leave me in Johannesburg in the company of Alan. "She's got a nice boy at home, a decent boy who respects her. I'd far rather see her just enjoying herself generally, with you young couples, while we're here." And there was always Per, the Swede, to even out the numbers; she knew he wasn't "exactly Jillie's dream of love". I suppose that made him safe, too. If I was no one's partner in our circle, I was a love-object, handed round them all, to whom it was taken for granted that the homage of a flirtatious attitude was paid. Perhaps this was supposed to represent my compensation: if not the desired of any individual, then recognized as desirable by them all. "Oh of course, you prefair to dance with Jeelie," Mireille, one of the young Belgians, would say to her husband, pretending offence. He and I were quite an act, at the *Au Relais*, with our cha-cha. Then he would whisper to her in their own language, and she would giggle and punch his arm.

Marco and I were as famous a combination on the squash court as Mireille's husband and I were on the dance floor. This was the

only place, if anyone had had the eyes for it, where our love-
making showed. As the weeks went by and the love-making got
better and better, our game got better and better. The response
Marco taught me to the sound of spilling grain the rain made on
the caravan roof held good between us on the squash court.
Sometimes the wives and spectators broke into spontaneous applause; I was following Marco's sweat-oiled excited face, antici-
pating his muscular reactions in play as in bed. And when he had
beaten me (narrowly) or we had beaten the other pair, he would
hunch my shoulders together within his arm, laughing, praising
me in Italian to the others, staggering about with me, and he
would say to me in English, "Aren't you a clever girl, eh?"; only
he and I knew that that was what he said to me at other times. I
loved that glinting flaw in his smile, now. It was Marco, like all
the other things I knew about him: the girl cousin he had been in
love with when he used to spend holidays with her family in the
Abruzzi mountains; the way he would have planned Tshombe's
road if he'd been in charge—"But I like your father, you
understand?—it's good to work with your father, you know?";
the baby cream from Italy he used for the prickly heat round his
waist.

The innocence of the grownups fascinated me. They engaged
in play-play, while I had given it up; I began to feel arrogant
among them. It was pleasant. I felt arrogant—or rather toler-
antly patronizing—towards the faraway Alan, too. I said to
Marco, "I wonder what he'd do if he knew"—about me; the
caravan with the dotted curtains, the happy watchman, the tips,
the breath of the earth rising from the wetted dust. Marco said
wisely that Alan would be terribly upset.

"And if Eleanora knew?"

Marco gave me his open, knowing, assured smile, at the same
time putting the palm of his hand to my cheek in tender paren-
thesis. "She wouldn't be pleased. But in the case of a man—"
For a moment he was Eleanora, quite unconsciously he mimicked
the sighing resignation of Eleanora, receiving the news (seated, as

usual), aware all the time that men were like that. Other people who were rumoured or known to have had lovers occupied my mind with a special interest. I chattered on the subject, ". . . when this girl's husband found out, he just walked out of the house without any money or anything and no one could find him for weeks," and Marco took it up as one does what goes without saying: "—Well of course. If I think of Eleanora with someone—I mean—I would become mad."

I went on with my second-hand story, enjoying the telling of all its twists and complications, and he laughed, following it with the affectionate attention with which he lit everything I said and did, and getting up to find the bottle of Chianti, wipe out a glass and fill it for himself. He always had wine in the caravan. I didn't drink any but I used to have the metallic taste of it in my mouth from his.

In the car that afternoon he had said maybe there'd be a nice surprise for me, and I remembered this and we lay and wrangled teasingly about it. The usual sort of thing: "You're learning to be a real little nag, my darling, a little nag, eh?" "I'm not going to let go until you tell me." "I think I'll have to give you a little smack on the bottom, eh, just-like-this, eh?" The surprise was a plan. He and my father might be going to the Kasai to advise on some difficulties that had cropped up for a construction firm there. It should be quite easy for me to persuade my father that I'd like to accompany him, and then if Marco could manage to leave Eleanora behind, it would be almost as good as if he and I were to take a trip alone together. "You will have your own room?" Marco asked. I laughed. "D'you think I'd be put in with Daddy?" Perhaps in Italy a girl wouldn't be allowed to have her own hotel room. Now Marco was turning his attention to the next point: "Eleanora gets sick from the car, anyway—she won't want to come on bad roads, and you can get stuck, God knows what. No, it's quite all right, I will tell her it's no pleasure for her." At the prospect of being in each other's company for whole days and perhaps nights we couldn't stop smiling, chattering and kissing, not with passion but delight. My tongue was loosened as if I *had* been drinking wine.

Marco spoke good English.

The foreign turns of phrase he did have were familiar to me. He did not use the word "mad" in the sense of angry. "I would become mad": he meant exactly that, although the phrase was not one that we English-speaking people would use. I thought about it that night, alone, at home; and other nights. Out of his mind, he meant. If Eleanora slept with another man, Marco would be insane with jealousy. He said so to me because he was a really honest person, not like the other grownups—just as he said, "I like your father, eh? I don't like some of the things he does with the road, but he is a good man, you know?" Marco was in love with me; I was his treasure, his joy, some beautiful words in Italian. It was true; he was very, very happy with me. I could see that. I did not know that people could be so happy; Alan did not know. I was sure that if I hadn't met Marco I should never have known. When we were in the caravan together I would watch him all the time, even when we were dozing I watched out of slit eyes the movement of his slim nostril with its tuft of black hair, as he breathed, and the curve of his sunburned ear through which capillary-patterned light showed. Oh Marco, Eleanora's husband, was beautiful as he slept. But he wasn't asleep. I liked to press my feet on his as if his were pedals and when I did this the corner of his mouth smiled and he said something with the flex of a muscle somewhere in his body. He even spoke aloud at times: my name. But I didn't know if he knew he had spoken it. Then he would lie with his eyes open a long time, but not looking at me, because he didn't need to: I was there. Then he would get up, light a cigarette, and say to me, "I was in a dream . . . oh, I don't know . . . it's another world."

It was a moment of awkwardness for me because I was entering the world from my childhood and could not conceive that, as adults did—as he did—I should ever need to find surcease and joy elsewhere, in another world. He escaped, with me. I entered, with him. The understanding of this I knew would come about for me as the transfiguration of the gold tooth from a flaw into a characteristic had come. I still did not know everything.

I saw Eleanora nearly every day. She was very fond of me; she was the sort of woman who, at home, would have kept attendant younger sisters round her to compensate for the children she did not have. I never felt guilty towards her. Yet, before, I should have thought how awful one would feel, taking the closeness and caresses that belonged, by law, to another woman. I was irritated at the stupidity of what Eleanora said; the stupidity of her not knowing. How idiotic that she should tell me that Marco had worked late on the site again last night, he was so conscientious, etc.—wasn't I with him, while she made her famous veal scaloppini and they got overcooked? And she was a nuisance to us. "I'll have to go—I must take poor Eleanora to a film tonight. She hasn't been anywhere for weeks." "It's the last day for parcels to Italy, tomorrow—she likes me to pack them with her, the Christmas parcels, you know how Eleanora is about these things." Then her aunt came out from Italy and there were lunches and dinners to which only Italian-speaking people were invited because the signora couldn't speak English. I remember going there one Sunday—sent by my mother with a contribution of her special ice-cream. They were all sitting round in the heat on the veranda, the women in one group with the children crawling over them, and Marco with the men in another, his tie loose at the neck of his shirt (Eleanora had made him put on a suit), gesturing with a toothpick, talking and throwing cigar butts into Eleanora's flower-trough of snake cactus.

And yet that evening in the caravan he said again, "Oh good God, I don't want to wake up . . . I was in a dream." He had appeared out of the dark at our meeting-place, barefoot in espadrilles and tight thin jeans, like a beautiful fisherman.

I had never been to Europe. Marco said, "I want to drive with you through Piemonte, and take you to the village where my father came from. We'll climb up to the walls from the church and when you get to the top—only then—I'll turn you round and you'll see Monte Bianco far away. You've heard nightingales, eh—never heard them? We'll listen to them in the pear orchard, it's my uncle's place, there."

I was getting older every day. I said, "What about Eleanora?" It was the nearest I could get to what I always wanted to ask him: "Would you still become mad?"

*Would you still become mad?*

*And now?*

*And now—two months, a week, six weeks later?*

*Now would you still become mad?*

"Eleanora will spend some time in Pisa after we go back to Italy, with her mother and the aunts," he was saying.

Yes, I knew why, too; knew from my mother that Eleanora was going to Pisa because there was an old family doctor there who was sure, despite everything the doctors in Milan and Rome had said, that poor Eleanora might still one day have a child.

I said, "How would you feel if Alan came here?"

But Marco looked at me with such sensual confidence of understanding that we laughed.

I began to plan a love affair for Eleanora. I chose Per as victim not only because he was the only presentable unattached man in our circle, but also because I had the feeling that it might just be possible to attract her to a man younger than herself, whom she could mother. And Per, with no woman at all (except the pretty Congolese prostitutes good for an hour in the rain, I suppose) could consider himself lucky if he succeeded with Eleanora. I studied her afresh. Soft white goose-flesh above her stocking-tops, breasts that rose when she sighed—that sort of woman. But Eleanora did not even seem to understand that Per was being put in her way (at our house, at the *Au Relais*) and Per seemed equally unaware of or uninterested in his opportunities.

And so there was never any way to ask my question. Marco and I continued to lie making love in the caravan while the roof made buckling noises as it contracted after the heat of the day, and the rain. Tshombe fled and returned; there were soldiers in the square before the post office, and all sorts of difficulties arose over the building of the road. Marco was determined, excitable, harassed and energetic—he sprawled on the bed in the caravan at the end of the day like a runner who has just breasted the tape. My father was nervous and didn't know whether to finish the road. Eleanora was nervous and wanted to go back to Italy. We made love and when Marco opened his eyes to consciousness of the road, my father, Eleanora, he said, "Oh for God's sake, *why* . . . it's like a dream. . . ."

I became nervous too. I goaded my mother: "The Gattis are a bore. That female Buddha." I developed a dread that Eleanora would come to me with her sighs and her soft-squeezing hand and say, "It always happens with Marco, little Jillie, you musn't worry. I know all about it."

And Marco and I continued to lie together in that state of pleasure in which nothing exists but the two who make it. Neither roads, nor mercenary wars, nor marriage, nor the claims and suffering of other people entered that tender, sensual dream from which Marco, although so regretfully, always returned.

What I dreaded Eleanora might say to me was never said, either. Instead my mother told me one day in the tone of portentous emotion with which older women relive such things, that Eleanora, darling Eleanora, was expecting a child. After six years. Without having to go to Pisa to see the family doctor there. Yes, Eleanora had conceived during the rainy season in E'ville, while Marco and I made love every afternoon in the caravan, and the Congolese found themselves a girl for the duration of a shower.

It's years ago, now.

Poor Marco, sitting in Milan or Genoa at Sunday lunch, toothpick in his fingers, Eleanora's children crawling about, Eleanora's brothers and sisters and uncles and aunts around him. But I have never woken up from that dream. In the seven years I've been married I've had—how many lovers? Only I know. A lot—if you count the very brief holiday episodes as well.

It *is* another world, that dream, where no wind blows colder than the warm breath of two who are mouth to mouth.

# THE BRIDE OF CHRIST

LYNDALL BERGER, at sixteen, wrote to her parents for permission to be confirmed.

"Are you mad?" Sidney's gaze was a pair of outspread arms, stopping his wife short whichever way she might turn.

"Well, I know. But it never enters your mind that for someone—I'm not saying for *her*—it could be necessary; real, I mean. When one says 'no,' one must concede that. Otherwise she must put the refusal down to rationalist prejudice. You see what I mean?"

"Saved them all the abracadabra at the synagogue for this. Mumbo jumbo for abracadabra."

It was Shirley who had agreed when the child went to boarding school that she could go to church with the other girls if she felt like it—just to see what it was all about. She bought her, at the same time, a Penguin on comparative religion; in the holidays she could read James Parkes on the origins of Judaism and Christianity, right-hand lower bookshelf near the blue lamp. Shirley did not know whether the child had ever read either; you were in the same position as you were with sex: you gave them the facts, and you left an unspoken, unanswerable question. How does it feel to want to perform this strange act? How does it feel to have faith?

"It's like cutting her skirts up to her thigh. She wants to be confirmed because her friends are going to be. The answer is no."

His wife's face winced in anticipation of the impact of this sort of dismissal. "Of course it's no. But we must show her the respect of giving her the proper reasons. I'll talk to her when she's home next Sunday."

Shirley had meant to take her daughter for a walk in the veld, but it wasn't necessary because Sidney and Peter, their other child, went off to play golf anyway. Shirley was not slow to take a stand on the one ground that stood firm beneath her feet. "You've been going to church for over a year now. I suppose you haven't failed to notice that all those nicely-dressed ladies and gentlemen of the congregation are white? A church isn't a cinema, you know—I say this because we get used to seeing only white people in public places like that, and it's quite under-standable that one begins to take it for granted. But a church is different, you know that; the church preaches brotherhood, and there's no excuse. Except prejudice. They pray to God, and they take the body of Christ into their mouths, but they don't want to do it next to a black man. You must have thought about it often."

"I think about it all the time," the girl said. They were peeling mushrooms; she didn't do it well; she broke off bits of the cap along with the skin she rolled back, but her mother didn't com-plain.

"That's why Sidney and I don't go to synagogue or church or anything—one of the reasons. Daddy wouldn't belong to any religion wherever he lived—that you know—but perhaps I might want to if I lived anywhere else, not here. I couldn't sit with them in their churches or synagogues here."

"I know." Lyndall did not look up.

"I wonder how you feel about this." No answer. Shirley felt there should be no necessity to spell it out, but to force the child to speak, she said, "How can you want to join the establishment of the Church when there's a colour bar there?"

"Well, yes, I know—" Lyndall said.

Her mother said of the mushroom stalks, "Just break them off; I'll use them for soup."

They returned to the silence between them, but a promising silence, with something struggling through it.

"I think about it every time I'm in church—I'm always— but it's got nothing to do with Christ, Mummy. It's not his fault"—she paused with shame for the schoolgirl phrasing before this woman, her mother, who inevitably had the advantage of adult articulateness—"not Christ's fault that people are hypocrites."

"Yes, of course, that's the point I'm trying to make for you. I can understand anyone being attracted to the Christian ethic, to Christ's teaching, to the idea of following him. But why join the Church; it's done such awful things in his name."

"That's got nothing to do with Christ."

"You associate yourself with them! The moment you get yourself confirmed and join the Church, you belong along with it all, from the Crusaders and the Spanish Inquisition to the good Christian Nazis, and the good Christians of the Dutch Reformed Church who sprinkle pious sentiments over the colour bar the way the Portuguese bishops used to baptize slaves before they were shipped from West Africa—you belong along with them just the way you do in church with the nice ladies in smart hats who wouldn't want a black child sitting beside theirs in school."

Lyndall was afraid of her mother's talk; often the constructions she had balanced in her mind out of her own ideas fell down before her mother's talk like the houses made of sticks and jacaranda feathers that used to turn to garden rubbish beneath the foot of an unrecognizing grownup.

She was going to be quite good-looking (Shirley thought so), but the conflict of timidity and determination gave her the heavy-jawed look of a certain old uncle, a failure in the family, whom Shirley remembered from her own childhood.

"What about Garth and Nibs." It was a statement not a question. The couple, Anglican ex-missionaries who had both been put under ban for their activities as members of the Liberal Party, were among the Bergers' closest friends.

"Yes, Garth and Nibs, and Father Huddleston and Bishop Reeves and Crowther and a lot of other names. Of course there are Anglicans and Catholics and Methodists who don't preach brotherhood and forget it when it comes to a black face. But the fact is that they're the rarities. Odd men out. The sort of people you'll be worshiping Christ with every Sunday are the people who see no wrong in their black 'brothers' having to carry a pass. The same sort of people who didn't see anything wrong in your great-grandparents having to live in a ghetto in Galicia. The same people who kept going to church in Germany on Sundays while the Jews were being shovelled into gas ovens."

She watched her daughter's face for the expression that knew *that* was coming; couldn't be helped, it had to be dragged up, again and again and again and again and again—like Lear's "nevers"—no matter how sick of it everyone might be.

But the child's face was naked.

"Darling"—the words found release suddenly, in helplessness—"I really can understand how you feel. I'm not just talking; I can tell you that if I had a religion at all it could only be Christ's; I've never been able to understand why the Jews didn't accept him, it's so logical that his thinking should have been the culmination—but I know I couldn't become a Christian, couldn't . . ."

The child didn't help her.

"Because of *that*. And the other things. That go with it. It's like having one drop of coloured blood in your veins. You'd always have to admit it, I mean, wouldn't you? You'd always want to tell people first. Everything'd have to begin from there. Well, it's just the same if you're a Jew. People like us—colour and race, it doesn't mean a damn thing to me, but it can only not mean a thing if I begin from there, from having it known that I'm Jewish. I don't choose to belong with the ladies who separate the meat and the milk dishes and wear their Sunday best to synagogue, but I can't not choose the people who were barred from the universities—they were, just like the Africans, here—and killed by the Germans—you understand?" Her voice dropped from an apologetic rise; she hadn't wanted to bring that in, again. Lyndall was rubbing rolls of dirt on her sweating hands. She blinked jerkily now and then as the words pelted her. "And you, you belong along with that too, d'you understand, you'll always belong with it. Doesn't matter if you're confirmed a hundred times over. And another thing—it's all part of the same thing, really. If you were to become a Christian, there would always be the suspicion in people's minds that you'd done it for social reasons."

In her innocence, the child opened her lips on a gleam of tooth, and frowned, puzzled.

Shirley felt ashamed at what was at once trivial and urgently important. "Clubs and so on. Even certain schools. They don't want to admit Jews. Oh, it's a bore to talk about it. When you think what Africans are debarred from. But at the same time— one wants *all* the pinpricks, one must show them one won't evade a single one. How can I explain—pride, it's a kind of pride. I couldn't turn my back on it."

The child moved her head slowly and vehemently in understanding, as she used to do, near tears, when she had had a dressing-down. "Lyndall," her mother said, "You'd have to be a real Christian, an every-minute-of-the-day, every-day-of-the-week Christian, before I could think of letting you be converted. You'd have to take all this on you. You'd have to know that the person kneeling beside you in church might make some remark about Jews one day, and you wouldn't be able to let it pass like a Christian; you'd have to say, I'm Jewish. I'd want you to take the kicks from both sides. It would be the only way."

"Oh, but I will, I promise you, Mummy!" The child jumped

clumsily, forgetting she was almost grown-up, forgetting her size, and gave her mother the hard kisses of childhood that landed on cheek and chin. The bowl of mushrooms turned over and spun loudly like a top coming to rest, and scrabbling for the mushrooms, looking up from under the hair that fell forward over her face, she talked: "Father Byrd absolutely won't allow you to be confirmed until you're sure you're ready—I've had talks with him three times—he comes to the school on Thursdays—and I know I'm ready, I feel it. I promise you, Mummy."

Shirley was left with the empty bowl; she urgently wanted to speak, to claim what had been taken out of her hands; but all she did was remove, by pressure of the pads of her fingers, the grit in the fungus dew at the bottom of the bowl.

Of course Lyndall had to be baptized, too. They hadn't realized it, or perhaps the child had wanted to break the whole business gently, one piece of preposterousness at a time. She had been named originally for that free spirit in Olive Schreiner's book, a shared feeling for which had been one of the signs that brought her parents together. Her mother attended both the baptismal and confirmation ceremonies; it was understood that Sidney, while granting his daughter her kind of freedom, would not be expected to be present. For the confirmation Lyndall had to have a sleeveless white dress with a long-sleeved bolero; all the other girls were having them made like that. "So's you can wear the dress for parties afterwards," she said.

"One never wears these dresses for anything afterwards," said her mother. Eighteen years in a plastic bag, the zipper made tarnish marks on the wedding dress.

Lyndall also had to have a veil, plain muslin, held in place with bronze bobby pins.

"The bride of Christ," said Sidney when, trying it on, she had left the room. At least he had managed not to say anything while she was there; Shirley looked up for a second, as if he had spoken to her thoughts. But he was alone in his own.

"She's not going into a nunnery," she said.

Yet why did she feel such a cheat with him over this thing? He could have stopped the child if he'd been absolutely convinced, absolutely adamant. The heavy father. How much distaste he had—they had—for the minor tyrannies. . . . It was all very well to set children free; he wouldn't compromise himself to himself by accepting that he might have to use the power of authority to keep them that way.

Lyndall was weeping when the bishop in his purple robes called her name and blessed her in the school chapel. The spasm on the rather large child's face under the ugly veil as she rose from her knees produced a nervous automatic counterspasm within her mother; the child was one of those who hadn't cried beyond the grazed-knees stage. Shirley stirred on her hard chair as if about to speak to someone, even to giggle . . . but she was alone: on the one side, somebody's grandmother with a pearl earring shaking very slightly; on the other, a parent in dark gray hopsack. Afterwards there was tea and cake and an air of mild congratulation in the school hall. Meeting over a communal sugar bowl, Shirley and another woman smiled at each other in the manner of people who do not know one another's names. "A big day in their lives, isn't it? And just as well to get it over with so they can settle down to work before the exams, I was just saying . . ." Shirley smiled and murmured the appropriate half-phrases. The white dresses swooped in and out among the mothers and fathers. Bobbing breasts and sturdy hams, or thin waists and blindly nosing little peaks just touching flat bodices—but nubile, nubile. That was Sidney's explanation for the whole thing: awakening sexuality finding an emotional outlet; they do not love Christ, they are in love with him, a symbolic male figure, and indeed, what about Father Whatnot with his pale, clean priest's hands, appearing every Thursday among three hundred females?

Father Byrd was gaily introducing the bishop to a parent in a blue swansdown hat. The bishop had disrobed, and now appeared in the assembly like an actor who has taken off his splendid costume and makeup. The confirmants were displaying presents that lay in cotton wool within hastily torn tissue paper;

they raced about to give each other the fancy cards they had bought. Lyndall, with a deep, excited smile, found her mother. They kissed, and Lyndall clung to her. "Bless you, darling, bless you, bless you," Shirley said. Lyndall kept lifting her hair off her forehead with the back of a mannered hand, and was saying with pleased, embarrassed casualness, "What chaos! Could you see us shaking? I thought I'd *never*—we could hardly get up the steps! Did you see my *veil*? Roseann's was down to her nose! What chaos! Did you see how we all bunched together? Father Byrd told us a million times . . ." Her eyes were all around the room, as if acknowledging applause. She showed her mother her cards, with the very faint suggestion of defiance; but there was no need—with heads at an angle so that both could see at the same time, they looked at the doggerel in gilt script and the tinsel-nimbused figures as if they had never wrinkled their noses in amusement at greeting-card sentimentality. Shirley said, "Darling, instead of giving you some little" (she was going to say "cross or something," because every other girl seemed to have been given a gold crucifix and chain), "some present for yourself, we're sending a donation to the African Children's Feeding Scheme in your name. Don't you think that makes sense?"

Lyndall agreed before her mother had finished speaking: "That's a much better idea." Her face was vivid. She had never looked quite like that before; charming, movingly charming. Must be the tears and excitement, bringing blood to the surface of the skin. An emotional surrogate, Sidney would have said, if Shirley had told him about it. But it was something she wanted to keep; and so she said nothing, telling the others at home only about the splendour of the bishop's on-stage appearance, and the way the girls who were not confirmants hung about outside the school hall, hoping for leftover sandwiches. Her son Peter grinned—he had disliked boarding school so much that they had had to take him away. Beyond this, they had had no trouble with him at all. He certainly had not been bothered by any religious phase; he was a year older than Lyndall, and as pocket and odd-job money would allow, was slowly building a boat in a friend's backyard.

When Lyndall was home for a weekend she got up while the rest of the house was still asleep on Sunday mornings and went to Communion at the church down the road. It was her own affair; no one remarked on it one way or another. Meeting her with wine on her breath and the slightly stiff face that came from the early morning air, her mother, still in a dressing gown, sometimes made a gentle joke: "Boozing before breakfast, what a thing," and kissed the fresh, cool cheek. Lyndall smiled faintly and was gone upstairs, to come clattering down changed into the trousers and shirt that was the usual weekend dress of the family. She ate with concentration an enormous breakfast: all the things she didn't get at school.

Before her conversion, she and Shirley had often talked about religion, but now when Shirley happened to be reading Simone Weil's letters and told Lyndall something of her life and thought, the girl had the inattentive smile, the hardly-patient inclinations of the head, of someone too polite to rebuff an intrusion on privacy. Well, Shirley realized that she perhaps read to much into this; Simone Weil's thinking was hardly on the level of a girl of sixteen; Lyndall probably couldn't follow.

Or perhaps it was because Simone Weil was Jewish. If Lyndall had shown more interest, her mother certainly would have explained to her that she hadn't brought up the subject of Simone Weil because of *that*, Lyndall must believe her; but given the lack of interest, what was the point?

During the Christmas holidays Lyndall went to a lot of parties and overslept on several Sunday mornings. Sometimes she went to a service later in the day, and then usually asked Shirley to drive her to church: "It's absolutely boiling, trekking there in this heat." On Christmas morning she was up and off to Mass at dawn, and when she came back, the family had the usual present-giving in the dining room, with the servants, Ezekiel and

Margaret and Margaret's little daughter, Winnie, and constant interruptions as the dustmen, the milkman, and various hangers-on called at the kitchen door for their *bonsella*, their Christmas tip. The Bergers had always celebrated Christmas, partly because they had so many friends who were not Jews who inevitably included the Bergers in their own celebrations, and partly because, as Sidney said, holidays, saints' days—whatever the occasion, it didn't matter—were necessary to break up the monotony of daily life. He pointed out, apropos Christmas, that among the dozens of Christmas cards the Bergers got, there was always one from an Indian Muslim friend. Later in the day the family were expected at a Christmas lunch and swimming party at the Trevor-Pearses'. After a glass of champagne in the sun, Shirley suddenly said to Sidney, "I'm afraid that our daughter's the only one of the Christians here who's been to church today," and he said, with the deadpan, young-wise face that she had always liked so much, "What d'you expect, don't you know the Jews always overdo it?"

The Bergers thought they would go to the Kruger Park over the Easter weekend. As children grew older, there were fewer things all the members of a family could enjoy together, and this sort of little trip was a safe choice for a half-term holiday. When they told Peter, he said, "Fine, fine," but before Shirley could write to Lyndall, there was a letter from her saying she hoped there wasn't "anything on" at half term, because she and her school friends had the whole weekend planned, with a party on the Thursday night when they came home, and a picnic on the Vaal on Easter Monday, and she must do some shopping in town on the Saturday morning. Since Lyndall was the one who was at boarding school, there was the feeling that family plans ought to be designed to fit in with her inclinations rather than anyone else's. If Lyndall wasn't keen to go away, should they stay at home, after all? "Fine, fine," Peter said. It didn't seem to matter to him one way or the other. And Sidney, everyone knew, privately thought April still too hot a month for the Game Reserve.

"We can go at our leisure in the August holidays," he said, made expansive and considerate by the reprieve. "Yes, of course, fine," Peter said. He had told Shirley that he and his friend expected to finish the boat and get it down for a tryout in Durban during August.

A friend at school had cut Lyndall's hair, and she came out of school as conscious of this as a puppy cleverly carrying a shoe in its mouth. Her mother liked the look of her, and Sidney said "Thank God" in comment on the fact that she hadn't been able to see out of her eyes before. Whatever reaction there was from her brother was elicited behind closed doors, like all the other exchanges between brother and sister in the sudden and casual intimacy that seemed to grow up between them, apparently over a record that Lyndall had borrowed and brought home. They played it over and over on Thursday afternoon, shut in Lyndall's room.

Lyndall's head was done up like a parcel, with transparent sticky tape holding strands of hair in place on her forehead and cheeks; she gave her fingernails a coating like that of a cheap pearl necklace and then took it off again. She had to be delivered to the house where the party was being held, by seven, and explained that she would be brought home by someone else; she knew how her mother and father disliked having to sit up late to come and fetch her. Her mother successfully prevented herself from saying, "How late will it be?"—what was the use of making these ritual responses in an unacknowledged ceremony of initiation to adult life? Tribal Africans took the young into the bush for a few weeks, and got it all over with at once. Those free from the rites of primitive peoples repeated plaintive remarks, tags of a litany of instruction half but never quite forgotten, from one generation to the next.

Lyndall came home very late indeed, and didn't get up until eleven next morning. Her brother had long gone off to put in a full day's work on the boat. It was hot for early autumn, and the girl lay on the brown grass in her pink gingham bikini, sunbathing. Shirley came out with some mending and said to her,

"Isn't it awful, I can't do that any more. Just lie. I don't know when it went." Whenever the telephone rang behind them in the house, Lyndall got up at once. Her laughter and bursts of intense, sibilant, confidential talk now sounded, now were cut off, as Ezekiel and Margaret went about the house and opened or closed a door or window. Between calls, Lyndall returned and dropped back to the grass. Now and then she hummed an echo of last night's party; the tune disappeared into her thoughts again. Sometimes a smile, surfacing, made her open her eyes, and she would tell Shirley some incident, tearing off a fragment from the sounds, shapes, and colours that were turning in the red dark of her closed lids.

After lunch her mother asked whether she could summon the energy for a walk down to the shops—"You'll have an early night tonight, anyway." They tried to buy some fruit, but of course even the Portuguese greengrocers were closed on Good Friday.

As they came back into the house, Sidney said, "Someone phoned twice. A boy with a French name, Jean-something, Frebert, Brebert?"

Lyndall opened her eyes in pantomime astonishment; last night's mascara had worked its way out as a black dot in the inner corner of one. Then a look almost of pain, a closing away of suspicion took her face. "I don't believe it!"

"The first time, I'd just managed to get Lemmy down on the bathroom floor," said Sidney. The dog had an infected ear and had to be captured with cunning for his twice-daily treatment. "You won't get within a mile of him again today."

"Jean? He's from Canada, somebody's cousin they brought along last night. Did he say he'd phone again, or what? He didn't leave a number?"

"He did not."

She went up to her room and shut the door and played the record. But when the telephone rang she was somehow alert to it through the noisy music and was swift to answer before either

Shirley or Sidney moved to put aside their books. The low, light voice she used for talking to boys did not carry the way the exaggeratedly animated one that was for girls did. But by the time Shirley had reached the end of the chapter they had heard her run upstairs.

Then she appeared in the doorway and smiled in on the pair.

"What d'you know, there's another party. This boy Jean's just asked me to go. It's in a stable, he says; everyone's going in denims."

"Someone you met last night?"

"*Jean.* The one Daddy spoke to. You know."

"Such gaiety," said Sidney. "Well, he's not one to give up easily."

"Won't you be exhausted?"

But Shirley understood that Lyndall quite rightly wouldn't even answer that. She gave a light, patronizing laugh. "He says he wanted to ask me last night, but he was scared."

"Will you be going before or after dinner?" said Shirley.

"Picking me up at a quarter past seven."

In Shirley's silences a room became like a scene enclosed in a glass paperweight, waiting for the touch that would set the snow whirling. The suburban church bells began to ring, muffled by the walls, dying away in waves, a ringing in the ears.

"I'll give you a scrambled egg."

Lyndall came down to eat in her dressing gown, straight out of the bath: "I'm ready, Ma." Sidney was still reading, his drink fizzling flat, scarcely touched, on the floor beside him. Shirley sat down at the coffee table where Lyndall's tray was and slowly smoked, and slowly rose and went to fetch the glass she had left somewhere else. Her movements seemed reluctant. She held the glass and watched the child eat. She said, "I notice there's been no talk of going to church today."

Lyndall gave her a keen look across a slice of bread and butter she was just biting into.

"I woke up too late this morning."

"I know. But there are other services. All day. It's Good Friday, the most important day in the year."

Lyndall put the difficulty in her mother's hands as she used to give over the knotted silver chain of her locket to be disentangled by adult patience and a pin. "I meant to go to this evening's."

"Yes," said Shirley, "but you are going to a party."

"Oh Mummy."

"Only seven months since you got yourself confirmed, and you can go to a party on Good Friday. Just another party; like all the others you go to."

A despairing fury sprang up so instantly in the girl that her father looked around as if a stone had hurtled into the room. "I knew it. I knew you were thinking that! As if I don't feel terrible about it! I've felt terrible all day! You don't have to come and tell me it's Good Friday!" And tears shook in her eyes at the shame.

Peter had come in, a presence of wood-glue and sweat, not unpleasant, in the room. Under his rough eyebrows bridged by the redness of an adolescent skin irritation, he stared a moment and then seemed at once to understand everything. He sat quietly on a footstool.

"The most important day in the year for a Christian. Even the greengrocers closed, you saw—"

"I just knew you were thinking that about me, I knew it." Lyndall's voice was stifled in tears and anger. "And how do you think I feel when I have to go to church alone on Sunday mornings? All on my own. Nobody knows me there. And that atmosphere when I walk into the house and you're all here. How d'you think I *feel?*" She stopped to sob dramatically and yet sincerely; her mother said nothing, but her father's head inclined to one side, as one offers comfort without asking the cause of pain. "And when you said that about the present—everyone else just got one, no fuss. Even while I was being confirmed I could feel you sitting there, and I knew what you were thinking—how d'you think it is, for me?"

"Good God," Shirley said in the breathy voice of amazement, "I came to the confirmation in complete sincerity. You're being unfair. Once I'd accepted that you wanted to be a real Christian, not a social one—"

"You see? You see? You're always at me—"

"At you? This is the first time the subject's ever come up."

The girl looked at them blindly. "I know I'm a bad Christian! I listen to them in church, and it just seems a lot of rubbish. I pray, I pray every night—" Desperation stopped her mouth.

"Lyndall, you say you want Christ, and I believe you," said Shirley.

The girl was enraged. "Don't say it! You don't, you don't, you never did."

"Yet you make yourself guilty and unhappy by going out dancing on the day that Christ was crucified."

"Oh, why can't you just leave her alone?" It was Peter, his head lifted from his arms.

His mother took the accusation like a blow in the chest.

Sidney spoke for the first time; to his son. "What's the matter with you?"

"Just leave her alone," Peter said. "Making plans, asking questions. Just leave people alone, can't you?"

Sidney knew that he was not the one addressed, and so he answered. "I don't know what you're getting hysterical about, Peter. No one's even mentioned your name."

"Well, we talk about you plenty, behind your back, to our friends, I can tell you." His lips pulled with a trembling, triumphant smile. The two children did not look at each other.

"Coffee or a glass of milk?" Shirley said into the silence, standing up.

Lyndall didn't answer, but said, "Well, I'm not going. You can tell him I'm sick or dead or something. Anything. When he comes."

"I suggest you ring up and make some excuse," said Shirley.

The girl gestured it away; her fingers were limply twitching. "Don't even know where to get him. He'll be on his way now. He'll think I'm mad."

"I'll tell him. I'm going to tell him just exactly what happened," said Peter, looking past his mother.

She went and stood in the kitchen because there was nobody there. She was listening for the voices in the livingroom, and yet there was nothing she wanted to hear. Sidney found her. He had brought Lyndall's tray. "I don't understand it," he said. "If the whole thing's half-forgotten already, why push her into it again? For heaven's sake, what are you, an evangelist or something? Do you have to take it on yourself to make converts? Since when the missionary spirit? For God's sake, let's leave well alone. I mean, anyone would think, listening to you in there—"

His wife stood against the dresser with her shoulders hunched, pulling the points of her collar up over her chin. He leaned behind her and tightened the dripping tap. She was quiet. He put his hand on her cheek. "Never mind. High-handed little devils. Enough of this God-business for today."

He went upstairs and she returned to the livingroom. Lyndall was blowing her nose and pressing impatiently at the betrayal of tears that still kept coming, an overflow, to her brilliant, puffy eyes.

"You don't know how to get hold of the boy?" Shirley said.

There was a pause. "I told you."

"Don't you know the telephone number?"

"I'm not going to phone Clare Pirie—he's her cousin."

"It would be so rude to let him come for you for nothing," said Shirley. Nobody spoke. "Lyndall, I think you'd better go." She stopped, and then went on in a tone carefully picking a way through presumption, "I mean, one day is like another. And these dates are arbitrary, anyway, nobody really knows when it was, for sure—the ritual observance isn't really the thing—is it?—"

"Look what I look like," said the girl.

"Well, just go upstairs now"—the cadence was simple, sensible, comforting, like a nursery rhyme—"and wash your face with cold water, and brush your hair, and put on a bit of makeup."

"I suppose so. Don't feel much like dancing," the girl added, offhand, in a low voice to her mother, and the two faces shared, for a moment, a family likeness of doubt that the boy Peter did not see.

# NO PLACE LIKE

THE RELIEF of being down, out, and on the ground after hours in the plane was brought up short for them by the airport building: dirty, full of up-ended chairs like a closed restaurant. *Transit? Transit?* Some of them started off on a stairway but were shooed back exasperatedly in a language they didn't understand. The African heat in the place had been cooped up for days and nights; somebody tried to open one of the windows but again there were remonstrations from the uniformed man and the girl in her white gloves and leopard-skin pillbox hat. The windows were sealed, anyway, for the air-conditioning that wasn't working; the offender shrugged. The spokesman that every group of travellers produces made himself responsible for a complaint; at the same time some of those sheep who can't resist a hole in a fence had found a glass door unlocked on the far side of the transit lounge—they were leaking to an open passage-way: grass, bougainvillea trained like standard roses, a road glimpsed there! But the uniformed man raced to round them up and a cleaner trailing his broom was summoned to bolt the door.

The woman in beige trousers had come very slowly across the tarmac, putting her feet down on this particular earth once more, and she was walking even more slowly round the dirty hall. Her coat dragged from the crook of her elbow, her shoulder was weighed by the strap of a bag that wouldn't zip over a package of duty-free European liquor, her bright silk shirt opened dark mouths of wet when she lifted her arms. Fellow-glances of indignance or the seasoned superiority of a sense of humour found no answer in her. As her pace brought her into the path of the black cleaner, the two faces matched perfect indifference: his, for whom the distance from which these people came had no existence because he had been nowhere outside the two miles he walked from his village to the airport; hers, for whom the distance had no existence because she had been everywhere and arrived back.

Another black man, struggling into a white jacket as he unlocked wooden shutters, opened the bar, and the businessmen with their hard-top briefcases moved over to the row of stools. Men who had got talking to unattached women—not much promise in that now; the last leg of the journey was ahead—carried them glasses of gaudy synthetic fruit juice. The Consul who had wanted to buy her a drink with dinner on the plane had found himself a girl in red boots with a small daughter in identical red boots. The child waddled away and flirtation took the form of the two of them hurrying after to scoop it up, laughing. There was a patient queue of ladies in cardigans waiting to get into the lavatories. She passed—once, twice, three times in her slow rounds—a woman who was stitching petit-point. The third time she made out that the subject was a spaniel dog with orange-and-black-streaked ears. Beside the needlewoman was a husband of a species as easily identifiable as the breed of dog—an American, because of the length of bootlace, slotted through some emblem or badge, worn in place of a tie. He sighed and his wife looked up over her glasses as if he had made a threatening move.

The woman in the beige trousers got rid of her chit for Light

Refreshment in an ashtray but she had still the plastic card that was her authority to board the plane again. She tried to put it in the pocket of the coat but she couldn't reach, so she had to hold the card in her teeth while she unharnessed herself from the shoulder-bag and the coat. She wedged the card into the bag beside the liquor packages, leaving it to protude a little so that it would be easy to produce when the time came. But it slipped down inside the bag and she had to unpack the whole thing— the hairbrush full of her own hair, dead, shed; yesterday's newspaper from a foreign town; the book whose jacket tore on the bag's zip as it came out; wads of pink paper handkerchiefs, gloves for a cold climate, the quota of duty-free cigarettes, the Swiss pocket knife that you couldn't buy back home, the wallet of travel documents. There at the bottom was the shiny card. Without it, you couldn't board the plane again. With it, you were committed to go on to the end of the journey, just as the passport bearing your name committed you to a certain identity and place. It was one of the nervous tics of travel to feel for the reassurance of that shiny card. She had wandered to the revolving stand of paperbacks and came back to make sure where she had put the card: yes, it was there. It was not a bit of paper; shiny plastic, you couldn't tear it up—indestructible, it looked, of course they use them over and over again. *Tropic of Capricorn. Kamasutra. Something of Value.* The stand revolved and brought round the same books, yet one turned it again in case there should be a book that had escaped notice, a book you'd been wanting to read all your life. If one were to find such a thing, here and now, on this last stage, this last stop . . . She felt strong hope, the excitation of weariness and tedium perhaps. They came round—*Something of Value, Kamasutra, Tropic of Capricorn.*

She went to the seat where she had left her things and loaded up again, the coat, the shoulder-bag bearing down. Somebody had fallen asleep, mouth open, bottom fly button undone, an Austrian hat with plaited cord and feather cutting into his damp brow. How long had they been in this place? What time was it where she had left? (Some airports had a whole series of clock-

faces showing what time it was everywhere.) Was it still yesterday, there? —Or tomorrow. And where she was going? She
thought, I shall find out when I get there.

A pair of curio venders had unpacked their wares in a corner.
People stood about in a final agony of indecision: What would he
do with a thing like that? Will she appreciate it, I mean? A
woman repeated as she must have done in bazaars and shops and
market-places all over the world, I've seen them for half the
price. . . . But this was the last stop of all, the last chance *to take
back something*. How else stake a claim? The last place of all the
other places of the world.

Bone bracelets lay in a collapsed spiral of overlapping circles.
Elephant hair ones fell into the pattern of the Olympic symbol.
There were the ivory paper knives and the little pictures of palm
trees, huts and dancers on black paper. The vender, squatting in
the posture that derives from the necessity of the legless beggar
to sit that way and has become as much a mark of the street professional, in such towns as the one that must be somewhere behind
the airport, as the hard-top briefcase was of the international
businessman drinking beer at the bar, importuned her with the
obligation to buy. To refuse was to upset the ordination of roles.
He was there to sell "ivory" bracelets and "African" art; they
—these people shut up for him in the building—had been
brought there to buy. He had a right to be angry. But she shook
her head, she shook her head, while he tried out his few words of
German and French (*bon marché, billig*) as if it could only be a
matter of finding the right cue to get her to play the part as-
signed to her. He seemed to threaten, in his own tongue, finally,
his head in its white skullcap hunched between jutting knees. But
she was looking again at the glass case full of tropical butterflies
under the President's picture. The picture was vivid, and new; a
general successful in a coup only months ago, in full dress uniform, splendid as the dark one among the Magi. The butterflies,
relic of some colonial conservationist society, were beginning to
fall away from their pins in grey crumbs and gauzy fragments.
But there was one big as a bat and brilliantly emblazoned as the

general: something in the soil and air, in whatever existed out
there—whatever "out there" there was—that caused nature
and culture to imitate each other . . . ?

If it were possible to take a great butterfly. Not take back; just
take. But she had the Swiss knife and the bottles, of course. The
plastic card. It would see her onto the plane once more. Once the
plastic card was handed over, nowhere to go but across the tarmac and up the stairway into the belly of the plane, no turning
back past the air hostess in her leopard-skin pillbox, past the barrier. It wasn't allowed; against regulations. The plastic card
would send her to the plane, the plane would arrive at the end of
the journey, the Swiss knife would be handed over for a kiss, the
bottles would be exchanged for an embrace—she was shaking
her head at the curio vender (he had actually got up from his
knees and come after her, waving his pictures), *no thanks, no
thanks*. But he wouldn't give up and she had to move away, to
walk up and down once more in the hot, enclosed course dic-
tated by people's feet, the up-ended chairs and tables, the little
shored-up piles of hand-luggage. The Consul was swinging the
child in red boots by its hands, in an arc. It was half-whimpering,
half-laughing, yelling to be let down, but the larger version of
the same model, the mother, was laughing in a way to make her
small breasts shake for the Consul, and to convey to everyone
how marvellous such a distinguished man was with children.

There was a gritty crackle and then the announcement in careful, African-accented English, of the departure of the flight. A
kind of concerted shuffle went up like a sigh: at last! The red-
booted mother was telling her child it was silly to cry, the Consul was gathering their things together, the woman was winding
the orange thread for her needlework rapidly round a spool, the
sleepers woke and the beer-drinkers threw the last of their foreign
small change on the bar counter. No queue outside the Ladies'
now and the woman in the beige trousers knew there was plenty
of time before the second call. She went in and, once more, unharnessed herself among the crumpled paper towels and spilt
powder. She tipped all the liquid soap containers in turn until she

found one that wasn't empty; she washed her hands thoroughly
in hot and then cold water and put her wet palms on the back of
her neck, under her hair. She went to one of the row of mirrors
and looked at what she saw there a moment, and then took out
from under the liquor bottles, the Swiss knife and the documents,
the hairbrush. It was full of hair; a web of dead hairs that bound
the bristles together so that they could not go through a head of
live hair. She raked her fingers slowly through the bristles and
was aware of a young Indian woman at the next mirror, moving
quickly and efficiently about an elaborate toilet. The Indian
back-combed the black, smooth hair cut in Western style to hang
on her shoulders, painted her eyes, shook her ringed hands dry
rather than use the paper towels, sprayed French perfume while
she extended her neck, repleated the green and silver sari that left
bare a small roll of lavender-grey flesh between waist and *choli*.

*This is the final call for all passengers.*

The hair from the brush was no-colour, matted and coated
with fluff. Twisted round the forefinger (like the orange thread
for the spaniel's ears) it became a fibrous funnel, dusty and obscene. She didn't want the Indian girl to be confronted with it
and hid it in her palm while she went over to the dustbin. But
the Indian girl saw only herself, watching her reflection apprais-
ingly as she turned and swept out.

The brush went easily through the living hair, now. Again and
again, until it was quite smooth and fell, as if it had a memory, as if it were cloth that had been folded and ironed a certain way, along the lines in which it had been arranged by professional hands in another hemisphere. A latecomer rushed into one of
the lavatories, sounded the flush and hurried out, plastic card
in hand.

The woman in the beige trousers had put on lipstick and run a
nail-file under her nails. Her bag was neatly packed. She dropped
a coin in the saucer set out, like an offering for some humble
household god, for the absent attendant. The African voice was
urging all passengers to proceed immediately through Gate B.

The voice had some difficulty with *l*'s, pronouncing them more like *r*'s; a pleasant, reasoning voice, asking only for everyone to present the boarding pass, avoid delay, come quietly.

She went into one of the lavatories marked "Western-type toilet" that bolted automatically as the door shut, a patent device ensuring privacy; there was no penny to pay. She had the coat and bag with her and arranged them, the coat folded and balanced on the bag, on the cleanest part of the floor. She thought what she remembered thinking so many times before: not much time, I'll have to hurry. That was what the plastic card was for —surety for not being left behind, never. She had it stuck in the neck of the shirt now, in the absence of a convenient pocket; it felt cool and wafer-stiff as she put it there but had quickly taken on the warmth of her body. Some tidy soul determined to keep up Western-type standards had closed the lid and she sat down as if on a bench—the heat and the weight of the paraphernalia she had been carrying about were suddenly exhausting. She thought she would smoke a cigarette; there was no time for that. But the need for a cigarette hollowed out a deep sigh within her and she got the pack carefully out of the pocket of her coat without disturbing the arrangement on the floor. All passengers delaying the departure of the flight were urged to proceed immediately through Gate B. Some of the words were lost over the echoing intercommunication system and at times the only thing that could be made out was the repetition, Gate B, a vital fact from which all grammatical contexts could fall away without rendering the message unintelligible. Gate B. If you remembered, if you knew Gate B, the key to mastery of the whole procedure remained intact with you. Gate B was the converse of the open sesame; it would keep you, passing safely through it, in the known, familiar, and inescapable, safe from caves of treasure and shadow. *Immediately. Gate B. Gate B.*

She could sense from the different quality of the atmosphere outside the door, and the doors beyond it, that the hall was emptying now. They were trailing, humping along under their burdens—the petit-point, the child in red boots—to the gate where the girl in the leopard-skin pillbox collected their shiny cards.

She took hers out. She looked around the cell as one looks around for a place to set down a vase of flowers or a note that mustn't blow away. It would not flush down the outlet; plastic doesn't disintegrate in water. As she had idly noticed before, it wouldn't easily tear up. She was not at all agitated; she was simply looking for somewhere to dispose of it, now. She heard the voice (was there a shade of hurt embarrassment in the rolling *r*-shaped *l*'s) appealing to the passenger who was holding up flight so-and-so to please . . . She noticed for the first time that there was actually a tiny window, with the sort of pane that tilts outwards from the bottom, just above the cistern. She stood on the seat-lid and tried to see out, just managing to post the shiny card like a letter through the slot.

*Gate B*, the voice offered, *Gate B*. But to pass through Gate B you had to have a card, without a card Gate B had no place in the procedure. She could not manage to see anything at all, straining precariously from up there, through the tiny window; there was no knowing at all where the card had fallen. But as she half-jumped, half-clambered down again, for a second the changed angle of her vision brought into sight something like a head—the top of a huge untidy palm tree, up in the sky, rearing perhaps between buildings or above shacks and muddy or dusty streets where there were donkeys, bicycles and barefoot people. She saw it only for that second but it was so very clear, she saw even that it was an old palm tree, the fronds rasping and sharpening against each other. And there was a crow—she was sure she had seen the black flap of a resident crow.

She sat down again. The cigarette had made a brown aureole round itself on the cistern. In the corner what she had thought was a date-pit was a dead cockroach. She flicked the dead cigarette butt at it. Heel-taps clattered into the outer room, an African voice said, Who is there? Please, are you there? She did not hold her breath or try to keep particularly still. There was no one there. All the lavatory doors were rattled in turn. There was a high-strung pause, as if the owner of the heels didn't know what to do next. Then the heels rang away again and the door of the Ladies' swung to with the heavy sound of fanned air.

There were bursts of commotion without, reaching her muffledly where she sat. The calm grew longer. Soon the intermittent commotion would cease; the jets must be breathing fire by now, the belts fastened and the cigarettes extinguished, although the air-conditioning wouldn't be working properly yet, on the ground, and they would be patiently sweating. They couldn't wait forever, when they were so nearly there. The plane would be beginning to trundle like a huge perambulator, it would be turning, winking, shuddering in summoned power.

Take off. It was perfectly still and quiet in the cell. She thought of the great butterfly; of the general with his beautiful markings of braid and medals. Take off.

So that was the sort of place it was: crows in old dusty palm trees, crows picking the carrion in open gutters, legless beggars threatening in an unknown tongue. Not Gate B, but some other gate. Suppose she were to climb out that window, would they ask her for her papers and put her in some other cell, at the general's pleasure? The general had no reason to trust anybody who did not take Gate B. No sound at all, now. The lavatories were given over to their own internal rumblings; the cistern gulped now and then. She was quite sure, at last, that flight so-and-so had followed its course; was gone. She lit another cigarette. She did not think at all about what to do next, not at all; if she had been inclined to think that, she would not have been sitting wherever it was she was. The butterfly, no doubt, was extinct and the general would dislike strangers; the explanations (everything has an explanation) would formulate themselves, in her absence, when the plane reached its destination. The duty-free liquor could be poured down the lavatory, but there remained the problem of the Swiss pocket-knife. And yet—through the forbidden doorway: grass, bougainvillea trained like standard roses, a road glimpsed there!

# OTHERWISE BIRDS
# FLY IN

Toni and Kate still saw each other regularly once or twice a year.

One would have quite expected Toni to be out of sight, by now; Kate would have accepted this as inevitable, if it had happened, and have looked up with affection at the bright passage of the little satellite among other worlds. Yet since Toni's extraordinary marriage, their alliance had survived their slummy bachelor-girlhood together, just as it had survived school. Perhaps it was because both had had no family to speak of, and had thought of themselves as independent rather than as good as orphaned. Certainly nothing else clung to either from the school in the Bernese Oberland where they had been part of an international community of five- to eighteen-year-olds displaced by war and divorce—their parents' war, and the wars between their parents. Kate was born in 1934, in Malta, where her father was an English naval officer. He was blown up in a submarine in the early forties, and her mother married an American major and went to live in St. Louis; somehow Kate was ceded to Europe, got left behind at the *Ecole Internationale*, and spent her holidays with her grandmother in Hertfordshire. Toni had a father somewhere—at school, when her mail arrived, she used to tear off the beautiful stamps from Brazil, for the collection of a boy she was keen on: days would go by before she would take her father's letter from the mutilated envelope. As she grew old enough to be knowing, she gathered that her English mother had gone off with someone her family loathed; though what sort of man that would be, Toni could not imagine, because her mother's family were English socialists of the most peace-proselytizing sort—indeed, this made them choose to let her grow up in an international school in a neutral country, their hostage to one world.

At the school, Toni and Kate were "friends" in the real, giggly, perfectly exclusive, richly schoolgirl sense of the word. Kate played the flute and was top in maths. Toni was the best skier in the school and too busy keeping up with her passionate pen-friend correspondence in four languages to do much work. The things they did well and in which each was most interested, they could not do together, and yet they were a pair, meeting in a euphoric third state each alone conjured up in the other. In their last year their room was decorated with a packing-case bar with empty vermouth bottles that Toni thought looked crazily homely. *Mutti* (Frau Professor) Sperber used to come and sniff at them, just to make sure; now and then, as women, Toni and Kate were reminded of things like this, but they were not dependent upon "amusing" memories for contact.

When Kate left school her grandmother paid for her to study music in Geneva. The two girls had always talked of Toni going off to ride about vast haciendas in Brazil, but as she grew up letters from her father came more and more irregularly— finally, one didn't know for certain whether he was still in Brazil, never mind the haciendas. She tried England for a few months; the English relatives thought she ought to take up nursing or work on a Quaker self-help project among the poor of Glasgow. She got back to Switzerland on a free air trip won by composing a jingle at a trade fair, and moved in with Kate, imitating for her the speech, mannerisms, and impossible kindness of the English relatives. In Geneva she seemed to attract offers of all kinds of jobs without much effort on her part. She met Kate several times a day to report, over coffee.

"To India? But who's this man?"

"Something to do with the UN delegation. His beard's trained up under his turban at the sides, like a creeper. He says I'd spend six months a year in Delhi and six here."

She and Kate shared a flat in Geneva for five years; at least, Kate was there all the time, and Toni came and went. She spent three months in Warsaw typing material for a Frenchman who was bringing out a book on the Polish cinema. Another time she accompanied an old Australian lady home to Brisbane, and came back to Europe by way of Tokyo and Hong Kong, eking out funds by working as a hotel receptionist. An Italian film director noticed her at an exhibition and asked her what she did; she replied in her good Italian accent, with her pretty, capable grin, "I live." He and his mistress invited her to join a party of friends for a week in Corsica. Toni met people as others pick up food poisoning or fleas—although she was without money or position, soon a network of friends-of-friends was there across the world for her to balance on.

Between times, life was never dull at home in the tiny Geneva flat; Toni took a job as a local tourist guide and the two girls entertained their friends on beer and sausage, and, coming home late at night, used to wake up one another to talk about their love affairs. Kate had dragged on a long and dreary one with a middle-aged professor who taught composition and had an asthmatic wife. They discussed him for hours, arranging and rearranging the triangle of wife, asthma, and Kate. They could not find a satisfactory pattern. Although this was never formulated in so many words, they had plumbed (but perhaps it had been there always, instinctive basis of their being "friends" against other indications of temperament) a touchstone in common: what finally mattered wasn't the graph of an event or human relationship in its *prog-*

*ress*, but the casual or insignificant sign or moment you secretly took away from it. So that they knew nothing would come of re-composing the triangle. Just as Kate understood when Toni said of the disastrous end of an affair in England with a bad poet—"But there *was* that day in Suffolk, when we went to see the old church at the sea and he read out just as he ducked his head under the door, 'Please close behind you otherwise birds fly in.' That was his one good line."

Kate had been the intellectual with talent and opportunity, when they left school. Yet it was Toni who moved on the fringe of the world of fashionable thinkers, painters, writers and politicians. Kate passed exams at the conservatoire, all right, but she was away down in the anonymous crowd when it came to scholarships and honours. Long after her days at the conservatoire were over she still dressed like a student, going happily about Geneva with her long, thick blond hair parting on the shoulders of her old suède jacket. She was content to teach, and to continue experiments with electronic music with a young man she was, at last, in love with. Egon was living in the flat with her when the cable came: "Arriving Sunday with friend. Take a deep breath." At the time, Toni had her best job yet—away commuting between Paris and New York as something called personal assistant to an elderly oil man with a collection of modern paintings. That Sunday night, she stood in the doorway, a carrier smelling of truffles balanced on her hip. Next to her, holding lilies and a bottle of *Poire William*, was a prematurely bald young man with a dark, withdrawn face that was instantly familiar. "Where're your things?" Egon said, making to go downstairs for the luggage. "We came as we were," said Toni, dumping her burden and hugging him, laughing.

Food, drink, and flowers lay on the old ottoman. That was to be Toni's luggage, in future. The young man's face was familiar because he was Marcus Kelp, a second-generation shipping magnate badgered by picture magazine photographers not only because his yacht and houses were frequented by actresses, but also because he conceived and financed social rehabilitation and land reclamation schemes in countries where he had no "interests." He and Toni were blazingly in love with each other. She was proud that he was not a playboy; she would have married him if he had been one of his own deck-hands. Yet her childlike pleasure in the things she could, suddenly, do and buy and give away, was intoxicating. When first Kate and Egon were married, Toni used to telephone Geneva at odd hours from all over the world; but in time she no longer needed to find ways to demonstrate to herself that she could do whatever she wanted, she grew used to the conveniences of being a rich woman. She was drawn into the preoccupations of life on Marcus's scale; she went with him on his business about the world (they had houses and apartments everywhere) not allowing even the birth of her daughter to keep her at home. Later, of course, she was sometimes persuaded to accept some invitation that he had to forgo because of the necessity to be somewhere dull, and gradually, since her responsibilities towards her child and various households were taken care of by servants, she acquired a rich woman's life of her own. Yet once or twice a year, always, she arrived at Kate's for a night or a day or two, with *Poire William* and flowers. Egon was still at the institute for musical research; he and Kate had a car, a daily cleaning-woman, and one of those Swiss houses withdrawn behind green in summer, shutters in winter.

Kate had owed Toni a letter for months when she wrote, mentioning in a general round-up of personal news that she and Egon hoped to go to France in the spring. She was surprised when at once a letter came back from London saying wouldn't it be fun to meet somewhere and spend part of the holiday together?

It was years since Kate had spent any length of time with Toni. "Toni and Marcus want to come with us!" she told Egon; they were very fond of Marcus, with his dry honesty and his rich man's conscience. But Toni drove alone up to the villa near Pont du Loup with her little daughter, Emma, standing beside her on the nanny's lap. "Oh Marcus can't leave the Nagas," Toni said. At once she went enthusiastically through the small rented house.

Later, in the content of lunch outdoors, Egon said, "What was that about Nagaland? Since when?"

"You know how Marcus takes the whole world on his shoulders. He went to Pakistan in July, that's how it started. Now they're absolutely depending on him. Well, he doesn't know what he's missing"—Toni was already in her bikini, and the strong muscles of her belly, browned all winter in Barbados and Tunisia, contracted energetically as she thrust out her glass at arm's length for some more wine, and Kate and Egon laughed. Emma ran about, tripping on the uneven flagstones and landing hard on her frilly bottom—something she found very funny. She spoke French and only a few words of English, because the nanny was French. "And what an accent!" Toni didn't bother for the woman to be out of earshot. "It wouldn't have done at the *Ecole Internationale*, I can tell you." And she picked up the child and wouldn't let her go, so that they could hear her furious protests in provincial French as she struggled to get down.

Toni wanted to go to the beach right away, that afternoon. They drove down the steep roads of the river gorge to the sea they knew, from the house's terrace, as a misty borderland between horizon and sky. Sitting or standing on the stony beach was putting one's weight on a bag of marbles, but Toni carried Emma astride her neck into the water, and the two of them floundered and ducked and gasped with joy. "I must teach her to swim. Perhaps I'll take her along to Yugoslavia this summer, after all." Toni came out of the sea looking like a beautiful little blond seal, the shiny brown flesh of her legs shuddering sturdily as she manoeuvred the stones. They were in their early thirties, she and Kate, and Toni was at the perfection of her feminine rounding-out. There was no slack, and there were no wrinkles; she had the physical assurance of a woman who has been attractive so long that she cannot imagine a change ahead. Kate's body had gone soft and would pass unnoticeably into middle-age; the deep concentration of her blue eyes was already a contrast to her faded face and freckled lips.

Kate and Egon were stimulated—and touched—that first

afternoon, by the fun of having Toni there, so quick to enjoy-
ment, so full of attack, a presence like a spot-light bringing out
colour and detail. It was exciting to find that this quality of hers
was, if anything, stronger than ever; hectic, almost. They were
slightly ashamed to discover how quiet-living they had become,
and pleased to find that they could still break out of this with
zest. They left the beach late, lingered at the fishing-harbour
where Toni and Emma got into conversation with a fisherman
and were given a newspaper full of fresh sardines, and half-way
home in the dark they decided to have dinner at a restaurant they
liked the look of. The food was remarkable, they drank a lot of
pastis and wine, and Emma chased moths until she fell asleep in a
chair. The nanny was disapproving when they got home and
they all apologized rather more profusely than they would have
thought necessary had they been sober.

In the days that followed they went to another beach, and
another—they would never have been so energetic if it had not
been for Toni. She anointed them with some marvellous unguent
everyone used in Jamaica, and they turned the colour of a nico-
tine stain, in the sun. But after three days, when Kate and Egon
were beginning to feel particularly drugged and well, Toni
began to talk about places farther away, inland. There was a Polish painter living near Albi—it might be fun to look him up?
Well, what about Arles then—had they ever eaten sausage or
seen the lovely Roman theatre at Arles? And the Camargue? One
must see the white horses there, eh? But even Arles was a long
way, Egon said; one couldn't do it in a day. "Why a day?" Toni
said. "Let's just get in the car and go." And the baby? "Emma
and Mathilde will stay here, Mathilde will love to have the place
to herself, to be in charge—you know how they are."

They went off in the morning, in the spring sun with the hood
of Toni's car down. It had rained and the air smelled of herbs
when they stopped to eat Kate's picnic lunch. They stood and
looked down the valley where peasants were spraying the vines
in new leaf, so thin, tender, and so brilliant a green that the sun
struck through them, casting a shivering yellow light on hands

and bare arms moving there. A long, chalky-mauve mountain rode the distance as a ship comes over an horizon. "Is it Sainte-Victoire?" said Kate. If so, it didn't seem to be in quite the right place; she and Egon argued eagerly. Toni sat on a rock between the rosemary bushes with a glass of wine in one hand and a chunk of crust thick with cheese in the other, and grinned at them between large, sharp bites.

Egon was, as Toni said delightedly, "quite corrupted" by the Jaguar and couldn't resist taking her up to ninety on the auto-route. Kate and Toni called him Toad and laughed to themselves at the solemn expression on his face as he crouched his tall body in the seat. They reached Arles in the middle of the afternoon and found a little hotel up in the old town. There was time to have a look at the theatre and the medieval cloister. In the Roman arena, as they walked past at dusk, a team of small boys was playing soccer. Toni stood watching the moon come up while Egon and Kate climbed to the stone roof of the church. Her back was quite still, jaunty, as she stood; she turned to smile, watching them come down out of the dark doorway. "I can't explain," Kate was saying, "it seems to me the most satisfying old town I've ever been in. The way when you're in the theatre you can see the pimply spires of the medieval buildings . . . and that figure on top of the church, rising up over everything, peering over the Roman walls. The boys yelling down in the arena . . ." "Kate darling!" Toni smiled. "Well, we'll see it all properly to-morrow," Kate said. And over dinner, Egon was earnestly ec-static: "What I can't believe is the way the farm buildings have that perfect rectilinear relationship with the size and perspective of the fields—and the trees, yes. I thought that was simply Van Gogh's vision that did it—?" He had driven very slowly in-deed along the road beneath the plane trees that led from Aix to Arles. Late that night Kate leant on the window in her night-gown, looking out into the splotchy moon-and-dark of the little courtyard garden and could not come to bed.

But they left next morning straight after coffee, after all.

"We buy a *saucisson d'Arles* and we're on our way, eh? Don't

you think so?" Toni drew deeply on her first cigarette and pulled
the sympathetic, intimate face of accord over something that
didn't have to be discussed.

Egon said, "Whatever you girls want to do"; and Kate
wouldn't have dreamt of getting them to hang on a second day
in Arles just because she wanted another look at things they'd already seen. It wasn't all that important. They drove rather
dreamily through the Camargue and didn't talk much—the wa-
tery landscape was conducive to contemplation rather than communication. A salt wind parted the pelt of grasses this way and
that and the hackles of the grey waters rose to it. Egon said he
could make out floating dark dots as waterfowl, but there was no
sign of the white horses Toni wanted to see, except in the riding
stables around Les Saintes-Maries-de-la-Mer. Toni disappeared
into one of the village shops there and came out in a pair of
skin-tight cowboy pants and a brillant shirt, to make them laugh.
The sun strengthened and they sat and drank wine; Kate wandered off and when she came back remarked that she had had a
look at the ancient Norman church. Toni, with her legs sprawled
before her in classic Western style, looked dashing by no other
effort than her charming indolence. "Should we see it, too?"
Egon asked. "Oh I don't think . . . there's nothing much," Kate
said with sudden shyness.

"It's nice, nice, nice, here," Toni chanted to herself, turning
her face up to the sun.

"I'm going to take a picture of you for Marcus," said Kate.

"Shall we have some more wine?" Egon said to Toni.

She nodded her head vehemently, and beamed at her friends.

When the wine came and they were all three drinking, Egon
said—"Then let's spend the night. Stay here. We can look at
the church. I suppose there's some sort of hotel."

Kate broke the moment's pause. "Oh I don't think we'd want
to. I mean the church is nothing."

They crossed the Rhone at Bac de Bacarin early in the afternoon. "We should go back to Saintes-Maries in the autumn,
there's something between a religious procession and a rodeo,

then—let's do that," said Toni; and Egon, just as if he could leave the institute whenever he felt like it and he and Kate had money to travel whenever they pleased, agreed—"The four of us."

"Yes let's. Only Marcus hates Europe. We're supposed to be going to North Africa in October. Oh, we can eat in Marseilles tonight," Toni had taken out the road map. "Must eat a bouilla-baisse in Marseilles. But we don't want to sleep there, mm?"

After she had bought them a wonderful dinner they lost their way in the dark making, as she suggested, for "some little place" along the coast. They ended up at Bandol, in a hotel that was just taking the dust covers off in preparation for the season. Before morning, they saw nothing of the place but the glitter of black water and the nudging and nodding of masts under the window. In the room Kate and Egon slept in, last season's cockroaches ran out from under the outsize whore of a bed behind whose padded head were the cigarette butts of many occupants. Kate woke early in the musty room and got Egon up to come out and walk. The ugly glass restaurants along the sea-front were closed and the palms rustled dryly as they do when the air is cold. Fishermen had spread a huge length of net along the broad walk where, in a month's time, hundreds of tourists would crowd up and down. Without them the place was dead, as a person who has taken to drink comes to life only when he gets the stuff that has destroyed him. When they walked back through the remains of the hotel garden—it had almost all been built upon in the course of additions and alterations in various styles—Egon pointed out a plaque at the entrance. *Il est trois heures. Je viens d'achever "Félicité" . . . Dieu sait que j'ai été heureuse en l'écrivant.—Katherine Mansfield. Jeudi 28 Févier 1918.* "My God yes, of course, I'd forgotten," Kate said. "It was Bandol. She wrote 'Bliss' here. This place." Kate and Toni as young girls had felt the peculiar affinity that young girls feel for Katherine Mansfield—dead before they were born—with her meticulously chronicled passions, her use of pet-names, her genius and her suffering. Somewhere within this barracks of thick carpets and air-conditioned bars were buried the old rooms of the hotel in a garden, in a village, where she had lain in exile, coughing, waiting for letters from Bogey, and fiercely struggling to work.

"We must show Toni," Egon said.

"No don't. Don't say anything."

Egon looked at Kate. Her face was anxious, curiously ashamed; as it had been the day before, in Les Saintes-Maries-de-la-Mer.

"I don't think she's enjoying . . . it all . . . everything, the way we are."

"But you're the one who said we shouldn't stay, in the Camargue. You were the one—"

"I have the feeling it's not the same for her, Egon. She can't help it. She can go everywhere she likes whenever she likes. The South Seas or Corinthia—or Zanzibar. She could be there now. Couldn't she? Why here rather than there?" Her voice slowed to a stop.

Egon made as if to speak, and the impulse was crossed by counterimpulses of objection, confusion.

"The world's beautiful," said Kate.

"You're embarrassed to be enjoying yourself!" Egon accused.

The whole exchange was hurried, parenthetic as they walked along the hotel corridors, and then suddenly suppressed as they reached their rooms and Toni herself appeared, banging her door behind her, calling out to them.

Kate said quickly, "No, for *her*. I mean if she were to find out . . . about herself."

They were back at the villa by evening, and all shared the good mood of being "home" again. For the next few days, Kate and Egon were not inclined to leave the terrace; they read and wrote letters and went no farther than the shops in the village, while Toni drove up and down to the beaches with Emma and the nurse. But on the day before Toni was to leave, Kate went along with her to the beach. She and Toni ate lobster in a beach restaurant, very much at ease; all their lives, there would always be this level at which they were more at ease with each other

than they would ever be with anyone else. The child and the
nanny had something sent down to them on the beach. Mathilde
had been promised that she would be taken into Nice to buy a
souvenir for her sister, but Toni couldn't face the idea of the
town, after lunch, and with the wheedling charm disguising command that Kate noticed she had learnt in the past few years,
asked the nanny to take the bus: she would be picked up later,
and could leave the child behind.

Wherever Toni went she bought a pile of magazines in several languages; the wind turned their pages, while the two
women dozed and smoked. At one stage Kate realized that Toni
was gone, and Emma. Being alone somehow woke her up; on her
rubber mattress, she rolled onto her stomach and began to read
antique and picture dealers' advertisements. Then the position in
which she was lying brought on a muscular pain in the shoul-
der-blade that she was beginning to be plagued with, the last few
years, and she got up and took a little walk towards the harbour.
She was rotating the shoulder gently as the masseuse had told
her and quite suddenly—it was as if she had thought of the
child and she had materialized—there was Emma, lying in the
water between two fishing boats. She was face-down, like a fallen
doll. Kate half-stumbled, half-jumped into the oily water a-wash
with fruit-skins—she actually caught her left foot in a rope as
she landed in the water, and, in panic for the child, threshed
wildly to free herself. She reached the child easily and hauled her
up the side of one of the boats, letting her roll over onto the
deck, while she herself climbed aboard. All the things that ought
to be done came back to her shaking hands. She thrust her forefinger like a hook into the little mouth and pulled the tongue forward. She snatched a bit of old awning and crammed it tight
under the stomach so that the body would be at an angle to have
the water expelled from the lungs. She was kneeling, shaking,
working frantically among stinking gut and fins, and the water
and vomit that poured from the child. She pressed her mouth to
the small, slimy blue lips and tried to remember exactly, exactly,
how it was done, how she had read about it, making a casual

mental note, in the newspapers. She didn't scream for help; there was no time, she didn't even know if anyone passed on the quay —afterwards she knew there had been the sound of strolling footsteps, but the greatest concentration she had ever summoned in all her life had cut her off from everything and everyone: she and the child were alone between life and death. And in a little while, the child began to breathe, time came back again, the existence of other people, the possibility of help. She picked her up and carried her, a vessel full of priceless breath, out of the mess of the boat and onto the quay, and then broke into a wild run, running, running, for the beach restaurant.

And that had been all there was to it; as she kept telling Toni. In twenty-fours Emma was falling hard on her bottom on the terrace again, and laughing, but Toni had to be told about it, over and over, and to tell over and over how one moment Emma was playing with Birgit Sorenson's dachshund (Toni had just that minute run into the Sorensons, she hadn't known their yacht was in the harbour) and the next moment child and dog were gone. "Then we saw the dog up the quay toward the boathouse end—" and of course the child had gone the other way, and they didn't know it. Marcus was flying back from Pakistan; but what Toni could not face was Mathilde: "She never looks at me, never, without thinking that it could not have happened with her; I see it in her face."

They were sitting on the terrace in the evening, letting Toni talk it out. "Then get rid of her," said Kate.

"Yes, let her go," Egon urged. "It could have happened with anybody, remember that."

Toni said to Kate in the dark, "But it was you. *That* couldn't have been anyone else."

This idea persisted. Toni believed that because it was her child who lay in the water, Kate had woken up and walked to the spot. No one else would have known, no one else could have given her child back to her. The idea became a question that demanded some sort of answer. She had to do something. She wanted to give Kate—a present. What else? As time went by

the need became more pressing. She had to give Kate a present.
But what? "Why shouldn't I give them the little house in
Spain?" As she said this to her husband Marcus, she instantly felt
light and relieved.

"By all means. If you imagine that they would strike such a
bargain." He had listened to her account of that day, many times,
in silence, but she did not know what he would say if she wanted
to take Emma away with her anywhere, again.

She thought of a new car; Egon had so enjoyed driving the
Jaguar. Yet the idea of simply arriving with the deed of a house
or a new car filled her with a kind of shyness; she was afraid of a
certain look passing between Kate and Egon, the look of people
who know something about you that you don't know yourself.
At last one day she felt impatiently determined to have done with
it, to forget it once and for all, and she went once again through
her jewellery, looking for a piece—something—something
worthy—for Kate. She arrived unannounced in Geneva with a
little suède pouch containing a narrow emerald-and-diamond collar. "I've smuggled this bauble in, Kate, you do just as you like
with it—sell it if you can't stand the sight of such things. But I
thought it might look nice round your long neck."

It lay on the table among the coffee cups, and Kate and Egon
looked at it but did not touch it. Toni thought: as if it might
bite.

Kate said kindly, "It's from Marcus's family, Toni, you must
keep it."

"Sell the damn thing!"

They laughed.

"Surely I'm entitled to give you something!"

They did not look at each other; Toni was watching them
very carefully.

"Toni," Kate said, "you've forgotten my *Poire William* and the
flowers."

# A SATISFACTORY
# SETTLEMENT

A SAGGING HULK of an American car, its body-work like coloured tinfoil that has been screwed into a ball and smoothed out, was beached on the axle of a missing wheel in a gutter of the neighbourhood. Overnight, empty beer cartons appeared against well-oiled wooden gates; out-of-works loped the streets and held converse on corners with nannies in their pink uniforms and houseboys in aprons. In dilapidated outbuildings dating from the time when they housed horses and traps, servants kept all sorts of hangers-on. The estate agent had pointed out that it was one of the quiet old suburbs of Johannesburg where civil servants and university lecturers were the sort of neighbours one had—but of course no one said anything about the natives.

The child was allowed to ride his bicycle on the pavement and he liked to go and look at the car. He and his mother knew none of their neighbours yet, and in the street he simply thought aloud: he said to a barefoot old man in an army greatcoat, "There's a dead rat by the tree at the corner. I found it yesterday." And the old man clapped his hands slowly, with the gum-grin of ancients and infants: "*S'bona*, my *baasie*, may the Lord bless you, you are big man." Under one of the silky oaks of the pavement the child said to a man who had been lying all morning in the shade with a straw hat with a Paisley band, over his eyes, and a brand-new transistor radio playing beside his head, "Did you steal it?"

The man said without moving, "My friend, I got it in town." The furze of beard and moustache were drawn back suddenly in a lazy yawn that closed with a snap.

"I saw a dead rat there by the corner."

"The crock's been pushed to Tanner Road."

"There's a native boy's got a ten transistor."

His mother was not interested in any of this intelligence. Her face was fixed in vague politeness, she heard without listening to what was said, just as he did when she talked on the telephone: ". . . no question of signing *anything* whatever until provision's made . . . my dear Marguerite, I've been fooled long enough, you can put your mind at rest . . . only in the presence of the lawyers . . . the door in his face, that's . . . cut out the parties he takes to the races every Saturday, and the flush dinners, then, if he can't afford to make proper provision . . . *and*, I said, I want a special clause in the maintenance agreement . . . medical expenses *up till the age of twenty-one* . . ."

When his mother was not talking to Marguerite on the telephone it was very quiet in the new house. It was as if she were still talking to Marguerite in her mind. She had taken the white bedside radio from her room in the old house—daddy's house —to a swop shop and she had brought home a grey portable typewriter. It stood on the dining table and she slowly picked out letters with her eyes on the typing manual beside her. The tapping became his mother's voice, stopping and starting, hesitantly and dryly, out of her silence. She was going to get a job and work in an office; he was going to a new school. Later on when everything was settled, she said, he would sometimes spend a weekend with daddy. In the meantime it was the summer holidays and he could do what he liked.

He did not think about the friends he had played with in the old house. The move was only across the town, but for the boy seas and continents might have been between, and the suburb a new country from where Rolf and Sheila were a flash of sun on bicycles on a receding horizon. He could not miss them as he had done when they had been in the house next door and prevented, by some punishment or other, from coming over to play. He wandered in the street; the rat was taken away, but the old man came back again—he was packing and unpacking his paper carrier on the pavement: knotted rags, a half-loaf of brown bread, snuff, a pair of boots whose soles grinned away from the uppers, and a metal funnel. The boy suddenly wanted the funnel, and paid the old man fifteen cents for it. Then he hid it in the weeds in the garden so that his mother wouldn't ask where he'd got it.

The man with the transistor sometimes called out, "My friend, where you going?" "My friend, watch out for the police!"

The boy lingered a few feet off while the man went on talking and laughing, in their own language, with the group that collected outside the house with the white Alsatian.

"Why d'you say that about the policeman?"

The man noticed him again, and laughed. "My friend, my friend!"

Perhaps the old man had told about the funnel; a funnel like that might cost fifty cents. In a shop. The boy didn't really believe about the policeman; but when the man laughed, he felt he wanted to run away, and laugh back, at the same time. He was drawn to the house with the white Alsatian and would have liked to ride past without hands on the handlebars if only he hadn't been afraid of the Alsatian rushing out to bite the tires. The Alsatian sat head-on-paws on the pavement among the night watchman and his friends, but when it was alone behind the low garden wall of the house it screamed, snarled and leapt at the women who went by in slippers and cotton uniforms gaping between the buttons, yelling "*Voetsak!*" and "*Suka!*" at it. There were also two women who dressed as if they were white, in tight trousers, and had straightened hair and lipstick. One afternoon they had a fight, tearing at each other, sobbing, and swearing in English. The Alsatian went hysterical but the night watchman had him by the collar.

The old car actually got going—even when the wheel was on, there was still the flat battery, and he put down his bike and helped push. He was offered a ride but stood shaking his head, his chest heaving. A young man in a spotless white golf-cap and a torn and filthy sweater wanted to buy his watch. They had been pushing side by side and they sat in the gutter, smiling like panting dogs. "I pay you five pounds!" The slim, sticky black hand fingered his wrist, on which the big watch sat a bit off-centre.

"But where have you got five pounds?"

"How I can say I buy from you if I can't have five pounds? I will pay five pounds!"

The impossible size of the sum, quoted in old currency, as one might talk wildly of ducats or doubloons, hung in credible bluff between them. He said of his watch: "I got it for Christmas." But what was Christmas to the other?

"Five pounds!"

A nanny pushing a white child in a cart called out something in their language. The hand dropped the skinny wrist and a derisive tongue-click made the boy feel himself dismissed as a baby.

He did not play in the garden. His toys all had been brought along but there was no place for them yet; they stood about in his room with the furniture that had been set here or there by the movers. His mother dragged his bed under the window and asked, Is that where you want it? And he had said, "I don't know where it's supposed to be."

The bicycle was the only thing he took out with him into the street. It was a few days before the car turned up again. Then he found it, two blocks away. This time it had two flat tires and no one did anything about them. But a house down there was one of those with grass planted on the pavement outside and the garden-boy let him go back and forth once or twice with the petrol-motor mower. He went again next day and helped him. The

garden-boy wanted to know if his father smoked and asked him
to bring cigarettes. He said, "My father's not here but when
we're settled I'll ask for some for you." He hardly ever went out
now without meeting the old man somewhere; the old man
seemed to expect him. He brought things out of his paper carrier
and showed them to the boy, unwrapped them from rags and the
advertising handouts that drift to city gutters. There was a tin
finger, from a cigar, a torch without switch or glass, and a broken plastic duck: nothing like the funnel. But the old man, who
had the lint of white hairs caught among the whorls on his head,
spread the objects on the pavement with the confidence of giving
pleasure and satisfaction. He took the boy's hand and put in it
the base of some fancy box; this hand on the boy's was strong,
shaky, and cold, with thick nails the colour of the tortoise's shell
in the old house. The box-base had held a perfume bottle and was
covered with stained satin; to the boy it was a little throne but he
didn't want it, it was a girl's thing. He said with an exaggerated
shrug, "No money." "Yes, my *baasie*, only shilling, shilling. The
Lord bless you, *Nkosana*. Only shilling."

The old man began to wrap it all up again; the base, the duck,
the torch and the tin finger. Afterwards, the boy thought that
next time he might take the tin cigar finger for, say, two-and-a-
half cents, or three. He'd have to buy something. As he rode
back to the new house, there was the angle of a straw hat with a
Paisley band in a little group chatting, accusing and laughing,
and he called out, "Hullo, my friend!"

"Yes, my friend!" the greeting came back, though the man
didn't look round at him.

Then he thought he saw, without the white cap, the one who
wanted to buy his watch, and with a hasty wobble of pleasurable
panic he rode off fast down the hill, lifting his hands from the
bars a moment in case somebody was looking, and taking a
chance on the white Alsatian.

When she was not at the typewriter she was on her knees for
hours at a time, sorting out boxes and suitcases of things to be got

rid of. She had gone through the stuff once when she packed up and left, setting aside hers from his and being brought up short when she came upon some of the few things that seemed indisputably theirs and therefore neither to be disposed of nor rightfully claimed by either. Now she went through all that was hers, and this time, on a different principle of selection, set aside what was useful, relevant and necessary from what was not. All the old nest-papers went into the dustbin: letters, magazines, membership cards, even photographs. Her knees hurt when she rose but she sometimes went on again after she and the child had eaten dinner, and he was in bed.

During the day she did not go out except for consultations with the lawyers and if Marguerite phoned at night to hear the latest, she sat down at the telephone with a gin and bitter lemon —the first opportunity she'd had to think about herself, even long enough to pour a drink. She had spoken to no one round about and awareness of her surroundings was limited to annoyance latent in the repetition of one worn, close-harmony record, mutedly blaring again and again from nearby—a gramophone in some native's *khaya*. But she was too busy getting straight to take much notice of anything; the boy was getting a bit too much freedom—still, he couldn't come to any harm, she supposed he wouldn't go far away, while out of the way. She hadn't seen any of the good friends, since she'd left, and that was fine. There'd been altogether too much talk and everyone ready to tell *her* what she ought to do, one day, and then running off to discuss the "other side of the story" the next—naturally, it all got back to her.

Marguerite was quite right. She was simply going ahead to provide a reasonable, decent life for herself and her child. She had no vision of this life beyond the statement itself, constantly in her mind like a line of doggerel, and proclaimed aloud in the telephone conversations with Marguerite, but she was seized by the preoccupations of sorting out and throwing away, as if someone had said: dig here.

She walked round the house at night before she went to bed,

and checked windows and doors. Of course, she was used to that; but when, as had so often happened, she was left alone in the other house, there were familiar servants who could be trusted. There was no one to depend on here; she had taken the first girl who came to the back door with a reference. It was December and the nights were beautiful, beautiful: she would notice, suddenly, while pulling in a window. Out there in the colour of moonstone nothing moved but the vibration of cicadas and the lights in the valley. Both seemed to make shimmering swells through the warm and palpable radiance. Out there, you would feel it on bare arms while you danced or talked, you could lie on your back on hard terrace stone and feel the strange vertigo of facing the stars.

It was like a postcard of somewhere she had been, and had no power over her in the present. She went to bed and fell asleep at once as if in a night's lodging come upon in the dark.

But after the first few days something began to happen in the middle of the night. It happened every night, or almost every night (she was not sure; sometimes she might have dreamt it, or run, in the morning, the experience of two nights into one). Anyway, it happened often enough to make a pattern of the nights and establish, through unease, a sense of place that did not exist in the light of day.

It was natives, of course; simply one of the nuisances of this quiet neighbourhood. A woman came home in the early hours of the morning from some shebeen. Or she had no home and was wandering the streets. First she was on the edge of a dream, among those jumbled cries and voices where the lines of conscious and subconscious cross. Then she drew closer and clearer as she approached the street, the house, the bed—to which the woman lying there was herself returning, from sleep to wakefulness. There was the point at which the woman in the bed knew herself to be there, lying awake with her body a statue still in the attitude of sleep, and the shadowy room standing back all round her. She lay and listened to the shouts, singing, laughter and sudden cries. It was a monologue; there was no answer, no response.

No one joined in the singing and the yells died away in the empty streets. It was impossible not to listen because, apart from the singing, the monologue was in English—always when natives were drunk or abusive they seemed to turn to English or Afrikaans; if it had been in their language she could have shut it out with a pillow over her ears, like the noise of cats. The voice lurched and rambled. Just when it seemed to be retreating, fading round a corner or down the hill, there would be a short, fearful, questioning scream, followed by a waiting silence: then there it was, coming back, very near now, so near that slithering footsteps and the loose slap of heels could be heard between the rise and fall of accusations, protests, and wheedling obscenities. ". . . telling LIARS. I . . . you . . . don't say me I'm cunt . . . and telling liars . . . L-I-A-R-S . . . you know? you know? . . . I'm love for that . . . LI-ARS . . . the man he want fuck . . . LI-A-A-RS . . . my darling I'm love . . . AHH-hahahahhahahoooooee . . . YOU RUBBISH! YOU HEAR! YOU RUBBISH . . ."

And then slowly it was all gathered together again, it staggered away, the whole muddled, drunken burden of it, dragged off somewhere, nowhere, anywhere it could not be heard any more. She lay awake until the streets had stifled and hidden it, and then she slept.

Until the next night.

The summons was out of the dark as if the voice came out of her own sleep like those words spoken aloud with which one wakes oneself with a start. YOU RUBBISH . . . don't say me . . . he want . . . L-I-A-R-S . . . don't say me.

Or the horrible jabber when a tape recorder is run backwards. Is that my voice? Shrill, ugly; merely back-to-front? L-I-A-R-S. The voice that had slipped the hold of control, good sense, self-respect, proper provision, the future to think of. My darling I'm love for that. Ahhhhhhhahahhaoooooeee. Laughing and snivelling; no answer: nobody there. No one. In the middle of the night, night after night, she forgot it was a native, a drunken black prostitute, one of those creatures with purple lips and a great backside in trousers who hung about after the men. She lay so that both ears were free to listen and she did not open her eyes on the outer dark.

Then one night the voice was right under her window. The dog next door was giving deep regular barks of the kind that a dog gives at a safe distance from uncertain prey, and between bouts of fisting on some shaky wooden door the voice was so near that she could hear breath drawn for each fresh assault. "YOU HEAR? I tell you I'm come find . . . YOU HEAR-R-R . . . I'm come give you nice fuck . . . YOU-OOO-HE-ARR?" The banging must be on the door of the servant's room of the next door house; the dividing wall between the two properties was not more than twenty feet from her bedroom. No one opened the door and the voice grovelled and yelled and obscenely cajoled.

This time she got up and switched on the light and put on her dressing gown, as one does when there is a situation to be dealt with. She went to the window and leant out; half the sky was ribbed with cloud, like a beach in the moonlight, and the garden trees were thickly black—she could not see properly into the neighbour's over the creeper-covered wall, but she held her arms across her body and called ringingly, "Stop that! D'you hear? Stop it at once!"

There was a moment's silence and then it all began again, the dog punctuating the racket in a deep, shocked bay. Now lights went on in the neighbour's house and there was the rattle of the kitchen door being unbolted. A man in pyjamas was in her line of vision for a moment as he stood on the back steps. "Anything wrong?" The chivalrous, reassuring tone between equals of different sex.

"In your yard," she called back. "Some drunk woman's come in from the street."

"Oh my God. Her again."

He must have been barefoot. She did not hear anyone cross the yard but suddenly his voice bellowed, "Go on, get out, get going. . . . I don't care what you've come for, just get on your feet and *hamba* out of my yard, go on, quickly, OUT!" "No master, that boy he—" "Get up!" "Don't swear me—" There was a confusion of the two voices with his quick, hoarse, sober one prevailing, and then a grunt with a sharp gasp, as if someone had been kicked. She could see the curve of the drive through the spaced shapes of shrubs and she saw a native woman go down it, not one of the ladies in trousers but an ordinary servant, fat and middle-aged and drunk, in some garment still recognizably a uniform. "All right over there?" the man called.

"Thanks. Perhaps one can get some sleep now."

"You didn't send for the police?"

"No, no I hadn't done that."

All was quiet. She heard him lock his door. The dog gave a single bark now and again, like a sob. She got into the cool bed and slept.

The child never woke during the night unless he was ill but he was always up long before any adult in the mornings. That morning he remembered immediately that he had left his bicycle out all night and went at once into the garden to fetch it. It was gone. He stared at the sodden long grass and looked wildly round from one spot to another. His mother had warned him not to leave anything outside because the fence at the lower end of the garden, giving on a lane, was broken in many places. He looked in the shed although he knew he had not put the bicycle there. His pyjamas were wet to the knees from the grass. He stuffed them into the laundry basket in the bathroom and put on a shirt and trousers. He went twice to the lavatory, waiting for her to get up. But she was later than usual that morning, and he was able to go into the kitchen and ask the girl for his breakfast and eat it alone. He did not go out; quietly, in his room, he began to unpack and set up the track for his electric racing cars. He put together a balsawood glider that somehow had never been assembled, and slipped off to throw it about, with a natural air, down the end of the garden where the bicycle had disappeared. From there he was surprised to hear his mother's voice, not on the telephone but mingled with other voices in the light, high way of grown-up people exchanging greetings. He was attracted to the driveway; drawn to the figures of his mother, and a man and woman dressed for town, pausing and talking, his mother politely making a show of leading them to the house without actually inviting them in. "No, well, I was saying to Ronald, it's all right if one's an old inhabitant, you know—" the woman began, with a laugh, several times, without being allowed to finish. "—a bit funny, my asking that about the police, but really, I can assure you—" "Oh no, I appreciated—" "—assure you, they're as much use as—" "It *was*, five or six years ago, but it's simply become a hang-out—" "And the women! Those creatures in Allenby Road! I was saying, one feels quite ashamed—" "Well I don't think I've had an unbroken night's sleep since I moved in. That woman yelling down the street at two in the morning." "I make a point of it—don't hang about my property, I tell them. They're watching for you to go out at night, that's the thing." "Every single morning I pick up beer cartons *inside* our wall, mind you—"

His mother had acknowledged the boy's presence, to the others, by cupping her hand lightly round the back of his head. "And my bicycle's been stolen," he said, up into their talk and their faces.

"Darling—where?" His mother looked from him to the neighbours, presenting the sensation of a fresh piece of evidence. "You see?" said the man. "There you are!"

"Here, in the garden," he said.

"There you are. Your own garden."

"*That* you must report," said the woman.

"Oh really—on top of everything else. Do I have to go myself, or could I phone, d'you think?"

"We'll be going past the police station on the hill, on our way to town. Ronald could just stop a minute," the woman said.

"You give me the particulars and I'll do it for you." He was a man with thick-soled, cherry-dark shoes, soaring long legs, an air-force moustache and a funny little tooth that pressed on his lip when he smiled.

"What was the make, again—d'you remember?" his mother asked him. And to the neighbours, "But please come inside—. Won't you have some coffee, quickly? I was just going to make myself—oh, it was a Raleigh, wasn't it? Or was that your old little one?" They went into the house, his mother explaining that she wasn't settled yet.

He told them the make, serial number, colour, and identifying dents of his bicycle. It was the first time he and his mother had had visitors in this house and there was quite a flurry to find the yellow coffee cups and something better than a plastic spoon. He ran in and out helping, and taking part in the grown-up conversation. Since they had only just got to know him and his mother, these people did not interrupt him all the time, as the friends who came to the other house always had. "And I bet I know who took it, too," he said. "There's an old native boy who just talks to anybody in the street. He's often seen me riding my bike down by the house where the white dog is."

# WHY HAVEN'T YOU WRITTEN?

Hᴵˢ ᴘʀᴏʙʟᴇᴹ was hardening metal; finding a way to make it bore, grind, stutter through auriferous and other mineral-bearing rock without itself being blunted. The first time he spoke to the Professor's wife, sitting on his left, she said how impossible that sounded, like seeking perpetual motion or eternal life—nothing could bear down against resistance without being worn away in the process? He had smiled and they had agreed with dinner-table good humour that she was translating into abstract terms what was simply a matter for metallurgy.

They did not speak now. He did not see her face. All the way to the airport it was pressed against his coat-muffled arm and he could look down only on the nest of hair that was the top of her head. He asked the taxi driver to close the window because a finger of cold air was lifting those short, overlaid crescents of light hair. At the airport he stood by while she queued to weigh-in and present her ticket. He had the usual impulse to buy, find something for her at the last minute, and as usual there was nothing she wanted that he could give her. The first call came

and they sat on with his arm round her. She dared not open her
mouth; misery stopped her throat like vomit: he knew. At the
second call, they rose. He embraced her clumsily in his coat, they
said the usual reassurances to each other, she passed through the
barrier and then came back in a crazy zigzag like a mouse threatened by a broom, to clutch his hand another time. Ashamed,
half-dropping her things, she always did that, an unconscious effort to make no contact definitively the last.

And that was that. She was gone. It was as it always was; the
joking, swaggering joy of arrival carried with it this reverse side;
in their opposition and inevitability they were identical. He was
used to it, he should be used to it, he should be used to never getting used to it because it happened again and again. The mining
group in London for whom he was consultant tungsten carbide
metallurgist sent him to Australia, Peru, and—again and again—
the United States. In seven or eight visits he had been in New
York for only two days and spent a weekend, once, in Chicago,
but he was familiar with the middle-sized, Middle West, middle-
everything towns (as he described them at home to friends in London) like the one he was left alone in now, where he lived in local
motels and did his work among mining men and accepted the standard hospitality of good business relations. He was on first-name
terms with his mining colleagues and their wives in these places
and at Christmas would receive cards addressed to his wife and him
as Willa and Duggie, although, of course, the Middle Westerners had
never met her. Even if his wife could have left the children and
the Group had been prepared to pay her fare, there wasn't much
to be seen in the sort of places in America his work took him to.

In them, it was rare to meet anyone outside the mining community. The Professor's wife on his left at dinner that night was
there because she was somebody's sister-in-law. Next day, when
he recognized her standing beside him at the counter of a drugstore she explained that she was on a visit to do some research in
the local university library for her husband, Professor Malcolm,
of the Department of Political Science in the university of another Middle Western town not far away. And it was this small

service she was able to carry out for the Professor that had made everything possible. Without it, perhaps the meetings at dinner and in the drugstore would have been the only times, the beginning and the end: the end before the beginning. As it was, again and again the Professor's wife met the English metallurgist in towns of Middle Western America, he come all the way from London to harden metal, she come not so far from home to search libraries for material for her husband's thesis.

It was snowing while a taxi took him back along the road from the airport to the town. It seemed to be snowing up from the ground, flinging softly at the windscreen, rather than falling. To have gone on driving into the snow that didn't reach him but blocked out the sight of all that was around him—but there was a dinner, there was a report he ought to write before the dinner. He actually ground his teeth like a bad-tempered child— always these faces to smile at, these reports to sit over, these letters to write. Even when she was with him, he had to leave her in the room while he went to friendly golf games and jolly dinners with engineers who knew how much *they* missed a bit of home life when they had to be away from the wife and youngsters. Even when there were no dinner parties he had to write reports late at night in the room where she lay in bed and fell asleep, waiting for him. And always the proprietorial, affectionately reproachful letters from home: . . . *nothing from you . . . For goodness' sake, a line to your mother . . . It would cheer up poor little mumpy Ann no end if she got a postcard . . . . . . nothing for ten days, now, darling, can't help getting worried when you don't . . .*

Gone: and no time, no peace to prepare for what was waiting to be realized in that motel room. He could not go back to that room right away. Drive on with the huge silent handfuls of snow coming at him, and the windscreen wipers running a screeching fingernail to and fro over glass: he gave the driver an address far out of the way, then when they had almost reached it said he had changed his mind and (to hell with the report) went straight to the dinner although it was much too early. "For heaven's sakes!

Of *course* not. Fix yourself a drink, Duggie, you know where
it all is by now . . ." The hostess was busy in the kitchen, a fat
beautiful little girl in leotards and dancing pumps came no farther
than the doorway and watched him, finger up her nose.

They always drank a lot in these oil-fired igloos, down in the
den where the bar was, with its collection of European souvenirs
or home-painted Mexican mural, up in the sitting-room round the
colour TV after dinner, exchanging professional jokes and anecdotes. They found Duggie in great form: that dry English sense
of humour. At midnight he was dropped between the hedges of
dirty ice shovelled on either side of the motel entrance. He stood
outside the particular door, he fitted the key and the door swung
open on an absolute assurance—the dark, centrally-heated smell
of Kim Malcolm and Crispin Douglas together, his desert boots,
her hair lacquer, zest of orange peel, cigarette smoke in cloth,
medicated nasal spray, salami, newspapers. For a moment he
didn't turn on the light. Then it sprang from under his finger and
stripped the room: gone; empty, ransacked. He sat down in his
coat. What had he done the last time? People went out and got
drunk or took a pill and believed in the healing sanity of morning. He had drunk enough and he never took pills. Last time he
had left when she did, been in some other place when she was in
some other place.

She had put the cover on the typewriter and there was a dust-
less square where the file with material for Professor Malcom's
thesis used to be. He took his notes for his report out of the briefcase and rolled a sheet of paper into the typewriter. Then he sat
there a long time, hands on the machine, hearing his own breathing whistling slightly through his blocked left nostril. His heart
was driven hard by the final hospitable brandy. He began to type
in his usual heavy and jerky way, all power in two forefingers.

In the morning—in the morning nothing could efface the
hopeless ugliness of that town. They laughed at it and made jokes
about the glorious places he took her to. She had said, if we
could stay with each other for good, but only on condition that

we lived in this town? She had made up the scene: a winter day five years later, with each insisting it was the other's turn to go out in the freezing slush to buy drink and each hurling at the other the reproach—it's because of *you* I got myself stuck here. She was the one who pulled the curtain aside on those streets of shabby snow every morning, on the vacant lots with their clapboard screens, on the grey office blocks with lights going on through the damp-laden smog as people began the day's work, and it was she who insisted—be fair—that there was a quarter-of-an-hour or so, about five in the evening, when the place had its moment; a sort of Arctic spectrum, the fire off a diamond, was reflected from the sunset on the polluted frozen river upon the glass faces of office blocks, and the evening star was caught hazily in the industrial pall.

In the morning frozen snot hung from the roofs of wooden houses. A company car drove him to his first appointment. Figures in the street with arms like Teddy bears, the elbow joints stiffened by layers of clothing. A dog burning a patch of urine through the snow. In the cafeteria at lunch (it was agreed that it was crazy, from the point of view of everyone's waist-line, to lay on an executive lunch for him every day) he walked past Lily cups of tuna fish salad and bowls of Jell-O, discussing percussive rock drilling and the heat treatment of steel. Some drills were behaving in an inexplicable manner and he was driven out to the mine to see for himself. A graveyard all the way, tombstones of houses and barns under snow. Sheeted trees. White mounds and ridges whose purpose could only be identified through excavation, like those archaeological mounds, rubbish heaps of a vanished culture silted over by successive ones. He did not know why the tungsten carbide-tipped drills were not fulfilling their promised performance; he would have to work on it. He lied to one generous colleague that he had been invited to dinner with another and he walked about the iron-hard streets of the downtown area (the freeze had crusted the slush, the crush was being tamped down by the pressure of feet) with his scarf over his mouth, and at last ended up at the steak house where they used to go. Because he was alone the two waitresses talked to each other near him as if he were not there. Each table had a small glass box which was a selector for the jukebox; one night she had insisted that they ought to hear a record that had been the subject of controversy in the newspapers because it was supposed to include, along with the music, the non-verbal cries associated with love-making, and they had laughed so much at the groans and sighs that the bloody slabs of meat on the wooden boards got cold before they ate them. Although he thought it senseless to fill himself up with drink he did finish the whole bottle of wine they used to manage between them. And every night, making the excuse that he wanted to "work on" the problem of the drill, pleading tiredness, lying about an invitation he didn't have, he went from brutal cold into fusty heat and out to brutal cold again, sitting in bars and going to the steak house or the Chinese restaurant and then back to bars again, until the final confrontation with cold was only half-felt on his stiff hot face and he trudged back along planes of freezing wind to the motel room or sat behind a silent taxi driver, sour to have to be out on such nights, as he had sat coming home alone from the airport with the snow flinging itself short of his face.

The freeze continued. The TV weatherman gabbling cheerily before his map showed the sweep of great snowstorms over whole arcs of this enormous country. On the airport she had left from, planes were grounded for days. The few trains there were, ran late. In addition, there was a postal strike and no letters; nothing from England, but also nothing from her, and no hope of a phone call, either, because she had flown straight to join the Professor at his mother's home in Florida, and she could neither telephone from the house nor hope to get out to do so from elsewhere at night, when he was in the motel room; they dared not risk a call to the Company during the day. He moved between the room—whose silence, broken only by Walter Cronkite and the weatherman, filled with his own thoughts as if it were some monstrous projection, a cartoon balloon, issuing from his mind —he moved between that room and the Japanese-architect-designed headquarters of the Company, which existed beneath blizzard and postal strike as an extraordinary bunker with contemplative indoor pools, raked-stone covered courtyards, cheerful rows of Jell-O and tuna fish salad. He woke in the dark mornings to hear the snow plough grinding along the streets. Men struck with picks into the rock of ice that covered the sidewalks a foot solid. The paper said all post offices were deep in drifts of accumulated mail, and sealed the mouths of all mail boxes. England did not exist and Florida—was there really anyone in Florida? It was a place where, the weatherman said, the temperature was in the high seventies, and humid. She had forgotten a sheet of notes that must have come loose from the file, and the big yellow fake sponge (it was what she had been buying when they found themselves together in the drugstore of that other Middle Western town) that she now always brought along. She would be missing the sponge, in Florida, but there was no way to get it to her. He kept the sponge and the sheet of paper on the empty dressing-table. Overnight, every night, more snow fell. Like a nail he was driven deeper and deeper into isolation.

He came from dinner with the Chief Mining Engineer and his party at the country club (the Chief Mining Engineer always took his wife out to eat on Saturday nights) and was possessed by such a dread of the room that he told the taxi driver to take him to the big chain hotel, that had seventeen floors and a bar on top. It was full of parties like the one he had just left; he was the only solitary. Others did not look outside, but fiddling with a plastic cocktail stirrer in the shape of a tiny sword he saw through the walls of glass against which the blue-dark pressed that they were surrounded by steppes of desolation out there beyond the feebly lit limits of the town. Wolves might survive where effluvia from paper mills had made fish swell up and float, and birds choked on their crops filled with pesticide-tainted seeds. He carried the howl somewhere inside him. It was as close as that slight whistling from the blocked sinus in his left nostril. When the bar shut he went down with those chattering others in an elevator that cast them all back into the street.

The smell in the motel room had not changed through his being alone there. He felt so awake, so ready to tackle something, some work or difficulty, that he took another drink, a big swallow of neat whisky, and, that night, wrote a letter to Willa. I'm not coming back, he said. I have gone so far away that it would be stupid to waste it—I mean the stage I've reached. Of course I am sorry that you have been such a good wife, that you will always be such a good wife and nothing can change you. Because so long as I accept that you are a good wife, how can I find the guts to do it? I can go on being the same thing—your opposite number, the good husband, hoping for a better position and more money for us all, coming on these bloody dreary trips every winter (why don't they ever send me in good weather). But it's through subjecting myself to all this, putting up with what we think of as these partings for the sake of my work, that I have come to understand that they are not partings at all. They are nothing like partings. Do you understand?

It went on for two more pages. When he had finished he put it in an airmail envelope, stamped it, went out again—he had not taken off his coat or scarf—and walked through the ringing of his own footsteps in the terrible cold to where he remembered there was a mail box. Like all the others, the mouth was sealed over by some kind of gummed tape, very strong stuff reinforced by a linen backing. He slit it with a piece of broken bottle he found in the gutter, and pushed the letter in. When he got back to the room he still had the bit of glass in his hand. He fell asleep in his coat but must have woken later and undressed because in the morning he found himself in bed and in pyjamas.

He did not know how drunk he had been that night when he did it. Not so drunk that he was not well aware of the chaos of the postal strike; everyone had been agreeing at the country club that most of the mail piled up at the GPO could never be expected to reach its destination. Not so drunk that he had not counted on the fact that the letter would never get to England. —Why, he had broken into the mail box, and the boxes were not being cleared.— Just drunk enough to take what seemed to him the thousand-to-one chance the letter might get there. Suppose the army were to be called in to break the strike, as they had been in New York? Yet, for several days, it did not seem to him that *that* letter would ever be dispatched and delivered— that sort of final solution just didn't come off.

Then the joke went round the Company headquarters that mail was moving again: the Company had received, duly delivered, one envelope—a handbill announcing a sale (already over) at a local department store. Some wit from the administration department put it up in the cafeteria. He suddenly saw the letter, a single piece of mail, arriving at the house in London. He thought of writing—no, sending a cable—now that communications were open again, instructing that the letter was to be destroyed unopened.

She would never open a letter if asked not to, of course. She would put it on the bedside table at his side of the bed and wait for a private night-time explanation, out of the hearing of the children. But suppose the letter had been lost, buried under the drifts of thousands, mis-sorted, mis-dispatched—what would be made of a mystifying cable about a letter that had never come? The snow was melting, the streets glistened, and his clothes were marked with the spray of dirty water thrown up by passing cars. He had impulses—sober ones—to write and tell the Professor's wife, but when she unexpectedly did manage to telephone, the relief of pleasure at her voice back in the room so wrung him that he said nothing, and decided to say nothing in letters to her either; why disturb and upset her in this particularly disturbing and upsetting way.

He received a letter from London a fortnight old. There must have been later ones that hadn't turned up. He began to reason that if the letter did arrive in London, he might just manage to get there before it. And then? It was unlikely that he would be able to intercept it. But he actually began to hint to the colleagues at the Company that he would like to leave by the end of the week, be home in England for the weekend, after all, after six weeks absence. The problem of the drill's optimum performance couldn't be solved in a day, anyway; he would have to go into the whole business back at the research laboratory in London. The Chief Mining Engineer said what a darned shame he had to leave now, before the greens were dry enough for the first eighteen holes of the year.

He forced himself not to think about the letter or at least to think about it as little as possible for the remaining days. Sometimes the idea of it came to him as a wild hope, like the sound of her voice suddenly in the room, from Florida. Sometimes it was a dry anxiety: what a childish, idiotic thing to have done, how insane to risk throwing everything away when, as the Professor's wife often said, nobody was being hurt: Professor Malcolm, the children, Willa—none of them. Resentment flowed into him like unreasonable strength—*I am being hurt!* Not so drunk, after all, not so drunk. Yet, of course, he was afraid of Willa, ranged there with two pretty children and a third with glasses blacked out over one eye to cure a squint. What could you do with that unreasonable, life-saving strength?—Against that little family group? And, back again to the thought of the Professor's wife, his being afraid disgusted him. He spoke to her once more before he left, and said, Why do we have to come last? Why do we count least? She accepted such remarks as part of the ragged mental state of parting, not as significant of any particular development. He put the phone down on her voice for the last time for this time.

He took the plane from Chicago late on Friday afternoon and by midnight was in early morning London. No school on Saturdays and Willa was there with the children at Heathrow. Airports, airports. In some times and places, for some men, it was the battlefield or the bullring, the courtroom or the church; for him it was airports. In that architectural mode of cheap glamour suited only to bathos his strongest experiences came; despair could not be distinguished from indigestion induced by time-change, dread produced the same drawn face as muscle cramp, private joy exhibited euphoria that looked no different from that induced by individual bottles of *Moët et Chandon*. These were the only places where he ever wanted to weep, and no places could have been more ridiculous for this to happen to him.

Willa had a new haircut and the children were overcome with embarrassment by the eternal ten yards he had to walk towards them, and then flung themselves excitedly at him. Willa hugged his arm and pressed her cheek against that coatsleeve a moment; her mouth tasted of the toothpaste that they always used at home. The last phone call—only nine hours ago, that's all it was—receded into a depth, a distance, a silence as impossible to reach down through as the drifts of snow and piled-up letters . . . No letter, of course; he saw that at once. His wife cooked a special lunch and in the afternoon, when the children had gone off to the cinema with friends, he did what he must, he went to bed with her.

They talked a lot about the postal strike and how awful it had been. Nothing for days, more than two weeks! His mother had been maddening, telephoning every day, as if the whole thing were a conspiracy of the wife to keep the mother out of touch with her son. Crazy! And her letters—had he really got only one? She must have written at least four times; knowing that letters might not arrive only made one want to write more, wasn't it perverse? Why hadn't he phoned?  —Not that she really wanted him to, it was so expensive . . . by the way, it turned out that the youngest child had knock knees, he would have to have remedial treatment.  —Well, that was what he had thought —such an extravagance, and he couldn't believe, every day, that a letter might not come. She said, once: It must have been quite a nice feeling, sometimes, free of everything and everyone for a change—peaceful without us, eh? And he pulled down his mouth and said, Some freedom, snowed under in a motel in that godforsaken town. But the mining Group was so pleased with his work that he was given a bonus, and that pleased her, that made her feel it was worth it, worth even the time he had had to himself.

He watched for the postman; sometimes woke up at night in a state of alarm. He even arranged, that first week, to work at home until about midday—getting his reports into shape. But there was nothing. For the second week, when he was keeping normal office hours, he read her face every evening when he came home; again, nothing. Heaven knows how she interpreted the way he looked at her: he would catch her full in the eyes, by mistake, now and then, and she would have a special slow smile, colouring up to her scrubbed little earlobes, the sort of smile you get from a girl who catches you looking at her across a bar. He was so appalled by that smile that he came home with a bunch of flowers. She embraced him and stood there holding the flowers behind his waist, rocking gently back and forth with him as they had done years ago. He thought—wildly again—how she was still pretty, quite young, no reason why she shouldn't marry again.

His anxiety for the letter slowly began to be replaced by confidence: it would not come. It was hopeless—safe—that letter would never come. Perhaps he had been very drunk after all; perhaps the mail box was a permanently disused one, or the letter hadn't really gone through the slot but fallen into the snow, the words melting and wavering while the ink ran with the thaw and the thin sheets of paper turned to pulp. He was safe. It was a good thing he had never told the Professor's wife. He took the children to the Motor Show, he got good seats for Willa, his mother and himself for the new "Troilus and Cressida" production at the Aldwych, and he wrote a long letter to Professor Malcolm's wife telling her about the performance and how much he would have loved to see it with her. Then he felt terribly depressed, as he often did lately now that he had stopped worrying about the letter and should have been feeling better, and there was nowhere to go for privacy, in depression, except the lavatory, where Willa provided the colour supplements of the Sunday papers for reading matter.

One morning just over a month after her husband had returned from the Middle West, Willa picked up the post from the floor as she brought the youngest home from school and saw a letter in her husband's handwriting. It had been date-stamped and re-date-stamped and was apparently about six weeks old. There is always something a bit flat about opening a letter from someone who has in the meantime long arrived and filled in, with anecdote and his presence, the time of absence when it was written. She vaguely saw herself producing it that evening as a kind of addendum to their forgotten emotions about the strike; by such small shared diversions did they keep their marriage close. But after she had given the little one his lunch she found a patch of sun for herself and opened the letter after all. In that chilly spring air, unaccustomed warmth seemed suddenly to become aural, sang in her ears at the pitch of cicadas, and she stopped reading. She looked out into the small garden amazedly, accusingly, as if to challenge a hoax. But there was no one to answer for it. She read the letter through. And again. She kept on reading it and it produced almost a sexual excitement in her, as a frank and erotic love letter might. She could have been looking through a keyhole at him lying on another woman. She took it to some other part of the garden, as the cat often carried the bloody and mangled mess of its prey from place to place, and read it again. It was a perfectly calm and reasonable and factual letter saying that he would not return, but she saw that it was indeed a love letter, a love letter about someone else, a love letter such as he had never written to her. She put it back in the creased and stained envelope and tore it up, and then she went out the gate and wandered down to the bus stop, where there was a lamp-post bin, and dropped the bits of paper into its square mouth among the used tickets.

# AFRICA EMERGENT

H E'S IN PRISON NOW, so I'm not going to mention his name. It mightn't be a good thing, you understand. —Perhaps you think you understand too well; but don't be quick to jump to conclusions from five or six thousand miles away: if you lived here, you'd understand something else—friends know that shows of loyalty are all right for children holding hands in the school playground; for us they're luxuries, not important and maybe dangerous. If I said, I was a friend of so-and-so, black man awaiting trial for treason, what good would it do him? And, who knows, it might draw just that decisive bit more attention to me. *He*'d be the first to agree.

Not that one feels that if they haven't got enough in my dossier already, this would make any difference; and not that he really was such a friend. But that's something else you won't understand: everything is ambiguous, here. We hardly know, by now, what we can do and what we can't do; it's difficult to say, goaded in on oneself by laws and doubts and rebellion and caution and—not least—self-disgust, what is or is not a friendship. I'm talking about black-and-white, of course. If you stay with it, boy, on the white side in the country clubs and garden suburbs if you're white, and on the black side in the locations and beerhalls if you're black, none of this applies, and you can go all the way to your segregated cemetery in peace. But neither he nor I did.

I began mixing with blacks out of what is known as an outraged sense of justice, plus strong curiosity, when I was a student. There were two ways—one was through the white students' voluntary service organization, a kibbutz-type junket where white boys and girls went into rural areas and camped while they built school classrooms for African children. A few coloured and African students from their segregated universities used to come along, too, and there was the novelty, not without value, of dossing down alongside them at night, although we knew we were likely to be harbouring Special Branch spies among our willing workers, and we dared not make a pass at the coloured or black girls. The other way—less hard on the hands—was to go drinking with the jazz musicians and journalists, painters and would-be poets and actors who gravitated towards whites partly because such people naturally feel they can make free of the world, and partly because they found an encouragement and appreciation there that was sweet to them. I tried the VSO briefly, but the other way suited me better; anyway, I didn't see why I should help this Government by doing the work it ought to be doing for the welfare of black children.

I'm an architect and the way I was usefully drawn into the black scene was literally that: I designed sets for a mixed colour drama group got together by a white director. Perhaps there's no urban human group as intimate, in the end, as a company of this kind, and the colour problem made us even closer. I don't mean what *you* mean, the how-do-I-feel-about-that-black-skin stuff; I mean the daily exasperation of getting round, or over, or on top of the colour bar laws that plagued our productions and our lives. We had to remember to write out "passes" at night, so that our actors could get home without being arrested for being out

after the curfew for blacks, we had to spend hours at the Bantu
Affairs Department trying to arrange local residence permits for
actors who were being "endorsed out" of town back to the villages to which, "ethnically," apparently, they belonged although
they'd never set eyes on them, and we had to decide which of us
could play the sycophant well enough to persuade the Bantu
Commissioner to allow the show to go on the road from one
Group Area, designated by colour, to another, or to talk some
town clerk into getting his council to agree to the use of a
"white" public hall by a mixed cast. The black actors' lives were
in our hands, because they were black and we were white, and
could, must, intercede for them. Don't think this made everything love and light between us; in fact it caused endless huffs
and rows. A white woman who'd worked like a slave acting as
PRO-cum-wardrobe-mistress hasn't spoken to me for years because I made her lend her little car to one of the chaps who'd
worked until after the last train went back to the location, and
then he kept it the whole weekend and she couldn't get hold of
him because, of course, location houses rarely have telephones
and once a black man has disappeared among those warrens you
won't find him till he chooses to surface in the white town again.
And when this one did surface, he was biting, to me, about white
bitches' "patronage" of people they secretly still thought of as
"boys". Yet our arguments, resentments and misunderstandings
were not only as much part of the intimacy of this group as the
good times, the parties and the love-making we had, but were
more—the defining part, because we'd got close enough to
admit argument, resentment and misunderstanding between us.

*He* was one of this little crowd, for a time. He was a dispatch
clerk and then a "manager" and chucker-out at a black dance
club. In his spare time he took a small part in our productions
now and then, and made himself generally handy; in the end it
was discovered that what he really was good at was front-of-
house arrangements. His tubby charm (he was a large young man
and a cheerful dresser) was just the right thing to deal with the
unexpected moods of our location audiences when we went on

tour—sometimes they came stiffly encased in their church-going best and seemed to feel it was vulgar to laugh or respond to what was going on, on stage; in other places they rushed the doors, tried to get in without paying, and were dominated by a *tsotsi*, street urchin, element who didn't want to hear anything but themselves. He was the particular friend—the other, passive half—of a particular friend of mine, Elias Nkomo.

And here I stop short. How shall I talk about Elias? I've never even learnt, in five years, how to think about him.

Elias was a sculptor. He had one of those jobs—messenger "boy" or some such—that literate young black men can aspire to in a small gold-mining and industrial town outside Johannesburg. Somebody said he was talented, somebody sent him to me —at the beginning, the way for every black man to find himself seems inescapably to lead through a white man. Again, how can I say what his work was like? He came by train to the black people's section of Johannesburg central station, carrying a bulky object wrapped in that morning's newspaper. He was slight, round-headed, tiny-eared, dunly dressed, and with a frown of effort between his eyes, but his face unfolded to a wide, apologetic yet confident smile when he realized that the white man in a waiting car must be me—the meeting had been arranged. I took him back to my "place" (he always called people's homes that) and he unwrapped the newspaper. What was there was nothing like the clumps of diorite or sandstone you have seen in galleries in New York, London, or Johannesburg marked "Africa Emergent," "Spirit of the Ancestors." What was there was a goat, or a goat-like creature, in the way that a centaur is a horse-like, man-like creature, carved out of streaky knotted wood. It was delightful (I wanted to put out my hand to touch it), it was moving in its somehow concretised diachrony, beast-man, coarse wood–fine workmanship, and there was also something exposed about it (one would withdraw the hand, after all). I asked him whether he knew Picasso's goats? He had heard of Picasso but never seen any of his work. I showed him a photograph of the famous bronze goat in Picasso's own house; thereafter all his beasts had sex organs as joyful as Picasso's goat's udder, but that was the only "influence" that ever took, with him. As I say, a white man always intercedes in some way, with a man like Elias; mine was to keep him from those art-loving ladies with galleries who wanted to promote him, and those white painters and sculptors who were willing to have him work under their tutelage. I gave him an old garage (well, that means I took my car out of it) and left him alone, with plenty of chunks of wood.

But Elias didn't like the loneliness of work. That garage never became his "place." Perhaps when you've lived in an over-crowded yard all your life the counter-stimulus of distraction becomes necessary to create a tension of concentration. No—well all I really mean is that he liked company. At first he came only at weekends, and then, as he began to sell some of his work, he gave up the messenger job and moved in more or less permanently—we fixed up the "place" together, putting in a ceiling and connecting water and so on. It was illegal for him to live there in a white suburb, of course, but such laws breed com-plementary evasions in people like Elias and me and the white building inspector didn't turn a hair of suspicion when I said that I was converting the garage as a flat for my wife's mother. It was better for Elias once he'd moved in; there was always some friend of his sharing his bed, not to mention the girls who did; some-times the girls were shy little things almost of the kitchenmaid variety, who called my wife "madam" when they happened to bump into her, crossing the garden, sometimes they were the be-wigged and painted actresses from the group who sat smoking and gossiping with my wife while she fed the baby.

And *he* was there more often than anyone—the plump and cheerful front-of-house manager; he was married, but as happens with our sex, an old friendship was a more important factor in his life than a wife and kids—if that's a characteristic of black men, then I must be black under the skin, myself. Elias had become very involved in the theatre group, anyway, like *him;* Elias made some beautiful *papier mâché* gods for a play by a Nigerian that we did—"spirits of the ancestors" at once amusing and frightening—and once when we needed a singer he surprisingly turned out to have a voice that could phrase a madrigal as easily as whatever the forerunner of Soul was called—I forget now, but it blared hour after hour from the garage when he was working. Elias seemed to like best to work when the other one was around; *he* would sit with his fat boy's legs rolled out before him, flexing his toes in his fashionable shoes, dusting down the lapels of the latest thing in jackets, as he changed the records and kept up a monologue contentedly punctuated by those soft growls and sighs of agreement, those sudden squeezes of almost silent laughter—responses possible only in an African language—that came from Elias as he chiselled and chipped. For they spoke in their own tongue, and I have never known what it was they talked about.

In spite of my efforts to let him alone, inevitably Elias was "taken up" (hadn't I started the process myself, with that garage?) and a gallery announced itself his agent. He walked about at the opening of his one-man show in a purple turtle-necked sweater I think his best friend must have made him buy, laughing a little, softly, at himself, more embarrassed than pleased. An art critic wrote about his transcendental values and plastic modality, and he said, "Christ, man, does he dig it or doesn't he?" while we toasted his success in brandy chased with beer—brandy isn't a rich man's sip in South Africa, it's made here and it's what people use to get drunk on. He earned quite a bit of money that year. Then the gallery owner and the art critic forgot him in the discovery of yet another interpreter of the African soul, and he was poor again, but he had acquired a patroness who, although she lived far away, did not forget him. She was, as you might have thought, an American lady, very old and wealthy according to South African legend but probably simply a middle-aged widow with comfortable stock holdings and a desire to get in on the cultural ground floor of some form of art collecting not yet overcrowded. She had bought some of his work while a tourist in Johannesburg. Perhaps she did have academic connections with the

art world; in any case, it was she who got a foundation to offer
Elias Nkomo a scholarship to study in America.

I could understand that he wanted to go simply in order to go:
to see the world outside. But I couldn't believe that at this stage
he wanted or could make use of formal art school disciplines. As
I said to him at the time, I'm only an architect, but I've had experience of the academic and even, God help us, the frenziedly
non-academic approach in the best schools, and it's not for people
who have, to fall back on the jargon, found themselves.

I remember he said, smiling, "You think I've found myself?"

And I said, "But you've never been lost, man. That very first
goat wrapped in newspaper was your goat."

But later, when he was refused a passport and the issue of his
going abroad was much on our minds, we talked again. He
wanted to go because he felt he needed some kind of general education, general cultural background that he'd missed, in his six
years at the location school. "Since I've been at your place, I've
been reading a lot of your books. And man, I know nothing. I'm
as ignorant as that kid of yours there in the pram. Right, I've
picked up a bit of politics, a few art terms here and there—I
can wag my head and say 'plastic values' all right, eh? But man,
what do I know about life? What do I know about how it all
works? How do I know *how* I do the work I do? Why we live
and die? —If I carry on here I might as well be carving walking
sticks," he added. I knew what he meant: there are old men, all
over Africa, who make a living squatting at a decent distance
from tourist hotels, carving fancy walking sticks from local
wood; only one step in sophistication below the "Africa Emergent" school of sculptors so rapturously acclaimed by gallery
owners. We both laughed at this, and following the line of
thought suggested to me my his question to himself: "How do I
know how I do the work I do?"—although in me it was a different line of thought from his—I asked him whether in fact
there was any sort of traditional skill in his family? As I imagined, there was not—he was an urban slum kid, brought up op-

posite a municipal beerhall among paraffin-tin utensils and abandoned motor-car bodies which, perhaps curiously, had failed to
bring out a Duchamp in him but from which, on the contrary, he
had sprung, full-blown, as a classical expressionist. Although
there were no rural walking-stick carvers in his ancestry, he did
tell me something I had no idea would have been part of the experience of a location childhood—he had been sent, in his
teens, to a tribal initiation school in the bush, and been circum-
cised according to rite. He described the experience vividly.

Once all attempts to get him a passport had failed, Elias's desire
to go to America became something else, of course: an obsessive
resentment against confinement itself. Inevitably, he was given no
reason for the refusal. The official answer was the usual one—
that it was "not in the public interest" to reveal the reason for
such things. Was it because "they" had got to know he was "living like a white man"? (Theory put to me by one of the black
actors in the group.) Was it because a critic had dutifully described his work as expressive of the "agony of the emergent African soul"? Nobody knew. Nobody ever knows. It is enough to
be black; blacks are meant to stay put, in their own ethnically ap-
portioned streets in their own segregated areas, in those parts of
South Africa where the government says they belong. Yet—the
whole way our lives are manœuvred, as I say, is an unanswered
question—Elias's best friend suddenly got a passport. I hadn't
even realized that *he* had been offered a scholarship or a study
grant or something, too; *he* was invited to go to New York to
study production and the latest acting techniques (it was the time
of the Method rather than Grotowski). And *he* got a passport,
"first try" as Elias said with ungrudging pleasure and admiration;
when someone black got a passport, then, there was a collective
sense of pleasure in having outwitted we didn't quite know what.
So they went together, *he* on his passport, and Elias Nkomo on
an exit permit.

An exit permit is a one-way ticket, anyway. When you are
granted one at your request but at the government's pleasure,

you sign an undertaking that you will never return to South Africa or its mandatory territory, South West Africa. You pledge this with signature and thumb-print. Elias Nkomo never came back. At first he wrote (and he wrote quite often) enthusiastically about the world outside that he had gained, and he seemed to be enjoying some kind of small vogue, not so much as a sculptor as a genuine, real live African Negro who was sophisticated enough to be asked to comment on this and that: the beauty of American women, life in Harlem or Watts, Black Power as seen through the eyes, etc. He sent cuttings from *Ebony* and even from *The New York Times Magazine*. He said that a girl at *Life* was trying to get them to run a piece on his work; his work?—well, he hadn't settled down to anything new, yet, but the art centre was a really swinging place, Christ, the things people were doing, there! There were silences, naturally; we forgot about him and he forgot about us for weeks on end. Then the local papers picked up the sort of news they are alert to from all over the world. Elias Nkomo had spoken at an anti-apartheid rally. Elias Nkomo, in West African robes, was on the platform with Stokely Carmichael. "Well, why not? He hasn't got to worry about keeping his hands clean for the time when he comes back home, has he?" —My wife was bitter in his defence. Yes, but I was wondering about his work—"Will they leave him alone to work?" I didn't write to him, but it was as if my silence were read by him: a few months later I received a cutting from some university art magazine devoting a number to Africa, and there was a photograph of one of Elias's wood sculptures, with his handwriting along the margin of the page—*I know you don't think much of people who don't turn out new stuff but some people here seem to think this old thing of mine is good*. It was the sort of wry remark that, spoken aloud to me in the room, would have made us both laugh. I smiled, and meant to write. But within two weeks Elias was dead. He drowned himself early one morning in the river of the New England town where the art school was.

It was like the refusal of the passport; none of us knew why. In the usual arrogance one has in the face of such happenings, I even felt guilty about the letter. Perhaps, if one were thousands of miles from one's own "place," in some sort of a bad way, just a small thing like a letter, a word of encouragement from someone who had hurt by being rather niggardly with encouragement in the past . . . ? And what pathetic arrogance, at that! As if the wisp of a letter, written by someone between other preoccupations, and in substance an encouraging lie (how splendid that your old work is receiving recognition in some piddling little magazine) could be anything round which the hand of a man going down for the second time might close. Because before Elias went under in that river he must have been deep in forlorn horrors about which I knew nothing, nothing. When people commit suicide they do so apparently out of some sudden self-knowledge that those of us, the living, do not have the will to acquire. That's what's meant by despair, isn't it—what they have come to know? And that's what one means when one says in extenuation of oneself, *I knew so little about him, really.* I knew Elias only in the self that he had presented at my "place"; why, how out of place it had been, once, when he happened to mention that as a boy he had spent weeks in the bush with his circumcision group! Of course we—his friends—decided out of the facts we knew and our political and personal attitudes, why he had died: and perhaps it is true that he was sick to death, in the real sense of the phrase that has been forgotten, sick unto death with homesickness for the native land that had shut him out forever and that he was forced to conjure up for himself in the parody of "native" dress that had nothing to do with his part of the continent, and the shame that a new kind of black platform-solidarity forced him to feel for his old dependence, in South Africa, on the friendship of white people. It was the South African government who killed him, it was culture shock—but perhaps neither our political bitterness nor our glibness with fashionable phrases can come near what combination of forces, within and without, led him to the fatal baptism of that early morning. *It is not in the private interest that this should be revealed.* Elias never came home. That's all.

But his best friend did, towards the end of that year. *He* came to see me after he had been in the country some weeks—I'd heard he was back. The theatre group had broken up; it seemed to be that, chiefly, he'd come to talk to me about: he wanted to know if there was any money left in the kitty for him to start up a small theatrical venture of his own, he was eager to use the know-how (his phrase) he'd learned in the States. He was really plump now and he wore the most extraordinary clothes. A Liberace jacket. Plastic boots. An Afro wig that looked as if it had been made out of a bit of karakul from South West Africa. I teased him about it—we were at least good enough friends for that—asking him if he'd really been with the guerrillas instead of Off-Broadway? (There was a trial on at home, at the time, of South African political refugees who had tried to "infiltrate" through South West Africa.) And felt slightly ashamed of my patronage of his taste when he said with such good humour, "It's just a fun thing, man, isn't it great?" I was too cowardly to bring the talk round to the point: Elias. And when it couldn't be avoided I said the usual platitudes and he shook his head at them —"Hell, man," and we fell silent. Then he told me that that was how he had got back—because Elias was dead, on the unused portion of Elias's air ticket. *His* study grant hadn't included travel expenses and he'd had to pay his own way over. So he'd had only a one-way ticket, but Elias's scholarship had included a return fare to the student's place of origin. It had been difficult to get the airline to agree to the transfer; he'd had to go to the scholarship foundation people, but they'd been very decent about fixing it for him.

He had told me all this so guilelessly that I was one of the people who became angrily indignant when the rumour began to go around that he was a police agent: who else would have the cold nerve to come back on a dead man's ticket, a dead man who

couldn't ever have used that portion of the ticket himself, because
he had taken an exit permit? And who could believe the story,
anyway? Obviously, *he* had to find some way of explaining why
he, a black man like any other, could travel freely back and forth
between South Africa and other countries. He had a passport,
hadn't he? Well, there you were. Why should *he* get a passport?
What black man these days had a passport?

Yes, I was angry, and defended him, by proof of the innocence
of the very naïveté with which—a black man, yes, and therefore used to the necessity of salvaging from disaster all his life,
unable to afford the nice squeamishness of white men's delicacy
—he took over Elias's air ticket because he was alive and needed
it, as he might have taken up Elias's coat against the cold. I refused to avoid him, the way some members of the remnant of our
group made it clear they did now, and I remained stony-faced
outside the complicity of those knowing half-smiles that accompanied the mention of his name. We had never been close friends,
of course; but he would turn up from time to time. He could not
find theatrical work and had a job as a travelling salesman in the
locations. He took to bringing three or four small boys along
when he visited us; they were very subdued and whisperingly
well-behaved and well-dressed in miniature suits—our barefoot
children stared at them in awe. They were his children plus the
children of the family he was living with, we gathered. He and I
talked mostly about his difficulties—his old car was unreliable,
his wife had left him, his commissions were low, and he could
have taken up an offer to join a Chicago repertory company if he
could have raised the fare to go back to America—while my
wife fed ice-cream and cake to the silent children, or my children
dutifully placed them one by one on the garden swing. We had
begun to be able to talk about Elias's death. He had told me how,
in the weeks before he died, Elias would get the wrong way on
the moving stairway going down in the subway in New York
and keep walking, walking up. "I thought he was foolin' around,
man, you know? Jus' climbin' those stairs and goin' noplace?"

*He* clung nostalgically to the American idiom; no African talks about "noplace" when he means "nowhere." But he had abandoned the Afro wig and when we got talking about Elias he would hold his big, well-shaped head with its fine, shaven covering of his own wool propped between his hands as if in an effort to think more clearly about something that would never come clear; I felt suddenly at one with him in that gesture, and would say, "Go on." He would remember another example of how Elias had been "acting funny" before he died. It was on one of those afternoon visits that he said, "And I don't think I ever told you about the business with the students at the college? How that last weekend—before he did it, I mean—he went around and invited everybody to a party, I dunno, a kind of feast he said it was. Some of them said he said a barbecue—you know what that is, same as a *braaivleis*, eh? But one of the others told me afterwards that he'd told them he was going to give them a real African feast, he was going to show them how the country people do it here at home when somebody gets married or there's a funeral or so. He wanted to know where he could buy a goat."

"A goat?"

"That's right. A live goat. He wanted to kill and roast a goat for them, on the campus."

It was round about this time that *he* asked me for a loan. I think that was behind the idea of bringing those pretty, dressed-up children along with him when he visited; he wanted firmly to set the background of his obligations and responsibilities before touching me for money. It was rather a substantial sum, for someone of my resources. But he couldn't carry on his job without a new car, and he'd just got the opportunity to acquire a really good second-hand buy. I gave him the money in spite of—because of, perhaps—new rumours that were going around then that, in a police raid on the house of the family with whom he had been living, every adult except himself who was present on that night had been arrested on the charge of attending a meeting of a banned political organization. His friends were acquitted on the charge simply through the defence lawyer's skill at showing the *agent provocateur*, on whose evidence the charge was based, to be an unreliable witness—that is to say, a liar. But the friends were promptly served with personal banning orders, anyway, which meant among other things that their movements were restricted and they were not allowed to attend gatherings.

*He* was the only one who remained, significantly, it seemed impossible to ignore, free. And yet his friends let him stay on in the house; it was a mystery to us whites—and some blacks, too. But then so much becomes a mystery where trust becomes a commodity on sale to the police. Whatever my little show of defiance over the loan, during the last year or two we have reached the stage where if a man is black, literate, has "political" friends and white friends, *and* a passport, he must be considered a police spy. I was sick with myself—that was why I gave him the money—but I believed it, too. There's only one way for a man like that to prove himself, so far as we're concerned: he must be in prison.

Well, *he* was at large. A little subdued over the fate of his friends, about which he talked guilelessly as he had about the appropriation of Elias's air ticket, harassed as usual about money, poor devil, but generally cheerful. Yet our friendship, that really had begun to become one since Elias's death, waned rapidly. It was the money that did it. Of course; he was afraid I'd ask him to begin paying back and so he stopped coming to my "place," he stopped the visits with the beautifully dressed and well-behaved black infants. I received a typed letter from him, once, solemnly thanking me for my kind cooperation and, etc., as if I were some business firm, and assuring me that in a few months he hoped to be in a position, etc. I scrawled a note in reply, saying of course I darned well hoped he was going to pay the money he owed, sometime, but why, for God's sake, in the meantime, did this mean we had to carry on as if we'd quarrelled? Damn it all, he didn't have to treat me as if I had some nasty disease, just because of a few rands.

But I didn't see him again. I've become too busy with my own work—the building boom of the last few years, you know; I've

had the contract for several shopping malls, and a big cultural
centre—to do any work for the old theatre group in its spo-
radic comings-to-life. I don't think he had much to do with it
anymore, either; I heard he was doing quite well as a salesman
and was thinking of marrying again. There was even a—yet
another—rumour, that he was actually building a house in
Dube, which is the nearest to a solid, bourgeois suburb a black
can get in these black dormitories outside the white man's city, if
you can be considered to be a bourgeois without having freehold.
I didn't need the money, by then, but you know how it is with
money—I felt faintly resentful about the debt anyway, because
it looked as if now *he* could have paid it back just as well as *I*
could say I didn't need it. As for the friendship; he'd shown me
the worth of that. It's become something the white man must
buy just as he must buy the cooperation of police stool pigeons.
Elias has been dead five years; we live in our situation as of now,
as the legal phrase goes; one falls back on legal phrases as other
forms of expression become too risky.

And then, two hundred and seventy-seven days ago, there was
a new rumour, and this time it was confirmed, this time it was no
rumour. *He* was fetched from his room one night and imprisoned. That's perfectly legal, here; it's the hundred-and-eighty-
day Detention Act. At least, because he was something of a per-
sonality, with many friends and contacts in particular among
both black and white journalists, the fact has become public. If
people are humble, or of no particular interest to the small world
of white liberals, they are sometimes in detention for many
months before this is known outside the eye-witness of whoever
happened to be standing by, in house or street, when they were
taken away by the police. But at least we all know where *he* is:
in prison. They say that charges of treason are being prepared
against him and various others who were detained at the same
time, and still others who have been detained for even longer—
three hundred and seventy-one days, three hundred and ten
days—the figures, once finally released, are always as precise as
this—and that soon, soon they will be brought to trial for

whatever it is that we do not know they have done, for when people are imprisoned under the Detention Act no one is told why and there are no charges. There are suppositions among us, of course. Was he a double agent, as it were, using his *laissez-passer* as a police spy in order to further his real work as an underground African nationalist? Was he just unlucky in his choice of friends? Did he suffer from a dangerous sense of loyalty in place of any strong convictions of his own? Was it all due to some personal, unguessed-at bond it's none of our business to speculate about? Heaven knows—those police spy rumours aside—nobody could have looked more unlikely to be a political activist than that cheerful young man, second-string, always ready to jump up and turn over the record, fond of Liberace jackets and aspiring to play Le Roi Jones Off-Broadway.

But as I say, we know where he is now; inside. In solitary most of the time—they say, those who've also been inside. Two hundred and seventy-seven days he's been there.

And so we white friends can purge ourselves of the shame of rumours. We can be pure again. We are satisfied at last. He's in prison. He's proved himself, hasn't he?